Dirty Cooking

Carley Mercedes

Literary Wanderlust | Denver Colorado

Dirty Cooking is a work of fiction. Names, characters, places, and incidents are the products of the author's imagination and have been used fictitiously. Any resemblance to actual events, locales, or persons, living or dead, is entirely coincidental.

Published in the United States by Literary Wanderlust LLC, Denver, Colorado. www.LiteraryWanderlust.com

ISBN Print: 978-1-942856-39-9
ISBN Digital: 978-1-942856-41-2

Cover design: Ruth M'Gonigle

Printed in the United States

Dedication

To the original Mercedes,
a more supportive grandmother there never was.

1

Melanie

"Did you find me a job that looks good?" Melanie asked her friend, Sheila, over the phone. She chopped veggies on her small, granite counter with her cell phone wedged between her shoulder and her cheek. Sheila worked as a career counselor at the local university, and she'd offered to help Melanie find a new job since she was currently employed at a heinous diner. She would've been thrilled to be jogging on the sunny Monday she had off, or if she was honest with herself, napping, but she needed to keep her spatula hand warm, or no one else would hire her.

"Well..." Sheila trailed off.

"Anything will do. Anything." Melanie was desperate. After graduating from one of the top culinary institutes in Phoenix, the only place that would hire her was a lousy diner called The Jivin' Diner. The restaurant even had a theme, or rather, a mascot. Fake, old Elvis with a wig would saunter from table to table, ahem-ing his way through a God-awful accent every day from noon to two p.m. and eight to midnight.

Even as the cook, Melanie had to dress up as a backup dancer in case she had to come out from the kitchen. For the past month, she'd slick back her black bob to tug on a blonde wig, only to work at a restaurant where the main ingredient was grease, and Elvis hit on her every night. One more forearm burn or cooking innuendo, and she was going to lose it. No one could blame her for her actions.

"C'mon, Sheila, tell me you've got something."

"Well, there is this guy in Scottsdale who's looking for a chef. He's got some big estate, and he's looking to hire a full staff. Apparently, he doesn't go out much. The pay is good but..."

"But what?"

"It's a live-in job. The staff lives there."

Melanie sighed. Her ideal job did not include moving to a new home. Then again, she had big plans, and they didn't involve spandex and sequins either. Ever since she'd been a kid, she'd wanted to open her own restaurant. She didn't just like cooking—she liked cooking for people. She loved watching people eat her food. The way her friends' faces filled with bliss after a bite of one of her soufflés made her day every time. She was a good cook, darn it. Her cousin's kids loved her asparagus soup. What kid likes anything with asparagus? Melanie didn't want to cook for just one person, she wanted her cooking to reach people, plural. She'd spent years honing that skill, and she didn't want to hide it at some estate.

"So, what do you think?" Sheila asked.

Melanie could feel the other woman's impatience across the phone line. "That's the only thing you've found?"

"Besides working at a fast food joint? Afraid so."

"All right, I'll give it a shot. Text me the info."

"You got it. I'll cross my fingers for you."

"I don't need luck, I've got skills."

"Glad to see you're so confident," Sheila said, laughing.

"Yep. I'm making too much soup, you want to come over for dinner?"

"Definitely, girl. I'll head over when I'm off work."

"Sounds good. Bye." Melanie looked at her fingers covered in tomato and wondered how to get rid of her phone.

"Bye," Sheila said.

Melanie heard the dial tone and edged over to her small living room. She kept her hands over the counter and swung her shoulder toward the light blue sofa, releasing her phone with a jerk of her head. "Come on, come on," she said, hoping it would land on the cushions. The phone flew left instead of right and hit the wall with a loud, clacking noise. It made a dull thud as it fell to the carpeted floor.

"Fantastic." A strand of her black, short hair fell from her barrette and into her eyes.

Erik

Erik sat at his mahogany desk in his brand new, six hundred square-foot office, wondering how he ended up with such an outrageously large space. He used a laptop, a TV, and sometimes a pad of paper. He had no idea what he was supposed to do with an entire office. His Aunt Stacie sat across the desk in a brown leather armchair. She stared at him over steepled fingers, her brown eyes sharp and her green skirt suit unwrinkled.

Having an aunt still seemed odd sometimes. Erik grew up an orphan and had been in and out of foster care until he was fifteen when he saw his foster dad try to hit his foster brother, Hunter, with a bat after the kid took some snacks from the kitchen without asking. That night he and the younger boy ran off, working their way from Nevada to Arizona. Erik would've been fine staying in Nevada, but Hunter wanted to get as far away from his past as possible. Erik didn't blame him. Once in Phoenix, Erik got his GED, and soon after, a business degree to support Hunter, who was eleven at the time. Getting Hunter to stick out high school had been a real struggle, but the education was worth it. The kid turned out to have a brilliant mind, and they'd come up with a video-editing app together that made millions while Hunter was in college. After, they'd worked as a team, and started a creative company. His brother created app ideas, they hired others to design and code them, and Erik handled the financing and marketing portion of their venture.

He'd found his aunt after they sold their first app. Erik hired a private detective to find his family.

He'd offered the same to Hunter, but his brother was uninterested. He wondered if Hunter would ever change his mind. The detective found out Erik's parents had passed away years ago, but he had an aunt who was still alive. His aunt hadn't even known he existed because her sister hid the pregnancy. Erik and Stacie hit it off right away. After a couple years, he hired her to handle his real estate investments.

"You don't like it," Stacie said, bringing him back to the present.

"It's not that I don't like it." Erik shifted in his seat. Normally he didn't have a problem expressing his dissatisfaction. He was accustomed to being in charge. He'd looked after Hunter as they grew up, and now he owned a business. He hadn't known his aunt for long though, and he was still unsure how to handle situations like this with family.

"But you don't like it," she said.

Erik chuckled and ran a hand through his thick, blond hair. "What am I supposed to do with the rest of the space in here?"

"Whatever you like. Use your imagination. Or if you can't find yours, use Hunter's imagination."

Erik glared at her. "He would suggest a basketball hoop in here."

"Nothing wrong with a few indulgences." She shrugged.

"This is an office."

"Do what you want."

"Do you know how many rooms are in this house?" he asked. The estate was ridiculous. He couldn't believe he'd let her talk him into buying this place. He felt like a pompous ass.

"Yes. I picked it, remember? Eighteen." She put a hand to her carefully coiffed blonde hair, and her brown eyes widened innocently.

"There are servants' quarters."

"Yes. Because you need a full-time staff if you're never going to leave the house."

"I leave the house a lot." He crossed his arms.

"Do you know how high the pile of Chinese food cartons in your last dining room was? It's a wonder you and Hunter survived as long as you did. I swear you boys are like animals."

"'Boys'? I am twenty-nine, you know. Do I need to remind you that I've been on my own for quite some time?" he asked, and then regretted it.

Stacie looked away, her dark eyes clouded. The similarity of their eyes was still odd, but he supposed that was part of having a relative. "I know, and I'm sorry for that."

"I didn't mean—"

"No, I understand. But let me help now, please?" she asked, her eyes wide.

He sighed. There was no way he could turn her down. "Fine, you win."

She grinned and bent over to her briefcase. She unclipped the black case and pulled out a file. "I printed off all the résumés for the manservant position, so you can't avoid reading them by saying it hurts your eyes to look at the computer screen."

His lips thinned, and his gaze hardened. "No. I'm sorry, but no. I draw the line at 'manservant.' There's no way."

Stacie burst out laughing. "I'm kidding. These are the cleaning and cooking staff applications."

He rolled his eyes skyward. That was much better. He grit his teeth and took the file from her. "Fine."

"You know Hunter's excited about this."

Erik nodded. Hunter's excitement was one of the only reasons he was going along with the whole house plan. "If he loses focus, I'm blaming you."

"I'll bring you the gardeners' résumés in a couple of days. Happy hiring." She grabbed her briefcase and left Erik alone in the gigantic office with a huge stack of résumés.

He looked at the pile and wondered if he should've hired someone to hire others. This was going to take so much time he didn't have. He groaned into his hands and then opened the folder.

Melanie

Melanie looked at herself in the mirror, trying to figure out if what she wore was both appropriate for an interview, and for preparing the four-course sample meal she needed to cook that afternoon. She'd applied for the job on the private estate with an anonymous employer and got a response right away. The call back came so fast, she'd wondered if the mystery person picked her file from the top of some stack. Whatever, she wasn't complaining. As long as this guy didn't dress up like Elvis or make her cook fifty grilled cheeses in an hour, she'd be fine.

She tugged at the orange button-down that lay tight

across her small breasts. She considered putting on an undershirt and unbuttoning the over shirt, but she was running out of time. Getting to the estate would take her at least twenty-five minutes, and she needed to be there in half an hour. She smoothed her dark jeans and looked at her heeled boots. They pinched a little, but she wanted to be taller for the interview. Three more inches gave her extra confidence. Her short stature could put her at a disadvantage for counter height. It was embarrassing but true.

Sitting at her upcycled vanity, she grabbed mascara and lip balm. She swiped the black mascara around her wide blue eyes and rubbed the lip balm over her full lips. Satisfied her black bob was behaving for once, she got up and grabbed a blue sweater from off her unmade bed. She'd already loaded her supplies into her navy-blue Jeep, but she'd left the vehicle in the apartment's loading dock.

She ran to her Jeep and turned the key in the ignition as the maintenance guy, Steve, yelled at her from the building. "It's been more than twenty minutes."

"Sorry," she shouted through the open window, waving a hand vaguely in his direction.

The drive to the estate took her twenty-three minutes going ten miles over the speed limit. Once she arrived though, she spent a couple extra minutes staring open-mouthed at the house from the road beside the gated entrance. The house was huge. It sat on the side of a mountain, with wall-height windows wrapped around the two-story building. A deck with a negative edge pool was built on the edge of a cliff, and a beautiful wrought iron fence wrapped around the property. She pulled up to the gate in front of a steep driveway. A man in the booth by the gate waved to her.

She unrolled the window, and he asked for her name. "Melanie Clark. I'm here for an interview."

"Yes, ma'am. Thank you," he said and closed the window.

The gate swung open and she drove up the driveway until she reached a mini parking lot around the side of the house. "Who lives here?" she muttered to herself. Nerves were setting in. She bit her lip and parked in a spot close to the huge oak door and walkway.

She turned off the car and opened her sun visor, checking her appearance in the mirror. No smudged mascara, no flyaway hairs—she was good to go if only her legs would start working. "C'mon, you can do this," she said to herself in the mirror. Nothing like a good pep talk to keep her hands from shaking.

She turned to the back of her Jeep to check on the food and a loud rapping sounded from her window. She jumped and screamed, whipping her head in the direction of her car door. Her heart pounded in her chest.

A man stood beside her Jeep. His arms were crossed over his broad chest, and he openly stared at her, his jaw sharp and hard, and his lips thin. His eyes were dark, and he had a straight nose and strong cheekbones. He wore jeans that hugged his thighs and a white T-shirt that clung to his torso. Even with the casual clothes, his body looked like it could have come directly from the cover of her runner's magazine.

Her gaze caught in his, and she couldn't look away. Her tongue stuck to the roof of her mouth, and her heartbeat wouldn't slow. The man was attractive—speech-incapacitatingly attractive.

Despite the window and door being closed, she had an urge to lean back. Who was this guy? She tore her gaze away and wondered at his behavior. Thinking he might be one of the newly hired staff, she unrolled her window and decided to try for polite despite her annoyance at this guy tapping on her window. She chuckled, but it came out sarcastic. "You startled me."

He continued to stare at her, his thick, blond hair whipping around his forehead in the wind. If he were one of the hired staff he'd need to learn some social skills fast. "Were you talking to yourself?"

Annoyance trumped her nerves. "Excuse me?" she asked, her eyes narrowing.

"Do you have trouble hearing? Were you talking to yourself?" He enunciated each word.

"No, I don't have trouble hearing. I just don't usually answer rude questions. Do you work here? Because I doubt your employer would appreciate your behavior." She grabbed the door handle, but he stood so close to the door that if she opened it, he would be hit. "Do you mind? I'm here for an interview."

He stepped back a foot, and she opened the door. "Thank you." She smiled as widely as she could.

"You're late," he said as she opened the door.

"Well, maybe you can inform this wished-to-remain-anonymous employer of yours I was late because you scared the bejeezus out of me." She jumped from the Jeep. Once she straightened, she looked up at the guy. Good Lord was he tall. She used her best intimidating stance, hands on hips and everything, but the guy still stared. He was a little unnerving.

"You would have been late anyway." He tucked his hands into his front pockets.

"I don't think so. If you'll excuse me, I need to get some stuff out of the back, and then I need to meet with the head of the house." Melanie turned her back to the man and opened the door to the backseat. She stacked Tupperware and tried to ignore the man's presence behind her. He was far too distracting. Relieved to be facing away from him, she took a deep breath to clear her head. She needed to calm down and prepare herself for the interview.

"So, what's this mystery person's name anyway?" she asked, her head in the back of the car.

"Erik. Do you need help carrying that?"

"No, no, I'm fine."

"All right."

She would not give the jerk the satisfaction of needing help. She'd carried all the food to her car; she could carry it out. Shoving her right hand under the mountain of containers, she put her left hand on the precarious top. She turned back to the guy with her arms full. Sighing, she realized she might end up working with him. Maybe she should start over. "I'm Melanie. What's your name?"

"Erik" His lips tugged upward the tiniest bit.

"That's a weird coincidence." She frowned. "Oh, shoot."

2

Erik

Erik watched Melanie's face, raised an eyebrow, and bit back a grin. Her bright blue eyes clouded in a scowl, but she kept her head held high, her black hair falling beneath her chin. He was impressed. He thought she might have left as soon as she discovered whom he was. He found he was a little excited by the prospect that he hadn't intimidated her enough to leave. Not that an obstinate employee would do him any good.

But he had to admit to himself that as soon as she assumed he was an employee of the estate, he had been dying for this moment. She'd been so stubborn, refusing to answer his reasonable questions, and then refusing his offer of assistance. He felt a little guilty for messing with her this way, but his amusement outweighed the guilt. She was adorable, her Tupperware piled from her hips to her chin, her button-down wrinkling around the food. If he were smart, he would tell her to go home now.

"Well, sir, would you like to show me your kitchen, so I can begin preparing the meal?" Her cheeks reddened, but she looked him directly in the eye.

"Yes, of course." Apparently, he wasn't that smart.

He walked with her to the house, opening the front door for her. She looked around the foyer, which opened to a grand room with spiral staircases to the left and the right. Her mouth fell open, and for the first time since he'd moved into the house, a prickle of pleased vanity ran through him. He clenched his jaw. This was a possible employee. He needed to maintain his professionalism.

He motioned past the staircases toward a hallway on the left. "After you."

"Thanks," she muttered and, walked ahead of him.

Her small ass rolled back and forth as she walked. He averted his eyes and cleared his throat. What was wrong with his libido? He'd slept with a woman a few nights ago, and he was reacting like a teenager to this lithe, small woman with a smart mouth. Maybe Hunter was right. Maybe he needed a new hobby. Something that would entertain him more than this woman's ass.

"The kitchen is ahead," he said.

Pushing through the doors, she entered the kitchen. She stopped short, and he'd been so focused on averting his gaze that he ran into her. She expelled breath and stumbled forward. He grabbed her shoulders and jerked her back, so she wouldn't fall. Her body fell in line against his, and he inhaled sharply. He could feel the heat of her even through their clothing. Her small curves molded against him. He stepped back and swallowed. "Are you all right?"

"I'm fine, fine," she said, her voice tight. She whirled around, her blue eyes wide. She licked her lips, and then glanced away.

So much for her confidence. Interesting. Her sharp change in behavior intrigued him. He had to hide a grin again; her face was an open book. The attraction he felt was clearly reciprocated. Not that he would do anything about it. Not only was she a potential employee, but she was also too innocent. His past was too dark, his worldview far too rough for a girl like this. "What do you think?"

Melanie

Melanie blinked, trying to clear her head. All she could think about was the way his firm thighs had felt against her behind. What was wrong with her? She'd had a boyfriend before, she'd had sex. She didn't have a ton of experience, but she'd had sex. She'd never reacted this way before. Maybe Sheila was right, maybe she needed to get out and date more, because she could not handle the distraction of being attracted to a possible boss. Seriously, she needed out of The Jivin' Diner. This was the only opportunity she'd found so far. She was not going to screw up her interview because she couldn't get her head out of her behind.

"Melanie?" he asked.

"What?" she said, the cobwebs clearing.

"I asked you what you thought the kitchen?"

She surveyed the kitchen. The place was amazing. It had every amenity she dreamed of buying for herself one day. A huge cutting board island, gorgeous granite counter tops, beautiful stoves, state-of-the-art ovens, and brand-new appliances of all kinds. The espresso maker was coffee shop ready. She cleared her throat. “Oh, sorry, I’m taking it all in. This is an incredible kitchen.”

“I’m glad you approve,” he said, his tone wry. He leaned against the counter and braced his hands on the granite. “So, I thought we could discuss your background first, and then you could get to cooking.”

“Sounds good.” She stood on her tiptoes and slid the Tupperware pile onto the counter. She smiled to herself, pleased she hadn’t dropped even one. Her balance had been touch-and-go there for a while.

“Great. So, you’re currently working at a place called The Jivin’ Diner?”

“That’s right.” Melanie stretched her lips into a smile, but the look probably appeared fake.

“And why do you want to leave that job?”

She nodded, trying to look earnest. She couldn’t talk about creepy Elvis, the grease, or the wig. Those stories would be for a therapist down the road. “I feel I’ve outgrown the position there.”

“And why are you interested in being a chef on a private estate?”

These were great questions, which she hated answering. She hated lying, even only partial lies. She was bad at misleading people and couldn’t keep lies straight anyway. “I thought it would be a great opportunity to diversify my culinary experience.”

Looking him in the eye was difficult.

He cocked his head to the side. "Practice much?"

She sighed. "A bit."

"How about we do this with some honesty?"

"What are you, a human lie detector? Those were both reasonable responses. And they're partly true," she said, putting her hands on her hips.

He raised a dark blond eyebrow and stared at her. "You could try the whole truth."

Melanie blinked. She knew practicing interview questions with Sheila would be overkill. "No one wants the whole truth," she muttered. "Fine. There's a creepy Elvis and my wig smells like grease. My friend recommended this job to me."

"It's the only one you could find, isn't it?"

"Did you interrogate all your staff members this way?" She wasn't going to back down. She needed this job. Panic inflated her lungs, and she took a deep breath. She could not stay at that diner. Although at this rate, she would need to work on being more personable for the rest of the interview.

"I find it's important to make sure everyone wants to be a part of the team here. Normally, they don't react this rudely."

"I'm rude? You accused me of lying. And I can be a part of the team. I would be a great team member. I bake cakes for co-workers. And my cooking is outstanding. Children eat my asparagus soup. Do you know how picky kids are about vegetables?" She was losing it, she could tell. Hysterics were not her usual M.O., and yet she could hear the shrillness in her voice. Lightheaded from rambling, she took deep breaths.

"I think I remember. All right. Let's see what you can do. I'll be in the dining room. Come get me when the food is ready," he said and left the room.

"Great, just great." She opened her Tupperware and got to work. He'd asked for fried chicken of all things, so she'd brought ingredients for soup, salad, chicken, mashed potatoes, green beans, and a cobbler. Hopefully, when he tasted her food, he'd lighten up. Everyone calmed down once they ate her fried chicken. Fattening food always made people lethargic.

Erik

Erik sat in the dining room with his laptop, going over marketing research for Hunter's new logo app concept. The app would be reasonably profitable, if not a huge seller. He leaned back in his chair wondering how long the meal would take Melanie to cook. She'd started humming about fifteen minutes ago, and within the last ten, it became loud singing. He was tempted to walk in and tell her he could hear her, but he was far too entertained. She had an awful singing voice.

Hunter walked into the dining room. His black hair curled around his ears and cut off just above the collar of the blue polo he wore. "Hey, who's making that awful noise?"

"That would be the auditioning chef," Erik said.

"I didn't know you were interviewing dying cats. I hope her cooking is better than her singing," he said, his grin bright white against his dark stubble and tan skin.

"One can only hope. Did you hire an assistant yet?"

"Not yet. I can't seem to find anyone with the right qualifications."

"Why do I get the feeling that these qualifications are ones you wouldn't be able to list in the classifieds?"

"Because you're reading the wrong section of the newspaper." Hunter sat beside Erik.

Erik sighed and placed his laptop aside. "Eventually you'll need to take the search seriously."

"If you say so. When will the food be ready?"

Melanie's singing quieted and Erik heard dishes clanging around. He winced and wondered if chefs knew how to handle fine china. Another purchase Stacie thought was necessary to civilize them.

"Soon or never, depending on what we hear next," Erik said.

The clanging stopped, and the door opened. Melanie walked into the dining room carrying soup and salad. Her pale skin seemed to be glowing, and she swayed as she walked. She looked satisfied with herself, her full lips curved in a smile and her blue eyes bright. She was beautiful, but her smile fell upon noticing Hunter. A rush of satisfaction surged through Erik. Normally women fawned over his brother, but Melanie's gaze was already back on Erik.

"I'm so sorry, I was under the impression I was cooking for one." She walked the length of the dining room table and set the dishes in front of Erik.

He opened his mouth to speak, but Hunter beat him to it. "You are, I'm just here to snag a few bites from my brother's plate. This looks fantastic, and it smells wonderful. Is this asparagus soup?"

Melanie smiled at Hunter. "Thanks. And it is."

"You know, I don't even like asparagus, but that looks amazing." Hunter bent over the bowl and inhaled.

She blushed. "Thanks again."

Erik's gaze snapped to his brother, who was still smiling and watching the chef. Annoyance shot through him. "Thank you, Melanie. You can bring the rest now. My brother and I will taste it all at once."

"All right," she said, her face turning serious.

"Thanks," Hunter said, his smile still baring teeth.

"You're welcome," she said, grinning back at him. She turned on her heel and walked back to the kitchen.

Hunter stared at her as she walked out.

"What are you doing?" Erik snapped.

Hunter's gaze jerked up. "What do you think I'm doing? Did you see those lips? And the rest of her?"

"Don't talk about her that way," Erik said, surprised by the hard quality of his own voice. What was wrong with him? He never spoke to his brother this way.

Hunter drummed the table with his fingers. "Well now, this is interesting."

"What's interesting?" Erik said through clenched teeth.

"Just that you—" he started, but Melanie walked back in carrying an entrée plate and a dessert plate.

"I have chicken, mashed potatoes, and green beans. For dessert, I made a peach cobbler." Melanie set the plates on the table.

The chicken was fried golden and the potatoes were garnished. The entire meal was presented well. Garlic from the green beans wafted toward Erik, and his mouth watered. "This looks great."

"Thank you." She stood beside the table with her

hands folded in front of her.

"Why don't you sit with us while we try everything?" Hunter asked.

"Oh, I don't want to intrude. I can wait in the kitchen."

"Nonsense. Please have a seat. I'm Hunter, by the way." He extended his hand across the table.

Melanie shook it, and Hunter slid a thumb over the back of her hand before he let go. Erik frowned at Hunter, but his brother wore a wide-eyed angelic expression.

"It's nice to meet you. I'm Melanie," she said, tucking her hair behind her ear.

Erik had a sudden urge to finger a strand of her hair. He cleared his throat and looked at the food in front of him. He couldn't wrap his head around why she distracted him this way. Normally, he was interested in women with rounder curves, but there was something appealing about Melanie's open face and small stature.

He shook off thoughts of her and picked up a fork to try the mashed potatoes.

Melanie

The two brothers picked up utensils to sample the food. Melanie sat across from Hunter and squeezed her hands together on her lap to still her jittering muscles. She loved watching people try her food, but the prospect they might not enjoy it was a painful one. And the nerves weren't going to go away sitting near two of the most attractive men she'd ever met. She couldn't believe such different-looking, but handsome, men had been born into the same family. She could imagine women swooning over Hunter with his dark, muscular build, and thick, black hair. He was polite and charming and put her at ease. Not at all like his intimidating brother.

Hunter tasted the asparagus soup and groaned. The sound was low and sensual. Pride filled her at his reaction.

"Mel, this is incredible."

"Her name is 'Melanie,'" Erik said, his dark eyes hard.

Hunter looked at Erik, and a smirk flitted over his face so fast that Melanie wondered if she'd imagined it. "Maybe Melanie doesn't mind the nickname."

"Maybe that's too informal for an interview." Erik's jaw looked tight, and his fork hung in midair, crowned with mashed potatoes. He still hadn't taken his first bite.

Melanie sat on the edge of her seat uncertain about what was going on between the two of them. She didn't mind the nickname, but she didn't want to butt into their discussion. She had happiness on the line here. The thought of trying to shimmy on spandex again later that week made her want to hit things or people. Fake Elvis especially.

Hunter took a bite of mashed potatoes. "This is delicious too, Mel."

Erik put his fork back on the plate and glared at his brother. "Melanie, bring the salt please."

Melanie's mouth dropped open. He hadn't tasted any food yet, but he had the nerve to ask for salt. She couldn't believe it. "It doesn't need salt," she said before she thought better of it.

They both swung their gazes to her, and her cheeks

warmed. She couldn't remember the last time she'd blushed so much. This was one of the most embarrassing days she'd had in a while. Well, okay, maybe it wasn't. But if she didn't have the dumbest job in the world, it would have been.

"Excuse me?" Erik said, his voice low.

"It doesn't need salt," she repeated, standing her ground. If she was going to be working here, she didn't want her work taken for granted. She may not have had anything to bargain with, but she still had dignity. "You should try it before adding salt. Salt is in my recipes. It doesn't need salt."

"I don't think it needs—" Hunter began, but Erik cut him off.

"You're interviewing for a position that requires you to cook as I tell you to." Erik leaned forward with narrowed eyes.

Melanie was tempted to shift back in her seat, but she didn't move. Her mouth went dry. His piercing stare held her gaze, and she licked her lips, trying to wet her mouth. She watched him follow the action with his eyes, and heat pooled in her lower belly.

"Bring me the salt," he said once more, his voice dangerous.

She cleared her throat. Where was her head today? His commanding tone struck a chord in her. Something feminine in her purred, and she had an immediate urge to do what he said. She started at the revelation, frustrated and wondering why they were arguing about salt. Could this really be all about salt? Well, she wouldn't be ordered around, and she wouldn't watch someone butcher her meal. "You'll ruin the meal. You are interviewing me because of my experience and expertise. You should defer to it."

Hunter made a choking noise, and she swung her gaze to him. He had a hand held to his mouth, and he was shaking. "Oh, Lord, are you ok?" Melanie asked.

He nodded. "I'm fine, fine."

Erik looked at him, his angular features hard. "Maybe you should go get some water."

"No, no, I'm fine. I can stay here. I'll just keep eating this delicious food you're not paying any attention to." Hunter took a bite of cobbler. "Oh, God, so good."

Erik frowned at Hunter and then turned back to Melanie. "If you're going to be my employee you'll be required to cook as I command. I do not tolerate insubordination from my employees."

Who was this guy? 'Cook as I command'? This was why she hated money. It made men entitled, arrogant jerks. She knew she should get up and just get the darn salt. Doing what he asked shouldn't have been a big deal, but she'd dealt with so many horrible customers demanding the most appalling substitutions for the past year at the diner that she just couldn't do it. Who commanded about seasonings anyway? Plus, there was something about him that made her want to challenge him. He looked domineering, leaning forward so he hovered over her, a feral energy building as he sat poised. Denying him was, well, thrilling. "Then hire a servant, not a chef," she said, proud her voice didn't shake.

"I'll give you one last chance, Ms. Clark." He crossed his arms over his chest, his biceps curving and tightening with the movement.

Her gaze caught on his chest, and she realized she

was ogling. She looked up and saw Erik had noticed, a tiny smile playing around the corners of his mouth. This day got better and better. Maybe she should've just got the stupid salt. She really wanted this job, but she couldn't let go of her pride or her principles. This was her area of expertise, and he wouldn't even try the food without salt. It was absurd. "I don't need one more chance. I haven't changed my mind."

Erik's gaze was inscrutable but trained on her face. What he was thinking? He nodded once. "Then I'll show you out."

Melanie nodded, dumbstruck by how the interview had gone. Salt. She couldn't believe it came down to salt. She walked to the kitchen to load up her Tupperware and racked her brain to remember when her next shift at the diner was.

Erik

"What's wrong with you? Do you realize you just didn't hire her because of salt? You didn't even taste the food, and you dismissed her because of salt." Hunter sat in front of the food, his fork still in hand.

Erik sat back down at the table, having come back from walking Melanie out, and stared at the leftover food. He rubbed the back of his neck and looked back at Hunter. "It was a simple request. I'd be her boss. If she can't even do a simple—"

"It was insulting. Just try the food."

Erik looked dubiously at his brother and picked up the fork again. He took a bite of the green beans with the mashed potatoes and stifled a groan at the rich taste. He couldn't understand how mashed potatoes could have such complex flavor.

"That's what you lost out on for the foreseeable future because of your stubbornness and salt. Can you even imagine what her stuffed French toast tastes like?" Hunter asked.

"Is that an innuendo?"

"No."

"I think you're getting too upset over food. We're not starving anymore." Although, now that he'd tasted the food, he did regret his rash behavior. He didn't know what had come over him. He sighed and picked up a drumstick. Crispy skin crunched between his teeth as he took a bite.

"Do you even know how you sounded with that poor girl?"

"I'm betting you're going to tell me even if I say 'yes.'"

"You were..." Hunter said, floundering. "Tyrannical."

"That seems extreme."

"Fine, you were bossy."

"I would have been her boss."

"Domineering."

"I'm used to being in charge." Erik shrugged, his shoulders tight. He was never questioned like this. His employees did what he told them to do. There were no questions asked, no challenge. Even Hunter usually deferred to his experience. Now he was being challenged over a tiny, mouthy chef. It was absurd.

"Okay, I'm going to say something awkward because I think you're unaware, and it's embarrassing for all of us." Hunter looked at the wall opposite and paused. "I wish Stacie was here instead of me. She's much better at this. Being in the room with you two was like watching, I don't know, two birds doing a mating dance, or two horny cheetahs testing each other, or—"

Erik held up a hand. "Stop. You're an inventor, not a writer, and it's apparent why. There was nothing sexual about what just happened. You're being ridiculous." He forced his features into a neutral expression. The insinuation that Melanie had been interested brought him an unnerving sense of satisfaction.

"So, you're not attracted to her. That's good," Hunter said with an innocent smile.

Erik took another bite of the chicken and didn't say anything. The number of times he had pictured her naked during that interview was appalling. As soon as she brought out the cobbler, he was a goner. All he could think about was laying her across the table and licking peach juice off her navel, her breasts, and her—

"Well then, maybe I'll ask her out. Since we're not hiring her and all."

Erik's nostrils flared, and he slammed his fist on the table without thinking. He clenched his jaw and swallowed. What was wrong with him? He had a tight reign over his emotions, and just thinking about the girl was making him nuts. His brother was right. He had been domineering. He enjoyed the way she disobeyed him and had been thinking about an opportunity in which she would do everything he told her to. "It's for the best that this didn't work out. I don't need a distracting employee."

"At least you're willing to admit you're attracted to her."

"I didn't say—"

"Whatever, Erik. Your life. I'm gonna go work out. And I'm taking the cobbler with me. You don't deserve her cobbler." Hunter grabbed the dessert plate as Erik reached for a bite.

The fork dropped out of his hand and he leaned back, telling himself it was for the best he hadn't hired her.

3

Melanie

Melanie stood in the old bathroom of The Jivin' Diner a couple days after the interview. During her break, she decided her scalp was in desperate need of a breather. She yanked the wig off in front of the mirror and looked at the thick powder on her made-up face and her red spandex shirt. Her makeup was in place, and while the look was over the top, now that her natural hair was showing, the whole ensemble wasn't as awful. The blood-red spandex top cut low to reveal as much cleavage as she could muster with her Bs and dipped low in the back too. The sleeves cut off at her forearms, and a sequined pattern of flames traced the bottom of her shirt. Her black pants were skin tight. She ran her hand through her hair to get rid of some tangles. Her phone vibrated in her front pocket as her fingers were snagged in a painful knot. She extricated her fingers, and then pulled out her phone. The screen showed Sheila's name and a picture of the voluptuous woman mid-dance step with her long, wavy, brown hair flipping around her tan shoulders.

An internal debate began as she decided whether to answer the call. She had avoided Sheila for days, not sure what to tell her about the interview. She still wasn't even sure what had happened. One minute, everything seemed fine, at least after she had confused Erik for an employee, and the next, she'd gotten into some weird contest of wills over salt. Well, she didn't want to ignore her friend forever. Since she was in her humiliating diner getup, she might as well get all the embarrassment out of the way for the day and admit the truth to Sheila.

"Hey. Where have you been? Is your phone broken?" Sheila asked when Melanie answered her phone.

"No, I've just been avoiding anyone who has any respect for me whatsoever."

"Uh-oh. You didn't get the job?"

"I didn't get the job," she confirmed.

"Oh, honey. What happened?" Sheila said, her voice dropping into sympathetic mothering mode.

"I don't know. Everything was going fine, and then I refused to get him salt, and he started talking about disobedient employees or something. It spiraled downward from there."

"Melanie. He's a rich guy with an estate. They're all eccentrics. I'm sure he didn't mean anything by it. Why didn't you just get him the salt?"

"I don't know. Ugh, I don't know what came over me.

He was being so unreasonable." His request had been unreasonable, but that hadn't been the only reason she hadn't got the salt. She wasn't sure why she'd said no. It had just been thrilling to deny this tall, domineering, and handsome man. Of course, now she was paying for it. Worse than that, she couldn't get the man out of her head. She'd been dreaming about him since she'd left the interview. His seductive, brooding eyes would peek out from the darkness in her bedroom, and she would turn on a lamp to see him shirtless and coming toward her. All kinds of carnal pleasures would follow. Yesterday the dreams even involved caramel sauce and certain parts of his anatomy. Her body heated thinking about it.

"Try to keep your spirits up. I'll keep looking."

Melanie cleared her throat and shook the lusty thoughts from her head. "Thanks, Sheila. I have to get back to work now. I'll call you later."

"Bye, hon."

"Bye," Melanie said, trying to sound bright. She dropped her phone in her pocket and put back on her wig. Her break was about over, so she walked back to the kitchen to start the fries. A couple of older women—the short-order chefs—milled around the stove cooking burgers.

The kitchen smelled like grease, and everything was covered in a thin film of grime. The appliances were outdated and an ugly lime color and made her miss Erik's amazing kitchen. She rolled her shoulders and heated the oil in the deep fryer. After waiting for a couple minutes, she dumped the fries in. Lunch rush would be starting soon, and she could hear fake Elvis's voice coming from the dining area. Maybe she'd get lucky, and he'd forget it was her shift. The oil bubbled, and the door to the kitchen opened.

"Hello, Melanie," a singsong voice called from behind her.

"Hey, Bob." Her shoulders sagged. She didn't bother to turn around. Fake Elvis had remembered her shift.

"We've discussed this, babe. The name is Elvis."

She wasn't in the mood for his harassment today. "How about this, you don't call me 'babe,' and I won't serve you poisoned food." She turned around to face him.

The man stood across the room wearing all white. His skin was leathery and wrinkled, and his beady, brown eyes sat too close together on his face. He giggled at her pronouncement and sauntered toward her. "How I do enjoy your sass."

"Seriously, Bob, this is dangerous. The grease is really hot. You should be out there singing to the paying customers." She lifted the tray of fries out of the grease.

"I'll sing to you, and you don't even have to pay. Come to my home after hours and I'll serenade you all night long," he said, wiggling his eyebrows.

That was it. She'd had it. She was done dealing with this tool. She dropped the tray of fries back into the grease. A few drops splashed out around the tray. "Look here, you little toad, I am so sick of your disturbing and disgusting come-ons."

"Um—" Bob bobbed on the balls of his feet.

"I'm not finished. You are a sad, little man who has nothing in life going for you, so you like to pretend you are Elvis. You can't even sing well."

The man was on his toes now. "But, Melanie—"

"I'm not done. Why you would think that your horrible sexual innuendos would work on me is something—"

"Oh my God, fire!" a woman shouted from behind Melanie.

She whipped her head around to see a paper towel on fire near the grease. The short-order chefs yelled and screamed. The flame was only a couple inches high, but the room dissolved into chaos. Two chefs ran from the room. Fake Elvis jumped up and down. The owner ran in, his cheap wig askew and his buggy, green eyes wide. "What the hell is going on?"

Melanie ran to the other side of the room to retrieve the fire extinguisher and prepared to shoot out the flame. Before she could put the fire out, fake Elvis grabbed a bottle of water and dumped the liquid over the fire. "No, you idiot! It's a grease fire," she shouted, but it was too late. The fire spread along the counter.

She ran up and shot the flame with the heavy white foam. The flames died, and the counter was covered in white. The room grew silent.

"What happened?" the owner asked, his voice a high-pitched squeal.

All three other chefs and Elvis pointed at Melanie. "She did it."

"Thanks, guys."

"Look at my kitchen," he shouted. His eyes were crazed, and his bulbous nose and wobbling cheeks were bright red.

She was about to get fired. She just knew it. Her time spent there flashed through her mind, and she didn't even care. The diner was an awful place where all her dreams went to die. As soon as she saw the fire, she knew she was done anyway. Now she had a plan. She would go buy a saltshaker to give to Erik and hope that he would be willing to give her a shot. No job could be as bad as this one.

Erik

"What do you think of the yard?" Erik asked his aunt. They sat in his office after getting brunch together like they did every two weeks. Normally, Stacie didn't go to his home afterward, but today she had said she wanted to see how he was settling into his new house. He wasn't sure why she felt she needed to see the place in person again though.

"It looks beautiful. I love what the groundskeeper is doing by the pool," Stacie said. The groundskeeper, Dan, had created an arrangement of cacti and desert native plants, which looked natural against the backdrop of the mountains.

Erik nodded, and the silence grew between them. "All right, Stacie, what's going on?"

She looked at her nails and cleared her throat. "Hunter tells me you still haven't hired a chef."

"And this is a cause of concern for you? Hiring people takes some time. Besides, I hired a grounds person, a housekeeper, and a personal assistant for Hunter. That all took time." He took a deep breath, willing the oxygen to ease the tension in his neck. He needed to find a way to get his brother to stop talking about him with Stacie. He tapped a pen against a pad of paper.

"I heard the first chef who applied was quite attractive."

Erik swallowed a groan and looked down. He tugged at the black collar on his shirt. It suddenly felt tight around his neck. "I'm going to kill Hunter. Her looks are irrelevant. She wasn't professional."

"I see."

"Is this why you felt the need to come over today?"

"If you don't want her in your employ, why haven't you found another candidate?" Stacie asked. "We could have discussed this over brunch..."

"I haven't found anyone suitable yet," he said, trying to keep his temper in check.

"Ah. Well, I know how seriously you take finding a staff." She stood and walked the length of the office.

Her poignant comment was not appreciated. He had picked everyone off the top of the résumé stack. She was right to question why he hadn't picked another chef. He hadn't even looked at the résumés of anyone else who'd applied yet. Every time he opened the folder of applicants, he couldn't help but think about Melanie. She still distracted him, and she wasn't even around. It was driving him nuts. He'd had one interaction with her, which hadn't lasted an afternoon, and now he was acting like some kid with a crush.

"I see you still haven't added anything to your office." Stacie surveyed the almost empty room. Only a desk, four chairs, and a TV sat in the room.

"I'm sure I'll think of something to add," he said, forcing himself to use a cheerful voice.

Stacie shook her head. "You're too young to be so stubborn. At least think about getting some artwork. I'll see you later, Erik. I love you," she said and walked out.

"Take care, Aunt Stacie." He was still unused to hearing "I love you." Each time she said it, he was sure he couldn't mask his surprise. He sat in the quiet and wondered if he should hand the job of finding a chef over to Hunter. The kid was here so often anyway. His home was a couple neighborhoods over, but Hunter seemed to enjoy hanging around and bugging him. Which was evident by Hunter's apparent discussion with Stacie. He would have to have to talk to his brother about that.

Melanie

As Melanie pulled up to the gate in front of Erik's home, a salt shaker in the passenger seat, she started to question her sanity. She had left the diner with elaborate makeup and her odd costume still on, and she'd run to a grocery store to buy a saltshaker to ask for a job she had blown during the interview. There was no way to know if Erik would even consider hiring her. He may not have even liked the food. She swallowed panic and straightened her shoulders. If he'd tasted the food, she was sure he'd want to hire her. Despite the skintight spandex. At least she'd removed the wig. She was a good cook, darn it, her appearance shouldn't matter. She lowered the window by the older man at the gate.

"Hi, I'm Melanie Clark, I'm here to see Erik," she said, trying to keep her voice steady.

"I don't have you on the list. I can call up to the house though." He picked up the telephone in the booth.

"Actually, put the call through to Hunter," she said,

changing her mind. Hunter had been so sweet; she figured she might have a chance getting in the door if he was around to let her in. She crossed her fingers that he was there today.

"Okay, ma'am." He sat quietly with the phone held up to his white hair. He spoke with someone, and then he turned back to Melanie. "I'll open the gate for you, miss."

"Thanks." She'd gotten through the gate, that was a good first step. Trying not to hyperventilate, she closed the window. She could do this. The worst that could happen was that Erik would say no and not hire her. The idea that he might not hire her was a painful notion though. She didn't normally take job rejection to heart. Food was to taste, she knew that, but imagining Erik disliking her food was a little upsetting.

She drove up the driveway, and Hunter stood in front of the house, the large windows gleaming blue behind him. He smiled and waved. His other hand was in his jeans pocket, and his tan skin was dark against his white shirt.

Melanie turned off the car, picked up the salt, and opened the Jeep door. "I brought the salt," she said with a sheepish grin.

Hunter let out a bark of laughter. "Hopefully that'll do it."

"It's worth a shot." She got out of the car and smiled up at him. He was nearly as tall as his brother and equally broad, but far less imposing.

Hunter surveyed her outfit and let out a low whistle. "Did you just come from comic convention?"

The temptation to cross her arms was strong but she

resisted. "It's the outfit I had to wear at my last job."

"Was the clothing the reason you're here?"

"Uh-huh, sure," she said and hoped he wouldn't press her on the partial truth. The kitchen fire she'd started an hour or so before wouldn't look great.

He shook his head and motioned her to the front door. "I hope he reconsiders. Your food is great."

"Thanks." She walked into the giant foyer.

"He's down that hall, second door on the left." He pointed to the right.

She was tempted to ask him to go with her. He was such a comforting presence, but she should do this by herself. "Thanks again."

Her shoes clicked against the tile, and she walked several feet down the hallway before coming to the second door on the left. The door was shut. She bit her lip and knocked on the door, clutching the salt in her right hand.

"Come in," Erik's voice called from inside the room.

She thought about turning right back around and leaving, but she'd made it this far, hadn't she? She resisted another urge to cover as much of herself as possible and walked into the room with even steps despite her pounding heart. Before he could say anything, she beelined for his desk and slammed the salt down. "I brought you salt," she said, finally looking up at Erik's stunned face.

He leaned back in his chair and rotated his pen through his fingers. He wore a black shirt that clung to his muscular shoulders and chest, and his blond, wavy hair hung over his forehead. She was glad she'd said her salt bit before she'd looked at him because now her mouth was dry. His piercing eyes were trained on hers, and a slow smile spread across his lips.

"I appreciate the gesture, Mel—" he started, but then he stopped as he looked over her form. His mouth clicked shut. His eyes darkened as he looked her over, his gaze catching on her cleavage, and her hips, and then moved down her legs and back to her face again.

A sudden heat filled her lower abdomen. She was positive that her cheeks must've been on fire. Simultaneously, she felt vulnerable and powerful. She wasn't sure if she wanted to cover herself or reveal more skin to the hunger in his stare. At that startling thought, she tried to swallow. Lord, help her. She was in way over her head if he did hire her.

"What are you wearing?" he asked. She could feel the rough edge in his voice, and she suppressed a shiver.

Licking her lips, she realized he watched the movement. "It's my work costume at The Jivin' Diner."

"You wear this to work?" The question sounded dangerous somehow.

There was clearly only one answer he wanted to hear, and she didn't have it. She shook the cobwebs from her head. What she wore was none of his business anyway. She held her head high. "Yes, I do. I'm Elvis's back up dancer."

"That's quite a distracting chef uniform." His gaze was back on her body.

She fought the desire to squirm under his intense scrutiny. "It's not like I have much to distract people with," she said without thinking. Cringing, she wondered what it was about this man that made her say the most inappropriate things.

"You have more than enough to be distracted by."

Was there a good response to that? She wasn't sure she could speak right then even if she'd thought of a great comeback so, she didn't say a word.

Erik

Erik tore his gaze from Melanie's petite curves. He wanted to peel the spandex away inch by inch to reveal what was beneath. He had to clear his head. Control was something he always had, and she was making him lose it.

"Would you like to take a seat?" he finally asked, motioning to a chair in front of his desk.

She nodded and rushed to the chair. If he weren't having such a hard time containing his own libido, he would have chuckled at her behavior. She'd been bright red since she'd walked in, her blue eyes wide, but her face determined. He could tell she'd been fighting the impulse to cover herself the entire time she'd been standing there. His theory was confirmed when she dropped into the seat, slouched low as possible, and leaned her hands on the desk so that her body was mostly shielded by the oak. He waited for her to speak.

"I'd like another chance. I'm sorry for the way I acted before. I feel strongly about my cooking. It's something I've worked hard at all my life," she said.

He could tell the apology cost her. The muscles in her neck strained, and she looked as if she'd swallowed a lemon. She was clearly not used to apologizing or following orders for that matter. Keeping her around would certainly be amusing. "Thank you for your apology. And your cooking was outstanding. I had some after you left."

"Really?" she asked, sitting up straighter.

He felt a measure of unexpected pleasure at her obvious joy. He was used to enjoying a woman's arousal; he was used to intriguing and beautiful women. He was not used to this level of satisfaction for making a girl smile. "Yes. I didn't even need salt."

A smug look flitted over her features. He raised an eyebrow at her, and she glanced away. "Well, I got some anyway."

"So, what brought you back here?" He intended to hire her. Consequences be damned. Attraction be damned, he wanted this woman around. She was... interesting. But he was also curious about her reasons for returning.

"I realized what a good opportunity I was passing up."

"Melanie, you're wearing your work makeup and you bought a salt shaker. What happened today?"

"Stupid fake Elvis and grease are a bad combination."

He had to bite his cheeks to keep from laughing. "Excuse me?"

She rolled her eyes skyward and sighed. "I'd prefer not to get into details right now, but today at work I realized how much I couldn't pass up the opportunity here."

"Did you get fired?" he asked darkly.

"No. Of course not. I mean, they didn't get that far before I left, but—fine, Bob was hitting on me, and I got angry and splashed some grease, and there was a small,

small, teeny, tiny fire. Then Bob splashed water on it, and you never splash water on a grease fire, and it spread. There's no major damage. And I put it out. It wasn't my fault. That wasn't any kind of coherent explanation, was it?" she asked, and her lips formed half a grin. "The point is that I really want this job."

He understood little of her explanation. Fire and a guy named Bob were the only things that registered. For some reason, he was much more fixated on this Bob, and how someone had got her so riled up that a fire started. He would have to ask her about the event in more detail later. He wondered if his lack of concern about that fire was foolish. "Your food makes you a great candidate. How about I go over the duties here?"

"Sounds great."

He counted the rational reasons for picking her as the chef. She was qualified, her food was delicious, and she was willing to live onsite. He also didn't want her going near any Bob in that spandex suit again. That sort of possessiveness was going to be a problem.

4

Melanie

Melanie looked around her apartment, trying to decide what she was going to take to her new job. She didn't intend to give up her apartment right away. After such a shaky start, she didn't feel ready to sublet the place yet. If she had a sudden urge to refuse him pepper, she might be right back here. Sheila had come over to help her pack the necessities about an hour before, but so far, she hadn't proved helpful. She kept picking clothes for Melanie to wear which were completely unprofessional.

She took a break from picking her books and went to the bedroom to see how Sheila was doing with the sheets. She walked through her small, bright living room and into the bedroom dominated by a cherry wood furniture set. Sheila's dress-clad back faced the door, and her brown hair fell in waves across her shoulders. She was picking through Melanie's underwear drawer.

"What are you doing?"

"I heard your description of the man. I am hoping that you are gonna need this." Off her tan, manicured finger, she dangled a black lace thong and matching bra she had given Melanie almost a year ago for her birthday.

"I'm not going to have sex with my boss." Melanie tugged the bra out of Sheila's hands. "I'm not a one-night-stand kind of girl, and I'm not a have-sex-with-the-boss kind of girl."

"When was the last time you had sex?" Sheila took the bra back and held it over her head—an effective play since she was several inches taller than Melanie.

Melanie didn't say anything. She wouldn't give Sheila the satisfaction of answering.

"Please tell me you hooked up with someone after your break up last year."

Melanie bit her lip. It had taken time, but she'd been with the guy for six years. It took time to get past the breakup.

"I know your ex, Mr. Scaredy Cat, did a number on you, but really? No sex? What the hell do you think the lingerie set was for?"

"Your personal amusement when I opened it in front of fifteen of my friends?"

"You deserved it. You didn't even have real cake. You had carrot cake. Who does that?"

"Carrot cake is real cake."

"If there's a vegetable in it, it isn't cake. I don't know what kind of bullshit they taught you at culinary school, but trust me on this, it wasn't cake."

Melanie shook her head. "I'm not going to argue this. Will you put the lingerie away and let this go?"

"I'd love to if you were going to make the right choice yourself."

"You can't be serious. I'm not picking up a cocaine habit; I'm choosing not to sleep with my boss. He probably doesn't want to have sex with me. Anyway, who says I want to sleep with him?" Not that she didn't think about sleeping with him but fantasizing in that direction didn't make a lot of sense. She needed this job, and if something happened, she'd have to go job hunting all over again. Besides, who knew if Erik was attracted to her anyway, so it was pointless to speculate. Or dream about.

"Honey, it's all over your face when you talk about him. You won't even use his name. And you seemed nervous through the entire explanation of your job interview. And—"

"Okay, okay, enough. I get it. Give me the damn underwear, and I'll stick it in my suitcase."

"It's just a contingency plan."

"My contingency plans involve my savings account and a car. They almost never involve lingerie."

"You're missing out."

Erik

Erik sat on the couch in his living room with Hunter. The room was large, and the black recliners and couch formed a semicircle around the glass coffee table at the center. A large TV sat on the opposite wall, but Erik looked through it. His senses were hyperactive since Melanie was moving into the house today. How long would his self-control last if he had to see her morning, afternoon, and evening? Part of him was hoping her terrible singing or other habits would begin to annoy him as soon as she moved in, but he didn't think that was likely. Every time he thought about her, the only thing he felt was desire. Not that he would do anything about it. He was her boss, and she was too sweet for a man with a past like his.

But right then, before she walked through the door and he had to give her a key, he needed to focus. Summer approached, and his outdoors program for the Phoenix area foster kids was coming along slowly. The process to start a program of this magnitude was tedious.

"Did you pick a park system or facility yet?" Hunter asked. He leaned forward, bracing his elbows on his knees. The gray slacks he wore rustled from the movement.

"We found a good basic park to do a sports league and an arts camp, but I also want to organize trips to the Jefferson Park and the Desert Botanical Garden. Figuring out staff for those kinds of trips will be more difficult, but I think it'll be worth it," Erik said. There were a few programs for foster kids depending on the organization, but he wanted to bring the kids together, so they could start making connections with their peers from around the city.

Hunter looked at his hands and smiled. "Do you remember the first time we went to that Park?"

"Yeah." Erik laid one arm across the back of the couch. When they got to Phoenix, he'd been sixteen and he'd worked waiting tables. He'd felt so lucky when he got that job. They only had a couple hundred dollars saved from their time in Nevada. As soon as he got his second paycheck, and he was certain the job was stable, he took Hunter to that park.

"You let me go on that train over and over again. I thought it was the coolest thing in the world. How'd you know?" Hunter asked, chuckling.

"How did I know what?"

"That I loved trains."

Erik grinned. "You weren't a stealthy kid. I saw you sneak that miniature train car from beneath your pillow and into your pocket on a regular basis."

"Oh yeah, I carried it everywhere."

"You still got it?"

"Of course. I can remember her giving it to me, you know. Her face is so blurry now, I can barely remember the color of her eyes, but I can remember her hands. Tan and smooth, orange nail polish..." Hunter drifted off.

Erik shifted in his seat. "Are you sure you don't want me to talk to that detective? I've still got his number."

His brother's head jerked up, and his eyes hardened for a second. "No. Thanks. But no. How's that activities director you hired working out?"

In moments like these, Erik had a hard time respecting Hunter's autonomy. He'd taken care of him for so long, it still felt strange when Hunter said no. The word wasn't the odd part. It was the part where Erik had to listen. He moved on though. "She's doing great. There's a lot to organize, but she sent out insurance forms and disclaimer forms to the facilities and foster parents. And she floated the sports options to the facilities. She's going to set up the sports leagues as soon as she gets the responses."

"That sounds great."

"Are you still willing to coach some of the basketball and soccer teams?"

"Yeah, but you should stick me with the younger teams. I haven't played basketball in a long time."

Erik surveyed his athletic, sports-obsessed brother. "I'm sure you'll do fine."

"Are people showing any interest in the banquet?" They were having a fundraising banquet before the summer camp to cover some of the expenses.

"Yeah. The numbers are looking good."

The doorbell rang, and Erik's jaw tightened.

"Are you going to get that?" Hunter asked.

"The housekeeper can get it," Erik said.

Hunter laughed. "You can't avoid her forever."

He grunted but didn't respond. He was pathetic. He knew it, but that didn't change anything.

"I'm going to go say 'hello.'" Hunter stood and stretched.

A sudden desire to tell Hunter to go away gripped him, but he suppressed the urge. "All right."

Hunter shook his head and left the room. Erik told himself to focus on his laptop, to look through the plan for the summer program, but he found himself listening for sounds coming from the other room.

The door opened and shut, and then Melanie's voice rang out. "Oh, hi, Hunter."

"Hey. Do you need help?"

"Oh yeah, that would be great. I can carry most of it, but I couldn't help myself, there are two boxes of books that are too heavy for me. Oh, shoot, my mom's calling."

"You can take the call. Give me your keys, and I'll get started."

"Are you sure?"

"Of course."

"Okay, thanks." Erik could hear the jingling of car keys, and then the door opened and closed again.

"Hi, Mother, how are you?" she said.

"Yes, I'm moving right now. I'll be fine." Silence reigned for a second. "He's not a serial killer. How do I know? Because serial killers have fewer acres. No. No. Of course, I'm not taking you seriously—you just asked if my boss was a serial killer."

She got quieter, and he strained to hear her next words. "Besides if serial killers looked this good, you'd want to work for one too."

Erik grinned. He almost felt bad about eavesdropping, but he couldn't help himself. This was starting to get interesting.

"I got the listing through Sheila. They check for that sort of thing. I should what? Mother, that's so violent. Where did you learn that?" There was silence once again, but it didn't last long. "I have to go. His brother will be back in a second. Yes, I'll see you next week. Love you. Bye."

The door opened and closed again. "Wow, you're carrying both? That's impressive."

"I have to put these massive guns to use at some point," Hunter said.

Erik could hear Melanie's easy laughter down the hallway. She was warming up to his brother so damn quickly. Maybe Hunter should spend more time at his own house.

Melanie

The day after she'd arrived, Melanie stood in Erik's kitchen surveying the space. Her first day and a half was simple, and she'd barely seen her boss. He had stopped by her new room for thirty seconds while she was unpacking to tell her she should take that afternoon to settle in. She didn't need to begin cooking until the following day.

She'd been thankful for the extra time. Being in another person's home was so weird. The protocol for this kind of position still made her nervous. Hunter helped her unpack and explained Erik was casual about his staff. They didn't have to walk around unseen or stay silent around other guests; they just needed to attend to their duties. Which was great because she wasn't great at being unseen or quiet.

So far, her first day on the job had been successful. She'd met the other staff, including Mary, an older woman who was the housekeeper. She offered to answer any questions Melanie might have and to help her settle in. Erik wanted breakfast at eight, so she was up early cooking. She'd barely said a word to him though—he ate while he was on a conference call.

Lunch was simple. Hunter and Erik requested sandwiches. After, she realized she needed to rearrange the kitchen. She was short, and the cabinets went up too high on the walls. The step stool she'd been given did nothing to help. She stood, hands in her jean pockets, trying to decide where to start and how to reorganize.

Cabinets lined the walls above every counter. Nothing was stored above the stove, microwave, or dishwasher thankfully. She didn't want to deal with spices that had gone bad. A pantry by one of the counters was filled to the ceiling. The only thing that didn't have to be rearranged was the refrigerator. She opened all the cabinets and the pantry, looking around. The highest shelves were way out of her reach. She decided to deal with those first.

Peeking around and listening to make sure no one was nearby, she shut the door to the kitchen and walked to the counter across from the sink. After bracing her hands on top of the granite, she swung her knees up. She clamored awkwardly onto the counter and decided a jogger should be more graceful than this. Up on her knees, she held onto the open cabinet with her left hand and lifted out pasta boxes one at a time with her right hand. Looking at the length of the counter, she realized this was going to take a while. She settled in and started to sing.

After about ten minutes, she'd got through only two cabinets and two Queen songs. Her knees started aching. She grabbed a washcloth to put underneath them and started again. She'd got two feet closer to the pantry and she'd found the breakfast oat selection. There were so many breakfast oats. Who on Earth had shopped for this man? It was like looking through an eighty-year-old woman's kitchen.

She sang "We Are The Champions" while pushing the oatmeal and grits to the side of the counter. Out of the corner of her eye, she saw something moving and whipped her head around.

"Eeep," she squealed when she saw Erik leaning against the counter by the sink. His muscular arms were crossed over his chest, and he stared at her, a hint of a smile on his lips. He wore a white T-shirt and jeans that clung to his thighs.

"Hello," he said, his voice husky.

Melanie face heated, and she wondered how wide her eyes must've been. She took a deep breath to slow her pounding heart. "How long have you been here?" she asked, her voice hushed.

He shrugged a shoulder. "A while."

"A while?"

"Yes."

The heat in her cheeks spread down her throat. "And were you ever going to tell me that you were standing there?"

"I intended to, at first. But I figured I should watch you in case you slipped."

Her eyebrows rose. His lips were straight, but he still might be making fun of her. Annoyance shot through her. "In case I slipped? So, you would've done a Superman and flown across the room if I'd fallen?"

His dark eyes narrowed. "I could stand closer and watch you if you'd like." He sauntered toward her.

Melanie's heart pounded again, and this time not from shock or fear. She could feel his presence as he approached; there was something feral in his walk. He stopped when he was less than a foot from her. Even on her knees on the counter, she was only a couple inches taller than him. His gaze locked onto hers. She couldn't look away if she'd wanted to.

"If I stood here, I could catch you," he said.

She licked her lips and his gaze dropped to watch her mouth. Hot awareness of him sizzled through her. She had a sudden urge to tug him closer. She gave herself a mental headshake. "It's rude to watch someone without them knowing," she said, her throat tight.

"I know."

Erik

Erik shouldn't be provoking her. He knew he should take a step back. She was innocent, there was no coyness or practiced flirtation in her behavior. Her big, blue eyes were open with longing, and her cheeks were red. He couldn't stop. He was attracted to this woman, and he wanted to keep her on her toes and watch her react to him. He wanted her so bad he ached. Finally, he took control of his impulses and took a step back. He almost groaned aloud at the disappointment he saw on her face when he did so.

"How about I help?" he asked, his tone lighter.

Her pink tongue darted out and wet her lips again. He caught himself before moving closer. She needed to stop doing that for both their sakes. "So, what do you say?"

"Is that your way of apologizing?" She crossed her arms over her chest, emphasizing her cleavage.

He cocked his head. "No."

She rolled her eyes.

"So, what are you trying to move around in here?" he asked.

Melanie looked skyward. "I can't reach the stuff on

the top shelf."

She looked so embarrassed that he forced his face blank. It wasn't easy, but he thought he managed. "Why don't you get down, and I'll pull everything out for you."

"I'd like to keep working on the cabinets. Maybe you could get the stuff off the top shelf from the pantry?"

"I can do that." He needed a way to distract himself from her presence. She still looked kissable, her lips plump, and her eyes drew him to her. He needed something else to focus on. "While I'm doing that, I want the full story of why you left your last job."

She sighed as he walked toward the pantry. "Fine. But first I should explain fake Elvis."

"I think a fake Elvis is pretty self-explanatory."

"You'd think so, but this guy wants even his co-workers to call him Elvis. And he leaves his wig everywhere."

Erik stopped walking mid-step to the pantry. "Why does he leave his wig everywhere? Doesn't he keep it on?"

Melanie started to giggle. Surprising warmth spread through his chest as he heard the noise. Not good. Distance. He needed distance. Once at the pantry, he started taking things down from the top two shelves.

"He tries. But it doesn't stay on. His head must be shaped weird or something. It slips off, even when he's performing. He catches it sometimes, but mostly it just falls to the ground. And since he's not paying attention, he doesn't pick it up."

Erik shook his head. He was curious about what happened to the wig. "What happens to it?"

"Well, none of the rest of the crew wants to touch it."

He could hear the shudder in her voice from across the room.

“I don’t blame you.”

“So, Matt, the guy who sweeps the floor—he’s a funny guy, still in high school and so energetic—well he sweeps up the wig and hides it around the restaurant. It annoys the heck out of fake Elvis and the boss.”

“They don’t know who does it?” Erik asked.

“Nope. Are you kidding? None of the rest of us would tell. It’s too funny.”

“So, did you wear a wig too?” Erik tried to imagine her with a different hair color but couldn’t. Her black hair framed her face too prettily to be anything else.

He heard her sharp inhale as he got to the soup stocks. “Yep. A stupid blonde one. It occasionally met with an accident, and then I’d go a week or two without one while I waited for another to arrive.”

He imagined her destroying a blonde wig and wondered what kind of accidents she was talking about. “Grease fire accidents?” Maybe the fire hadn’t been a one-time deal. Maybe he should only request grilled foods.

“Oh, no,” she said, sounding surprised, “I mean the wig just gets run over or dropped in the dumpster.”

“I don’t suppose there are Jeep tire prints on the wigs.” He placed the flour and salt on the island in the kitchen.

She had her hands on her hips and was grinning. “Erik, your insinuation is insulting.”

“Uh-huh.”

“Besides, my clumsy friend runs it over with her Toyota. It’s not my fault. Thank goodness for Sheila.”

He had no idea how she could go off on so many tangents when trying to tell one story. Wondering if she still remembered she was supposed to be telling him the story about the fire, he leaned against the island and waited to prompt her.

"So, back to the fire," she said.

He nodded and walked back to the pantry.

"Fake Elvis thinks he's very suave. He also seems to think he's twenty-five years younger than he is because he hits on...a few of us...a lot."

He looked around the door and noticed she looked disgruntled. She was bad at even telling even half-truths. It was almost sad. "You're the only one he hits on."

Ducking her head, she nodded. "Yep. Well, that I know of. He's very sleazy. I'm sure he hits on a lot of people while he's not at work. Anyway, I got sick of it. I was having a frustrating day, and he came back to the kitchen, which was my greasy little haven, and starts hitting on me. I couldn't handle it. I wasn't paying attention, and I dropped the tray of fries I had in my hand and grease splattered on a nearby paper towel. It caught fire. It was very small..."

"That doesn't sound too bad."

"At first. Then bright Elvis decided to pour water on it."

Erik cringed. That was a dumb thing for someone in the restaurant business to do.

"The fire got a little bigger." She paused in the middle of taking down cereal boxes. The box she held had a picture of a cartoon child playing with fish on the front. "Seriously? You eat this?"

"It's Hunter's. What happened with the fire?"

"I grabbed the extinguisher and put the fire out." She shrugged and pointed to the accumulated pile of cereal boxes on the counter. "All of these can't be for Hunter. He doesn't even live here."

"You're going to tell me you don't ever eat cereal?" Erik stepped out of the pantry. The top two shelves were empty. He'd put some foods on the lower shelves and the rest were strewn on the island.

"I'm an adult," she said, smirking.

He looked her over, his gaze catching on her curves, and when he looked up he was satisfied that she was blushing again. "I'm aware."

"I'm also a chef." She scowled.

He shrugged. "So, you put the fire out and they still fired you?"

She shook her head so fast that her bob whipped around her face. "They didn't fire me."

"Then why did you come back? It couldn't have been easy for you. You were adamant about the salt before."

Distracted from clearing off the shelves, she repositioned her legs. They dangled over the edge of the counter. "Their main ingredient is grease. And did you see the outfit?"

"Yes, I saw the uniform. You came over wearing it."

"Oh, right. The comical humiliation continues."

That was not a word that came to mind when he thought about the outfit. Remembering how the spandex wrapped around her body evoked a completely unfunny response. He felt a sudden need to assuage her concerns. He walked toward her. "There was nothing comical about what you were wearing."

He stood right in front of the counter she sat on. She

looked at him, her black eyelashes fluttering, her mouth barely open. She was beautiful. "There wasn't?"

He shook his head and bent over her, bracing his hands on the counter around her. She leaned back, and her pulse fluttered in her neck. He thought about doing the right thing and backing off, but then she tilted her head up at him defiantly.

"What did you think about what I was wearing?"

5

Melanie

Melanie couldn't believe she'd asked him what he thought of her old uniform. Such a question was an inappropriate thing to ask her boss of all people, and she was not that kind of forward anyway. But the way he was looking at her...she had to know. She bit her lip and waited, trying not to shy away. His dark eyes were trained on hers, and the intensity of his gaze shot electricity through her body.

He inclined his head. She could feel his hot breath against her neck. Tingling started just below her ear and spiraled outward. "Sexy. The outfit was damn hot."

"Sexy?" she asked, her voice breathy.

He leaned back, a small grin pulling at his lips. "This surprises you? You were wearing spandex so tight it looked painted on."

"Oh, yeah, I mean I know how tight it is, I'm the one wearing it after all. I just meant that...I was surprised you found it sexy," she said without thinking. Well, no coming back from her honesty now. The idea that a man as arousing as Erik found her attractive was too heady a concept.

"Why?" he asked, his voice commanding.

She was so immediately persuaded to tell him, she wondered where her self-control was. "You're practically cut from stone. Even with the T-shirt on. I know I get by. I run, and I can't complain. But...I can only imagine how chiseled you are without the clothing."

He raised his eyebrow as soon as she said it. Once again, she'd realized what she said only after she'd said it. She was sure her face must be in flames. "Not that...I didn't mean...oh God. Not that I spend my time imagining you without clothing on. I always imagine you with some clothes on. All! All clothing. I'm going to try to melt off the counter now."

She squeezed her eyes shut, hoping one of them would disappear, but then she heard a low chuckle coming from the man in front of her. Her eyes snapped open. Her embarrassment sizzled out at the chuckle. Not only was it rude to laugh, but did his chuckle also have to be sexy as heck? It wasn't fair. She glowered and fisted her hands on the counter. "You think this is funny?"

"It's a little amusing." His eyes narrowed.

She would not be intimidated. She would hold her ground. "Uh-huh."

"If you want to think about me while you're not wearing clothes, that's fine with me," he said, his voice husky.

Melanie clapped a hand over her mouth, and she leaned back. "That is not what I meant. I meant that you had only some clothing on, not that I imagined you while I'm naked."

Erik inhaled, his nostrils flaring. "You're making things difficult, Melanie. You're attracted to me."

She blinked at him, uncertain what to say. Was it obvious? She wasn't sure if she wanted a way out of this conversation, or a way to get in deeper. But oh boy, did she love the way he said her name. "Um," was the only thing she could get out. Her tongue wasn't working well.

"I'm going to kiss you until you forget where you are unless you tell me to stop now."

Her breathing caught in her chest. There wasn't anything she wanted more than for him to kiss her right then. She licked her lips, and he groaned. His eyes were molten dark chocolate, and his jaw was clenched.

"Consequences be damned." He stepped in between her dangling legs and grabbed her waist with his right hand and her nape with the other, and then hauled her to him. She shuddered as she felt the hard planes of his stomach and chest through his shirt. He tilted his head over her so that his face was an inch from hers and stopped, watching her.

She wanted him to bridge the space between their lips, and for the moment, she didn't give a flying fig that her body strained to get even closer to his. Finally, he bent over her, his lips capturing hers. Heat spread through her in a surge, and she clutched his shoulders. She was sure her nails bit into his shoulder muscles, but she didn't care.

He nipped her bottom lip and her mouth fell open on a moan. His tongue swept between her lips, tangling with hers, robbing her of conscious thought. His hands slid down her arms until they encircled her waist underneath her shirt. He held her tighter against him, and she could feel the wonderful pressure of his hardness against the apex of her thighs. She tore her mouth away, gasping, and he kissed along the underside of her jaw and his teeth grazed her chin.

She moaned, and then he kissed his way down to her collarbone. She writhed against him, her body searching for some kind of relief against his, but there were too many clothes between them. She dragged her hand down his muscular chest, humming in appreciation as her fingers ran along the contours of his abs. Her hands found his belt, and she tugged at the buckle without giving it any thought.

Erik stilled at the action. His lips stopped moving and he caught her nimble fingers with his hands. She heard his ragged breathing against her neck. He leaned back and looked into her eyes, his gaze was so hot she thought the look could burn through metal. "As much as I want to fuck you right here on the counter, I'm not sure it's the best idea."

Melanie blinked a few times trying to take in her surroundings. She looked down at her hands on his belt, and embarrassment flooded through her. She had been about to take off his pants. She didn't disrobe men in kitchens. Although, if she were being honest with herself, she wouldn't have minded trying right about then. She cleared her throat and looked away, chagrined by the utter wantonness of her actions. He was her boss for goodness sake. Sure, he kissed her, but he hadn't tried to remove her pants.

Erik

A series of emotions flitted over Melanie's face. Arousal was evident in her unfocused eyes and her flushed skin, but embarrassment followed in her pressed lips. Erik frowned. Embarrassment was the last thing he wanted to cause. He was thrilled at her responsiveness. More than anything, he wanted to let her take his pants off. It had taken all of his willpower not to strip her down and take her there in the kitchen. He was her employer, and he couldn't take advantage of her like that.

He took a deep breath and stepped back. His arousal was still obvious, and Melanie was certainly fascinated by that. She followed him with her gaze, staring at his erection. If resisting her weren't so hard, he would have been amused, but as it was, she was making things exponentially more difficult. "You're going to have to stop staring."

Her wide eyes peeked up to meet his, and then she averted her gaze, her face bright red. He shook his head in disbelief. Not two minutes ago she tried to unbuckle his belt, and now he caught her looking, she was blushing again. She was such an intriguing mix of seductive and sweet.

Closing his eyes, he pulled himself together. This couldn't happen again. Kissing her like that wasn't fair to her. She probably wanted things like relationships and love, and he wasn't in a place where he could give her either. He wasn't sure he ever would be. He opened his eyes and she straightened her clothes. "We can't do this again."

She held her arms over her waist. "I didn't start this. You kissed me."

"I know and I'm sorry I did. Now I'm saying it won't happen again."

A look of hurt passed over her eyes, but then it was gone, and he thought he'd imagined it. "Oh, okay, I get it."

Unsure about what there was to 'get' he nodded. "All right, good."

She looked at the ground and turned away from him. "I have to go freshen up," she said and rushed from the kitchen.

He ran a hand through his hair. How he was going to deal with the temptation of her every day in his home, he sure as hell didn't know.

Melanie

As soon as Melanie got to her room, tears welled up behind her eyes. She was so embarrassed, she wished she could quit the job right then and there. There she was getting all hot and heavy and offering herself to him, and he regretted kissing her. She couldn't believe she'd thought he'd been into it. Humiliating as that was, she couldn't give up the job. It paid too well and offered her more happiness—at least, before two minutes ago it had—than her last job. She would just have to suck it up and act professional and aloof. For the next fifteen minutes though, she would allow herself time to feel disappointed at his reaction. She was human after all. She would wallow and then throw herself back into her cooking and jogging, and she'd feel better in no time.

But before any of that, she deserved some sympathy. She slid her phone from her pocket and speed-dialed Sheila.

"Hey, Mel. Hold on a second," Sheila said when she answered, but her muffled voice continued. "No, they didn't fire you from the internship because they have a thing against white people, they kicked you out because they caught you on video touching the paintings. Now if you'll excuse me, I have to take care of this phone call. Sure, an apology would help. Not to me. To the museum. Okay, bye."

Melanie smiled despite her embarrassment and frustration. She could always count on Sheila's work interactions to make her laugh. There were people who had it even less together than she did. It may have been selfish, but it was a relief.

"Sorry about that," Sheila said.

"No problem." Melanie lay back on her bed.

"How's the job going?"

Melanie wasn't sure how to handle the conversation or figure out where to start. She wasn't even sure why she was so upset over one kiss. "It's fine."

"You can't even lie over a phone. It's sad. What happened?"

She rubbed a hand over her face. "Erik and I kissed."

"Oh no, and it was bad? Is he a slobberer? Too big of a tongue?"

"No. It's just, I think he was disappointed by it." She

heard the strain in her own voice, and she was disgusted with herself. She wanted to chuck her phone across the room. It was just a dumb kiss.

"Are you sure?"

"He made it very clear he didn't want it to happen again."

"What a jackass. Don't let it get to you. It sounds like he's a jerk."

"Okay, but I'm going to go ahead and ask you a dumb question now. Because, you know, it has been a while for me." And if she was being honest, her ex and she didn't get it on all that often. She decided to leave that part out. "Is it possible I did something wrong? Is there, like, a thing that guys don't like that I could've done?"

"Did you kick him in the balls?"

"What? No. Of course not."

"Then no. I'm not saying all guys are like cars, but moan and show some cleavage, and you've pretty much turned on the ignition."

"Okay, I do not believe that. Also, where the heck do you get your metaphors?"

"I might be exaggerating a little. And a student left a car magazine behind. I got bored between meetings with students because they've restricted our internet access for a while. Some tool was looking at porn."

"Eww."

"No kidding." They sat in silence for a minute before Sheila spoke again. "Are you going to stay there?"

"Yeah. I don't want to give up on this job so soon. But will you let me know if you find something else? Just in case."

"Of course."

"By the way, I have to go to dinner at my parents' house this Friday. Want to go?"

"I haven't seen Mr. and Mrs. Clark in forever. Sure."

"You saw them last month."

"Whatever. It was great. I love your parents. It's like they're from a different era."

"They are from a different era," Melanie said.

"You know what I mean. They're pretty old."

She knew exactly what Sheila meant. Her parents were at least ten years older than all her friends' parents. They'd had Melanie later in life. Her father was retired, and her mother was on a different plane from the rest of humanity in general. Melanie always invited Sheila as a buffer. Her mother tended to be less offensive when others were around.

6

Melanie

The few days following Melanie's interlude with Erik in the kitchen were awful. She couldn't sleep because she kept thinking about the darn kiss, and at random times throughout the day, she would imagine him naked. For the first time since she'd been sixteen, she burned chicken. Dinner was late. The only consolation was that Erik was avoiding her. He'd gone to great lengths to do so. She would prepare food at the time he'd requested, and then he would have to run to a meeting or deal with a conference call when she was serving it. He would tell the housekeeper, Mary, to tell Melanie to leave the food out, and he would come by and grab some later. If she hadn't been so hurt, his avoidance would've been funny. As it was, she was still confused. The best kiss of her life had appalled Erik.

She'd taken to getting up an hour and a half before she started breakfast to go for prolonged runs, trying to work out her aggravation. At least the neighborhood he lived in was gorgeous. Even when she ran along the road, the view of the city to one side and the desert to the other, was remarkable, more so at sunrise. She'd even done some trail running. She didn't have the right shoes for it but jumping over rocks and dodging branches was exhilarating.

The cold showers she took after her jogs helped calm her as well. She was sure the feelings would go away soon. She just had to get past them, and then she could enjoy her job more. The kitchen was now organized to her satisfaction, and the staff was nice. Mary was older but sweet, and she was always excited to see what Melanie was cooking. Hunter was kind when he visited. For a rich sophisticate, he was friendly with staff and wasn't a snob. Not that he was particularly sophisticated. He was down to earth and funny.

Despite how well everything else was going, she was relieved when Friday rolled around, and she had the day off. She needed a day away from Erik's home. Even when he wasn't in the same room, she could feel his presence. A slow, calm dinner with her parents would be a much-needed reprieve.

She spent her day shopping with Sheila, and then they drove to Melanie's parents' house a little after five. Her parents lived in Glendale near the country club where her father golfed—west of central Phoenix—so it took some time getting there from Scottsdale, which was much farther north. Normally, the drive was under thirty-five minutes, but Sheila rode her brakes.

They arrived at her family's place a few minutes before six. The large, eggshell-colored house was set back from the road. An open yard with desert landscaping and a flagstone pathway met the sidewalk that connected neighboring houses. The neighborhood looked rather boring, but her parents liked how calm the community was. She enjoyed the quiet area as a child, but once she'd gone to culinary school, she'd been excited to be closer to the city center.

Sheila parked behind her dad's beige car along the road, and they walked up a sidewalk to the two-story house. Melanie's knock was met with her mother's yells through the door. She wasn't sure how her mother's voice could get so loud. The house was large. "Howard? I'm stirring, Howard. Can you get that?" Melanie cringed, wishing she'd remembered her key.

Her father answered the door wearing khaki shorts and a striped polo. He peered at her through low-hung glasses perched low on his small nose. "How are you, honey?" he asked, hugging her.

"I'm good, Dad."

"Come on in. Hi, Sheila, how are you?" he asked and stepped inside.

"I'm great, Mr. Clark."

They walked through the foyer, where Melanie avoided looking at awkward teenage photos of herself, and into the living room where her dad's big screen TV was lit up. The news was on, and the weatherman's voice boomed from the speakers. Her dad grabbed the controller off the large leather sofa, and turned off the TV.

"Your mother is still cooking. Food should be done in a couple minutes." Howard guided them to the dining room.

A chandelier hung in the middle of the dining room above the center of a large, rectangular wood table. The table was set with rose-patterned fine china plates, which rested on lace placemats, and her mother's best silverware had been put out. Steaming sides of potatoes and various vegetables were set out as well. As always, Melanie felt underdressed in her sundress. She disliked dresses but wore them when she visited her parents' house. Out of habit, she looked to Sheila to make sure she was all right. Her friend had been coming over since they were in middle school, but Melanie couldn't help it. Other people always seemed a little uncomfortable in her parents' home.

"Mother, do you need any help?" she asked through the kitchen door.

"I'm fine, dear. You can serve the wine and have a seat."

Melanie picked up the wine from where it was being chilled near the middle of the table and filled four glasses. Her father sat at one end, and she sat next to him. Sheila chose the seat next to Melanie.

"How do you like your new job?" Howard asked.

"It's great."

"What does your employer do?"

"He has a company that makes apps." She waited for her father's age to show.

"Apps?"

There it was. "Applications for phones."

Her mother, Diane, walked in, wearing a floral-patterned dress. She carried a platter of chicken to the table, and then tucked a loose strand of her dyed red hair into her bun.

"Are we talking about the new employer? What does he do?" Diane asked.

"She just said. He makes phones," Howard said.

Melanie looked over at Sheila and shook her head. Sheila turned her head away as she smiled and brushed her brown hair in front of her face.

"He doesn't make phones, Dad. He's an app developer."

"Uh-huh. So, that makes good money?" He picked up the platter of chicken.

"Apparently. He has a full staff," Melanie said.

"Howard, we haven't said grace yet. Put that down," Diane said.

Melanie didn't consider herself a religious person. She was still figuring out her livelihood, so it might take longer to figure out her spirituality. At that moment, she just wanted to eat. She leaned back to get comfortable. Her mother's grace took some time.

"Dear Lord, thank you for this food. It's so bountiful and fresh, and we are fortunate for the nutrition we are about to receive. Bless Howard who is sitting across from me. That he may remain in good health despite the fact that he's getting old. Bless Sheila, Melanie's oldest, and possibly only, friend. Sheila, dear, what are we praying about for you today?"

"Good health would be great."

"Bless Sheila with good health," Diane said.

Sheila winked at Melanie and mouthed "A sexy boy toy" through full, glossed lips. Diane's blue eyes were always closed during grace, but Melanie checked before turning back to her friend. Melanie mouthed "Sorry" back. Not that her friend wasn't used to it but being put on the spot was annoying.

"And bless our daughter. We are lucky when she comes to see us, even if the visits are rare. We hope this job is better than the last, that the uniform affords her some dignity. Lord help her to never wear spandex again. It is the devil's choice of material."

Sheila put a fist to her mouth to stop from laughing.

Yeah, this would be a calming dinner. That was realistic. Although with any luck, she might get Erik out of her head for a couple of hours.

"Amen. Now, tell us about your job, dear," Diane said, serving herself Brussels sprouts.

Or maybe not.

Erik

Erik and Hunter sat in Cafe Cardinal, waiting for Jennifer, the activities director for the summer, to join them. Upon looking around the establishment, Erik couldn't figure out why his brother chose the spot. The restaurant looked too romantic for a business meeting. At 7:30 p.m. on a Friday night, the intimate dining room, with wood paneling on the lower half of the walls and butterflies in frames on the upper half, was filled with young couples holding hands across the table. The outdoor seating area, which could be seen through the window they were seated next too, looked even more romantic with its soft candle and sconce lighting, and an array of greenery surrounding the tables.

Despite the oddity in restaurant choice, he was relieved to get out of the house. Avoiding Melanie was taking all his self-control. Her lips were always on his mind. He wanted to watch her melt in his arms again, but it wouldn't be right. He couldn't believe a kiss affected him this much. Disgusted that he felt like a horny teenager, he took a sip of the wine Hunter had ordered. Erik slept with women all the time. Why this one would affect him so much more than any other was beyond him. The romantic nature of the restaurant was not making him feel any better.

"Why did you pick this—Oh, of course," Erik said, raising an eyebrow at the back of Hunter's head. His brother was watching a voluptuous waitress with silky blonde hair and a short skirt walk by. The woman smiled and batted her thick, black eyelashes. Hunter's head turned as the woman walked by, and he winked.

"I'm sorry, Erik, did you say something?" Hunter turned back to the table.

"You do realize we're here on business, right?"

"I'll be taking her home when her shift is over."

"You know her?"

"Not exactly. I brought a girl here on a date two weeks ago and saw that waitress," Hunter said, tipping back in his chair.

"You think she's going home with you after that?"

"Yes." He looked past Erik and grinned.

"She's standing behind me, isn't she?"

"Yes."

"You know, maybe you shouldn't screw where you eat."

"You're one to talk."

"What are you referring to?"

"That hot, little chef you got yourself. I see the way she looks at you, and I see the way you look at her when she's not looking. It's like she's a candy bar, and you're a kid at fat camp."

"We talked about the metaphors."

Hunter shrugged and took a sip of wine. "I also heard her moaning in the kitchen a few days ago. For everyone's sake, I can only hope you were the other person in there with her. Unless you think she was alone? God, that would be hot."

Erik clenched his jaw until his teeth hurt. For the first time since he was eighteen, he wanted to punch his brother. "You're treading a fine line, brother."

One corner of Hunter's mouth tipped up. "I knew you liked her. This is fun. I've never seen you get upset over a girl like this."

Erik opened his mouth to call Hunter an idiot, but he caught sight of Jennifer. She stood near the entrance wearing a black pantsuit and low beige heels. Her blonde hair was in a tight ponytail, sharpening her delicate features. She wore large glasses over her hazel eyes. He waved to her, and she smiled and walked over.

Both brothers stood as she approached. "Jennifer, good to see you again." Erik shook her hand and turned to Hunter. "This is my brother, Hunter. He'll be coaching some of the sports teams."

They shook hands, but Hunter maintained eye contact briefly before looking over her shoulder. "It's nice to meet you, Jennifer."

Jennifer's forehead wrinkled in confusion, and she

looked behind her. After a second, she turned back to Hunter and spoke. "Nice to meet you too." She sat between the two men.

"I appreciate you meeting us on a Friday night. I've had a busy day. We're dealing with a logo concept, and we're trying to get it done quickly," Erik said.

As the voluptuous waitress with a nametag that read Tina approached, carrying water, Jennifer nodded. "It's no trouble. I was just—"

Hunter cut her off as Tina picked up his water glass. "Yeah, the logo app has been tough, but it should make a fair amount of money." He cocked his head, smiling at Tina.

Jennifer cut her gaze to him and watched as he stared at the other woman. Erik cleared his throat. He couldn't believe how rude his brother was being. The guy got laid on almost a nightly basis. Did he need to do this during a business meeting?

"That's excellent to hear. I'm sure you could use some money to pay for your ginko," Jennifer said.

Tina jerked up and stared at Jennifer. Hunter turned to blink at Jennifer. "I'm sorry?"

"Well, I mean, you probably need a supplement to deal with your little focus issue. I'm sure it will help you in other business meetings. Like this one." She shoved her glasses up the bridge of her nose with her forefinger.

Erik put a hand to his face to cover his grin. Tina turned on her heel and walked away. Hunter's face tightened. "Or at least it will help me in business meetings with people who matter."

Hurt flashed through Jennifer's eyes, but a forced smile crossed her lips. "Yes, I suppose working at a residential treatment center for foster kids doesn't make me someone who matters."

Red slashed across Hunter's cheekbones, but he remained silent. Erik glared at his brother, and then looked at Jennifer. "You know I, of all people, don't believe that. I wouldn't have contacted you if I did."

Jennifer nodded. "Yes, on to the children then. They're who matter in this discussion."

"Of course," Erik said. He looked across the table and was surprised to see his brother, who was normally so charming, scowling at his plate. Well, he deserved to be upset after the things he'd said. Erik hoped it wouldn't lead to an uncomfortable meeting though. They had a lot of work to cover. Especially with the fundraising banquet coming up so soon.

Melanie

Late Sunday morning, Melanie stood in Erik's kitchen, grilling pancakes on a portable griddle. She loved watching the bubbles sprout up through the thick batter, but this morning she couldn't wait. She was impatient to finish cooking. This morning was the first in days that she knew Erik was sitting in the dining room because Hunter was there with him. As soon as she'd realized this, she'd run to her bathroom to put on lipstick, mascara, and a bra that made her breasts look perkier than usual. It was pathetic, but she wanted him to eat his heart out. At the very least, she didn't want to look like a hag after he rejected her. She had her pride. Most of the time.

She tapped her low-heeled, black boot and slowed her flipping impulse by counting to ten. Staring at the unmoving batter puddles, she willed them to bubble. Finally, air pockets rose, and she flicked the cakes over. After she had two-dozen pancakes on a platter, she carried them out to the dining room where there were plates of bacon, sausage, Canadian bacon, scrambled eggs, fresh fruit, and a bowl of cheesy grits on the table. She may have gone a little overboard.

She walked into the dining room to find Erik and Hunter glaring at one another.

"That's why you've been acting pompous? Because you think I was rude at dinner?" Hunter asked, rubbing his stubble.

"It was important. Your behavior was embarrassing." Erik turned to Melanie as she approached. "This looks delicious," he said, his voice softening.

Shocked, she had to tell herself to smile. He hadn't talked to her in days. "Thanks."

"I apologized," Hunter said.

"To me. Not to her. I think you hurt her feelings," Erik said.

"She basically said I have the attention span of a goldfish, and you think I should apologize?"

"Yes."

Melanie placed the pancakes on the table and then walked back to the kitchen to get fresh coffee for their mugs. What would lead Erik to be more concerned about politeness than Hunter? Maybe business?

She walked to the coffee pot and poured its contents into a white carafe. Before she could turn around, she heard the door to the kitchen open. A part of her she rather hated hoped that the person walking in was Erik.

"Hey, Mel," Hunter said.

"Hey," she said, turning around.

"How are you?"

"I'm fine." She opened the fridge to get the cream.

"You look a little tired, is my brother working you too hard?"

"That would be impossible since your brother doesn't see me enough to assign tasks," Melanie said and rolled her eyes. She looked at Hunter, and then froze, realizing what she'd said was probably unprofessional. "I'm sorry, I overstepped. I didn't—"

Hunter shook his head. "It's fine. You didn't overstep. I prefer you be real. I'm not used to the whole having a staff thing. It makes me a lot more comfortable."

"Oh, good, phew," she said, grinning.

"So, Erik has been avoiding you?"

Melanie shrugged and took the cream out of the fridge.

"I have a favor to ask you," Hunter said.

She poured cream into the saucer she set beside the counter. "What's the favor?"

"Will you teach me how to cook something date-worthy?" He leaned against the counter.

"Hunter, are you trying to impress a girl?" She grinned at the thought of this muscular man wearing an apron and cooking up something in the kitchen. Whatever girl would be thrilled.

"As a matter of fact, I am," he said, rubbing the back of his neck.

Melanie ducked into the pantry to find sugar. After rooting around for a few seconds, she walked back out.

"So, what are you thinking? An entrée? Something known for being an aphrodisiac? Or are you looking for the works? Ooh, or maybe some smooth, silky, chocolaty dessert."

He laughed and held his hands up in surrender. "I haven't given it much thought. You'll have to help me pick."

"I can do that." She put the saucer, sugar dish, and coffee on a silver tray. "When are you thinking?"

"I know it's short notice, but I was thinking in the next couple days."

"That would be a quick impression."

"Is it doable?"

"I don't have time off coming up, but as long as your brother doesn't care, you could shadow me. I don't mind having company in the kitchen. The last time I taught someone anything about cooking was two years ago. I taught my friend, Gary, how to make a lamb chop. That's how he landed his husband."

"Impressive. Although, maybe we should tone it down a bit. I'm not looking for a spouse."

"No kidding. You just have to promise one thing."

"What's that?"

"You can't use the power of my cooking for evil," she said, lifting the tray.

"What evil?"

"Oh, come on. It's obvious you're a lady's man. No hurting unsuspecting women."

"I think I'm flattered and insulted at the same time."

"Good, then your head won't get any bigger."

Melanie walked to the door, but Hunter got there first, holding it open. "Thanks." She headed to the dining room table, where Erik was filling his plate with more bacon. It was silly, but she was thrilled he was eating seconds of her food.

Erik looked at her and smiled. “Thanks again. Everything tastes great.”

Her cheeks burned, and she wanted to groan. Compliments on her cooking were not hard to come by, but there she was acting like a silly kid. “You’re welcome.” She set the tray on the table, and then rushed from the room to begin cleanup, hoping he hadn’t noticed her blush.

Erik

“You and Melanie were chatting for quite some time,” Erik said, pouring more coffee.

Hunter glanced at his brother and grabbed a strip of bacon. “You know what I find interesting? She blushed when you thanked her.”

Erik smoothed the napkin on his lap. He’d noticed her blush all right. He loved watching her get flustered, knowing he got under her skin. It was sad the way he couldn’t help himself. He had done so well staying away from her for a few days, but he’d gotten sick of it. He wanted to be around her again, and what he got for his weakness was a fresh batch of temptation. Erik took a drink of coffee.

“You know she called me a ‘lady’s man,’” Hunter said, taking a bite of the bacon.

Erik choked on his coffee. “A what?”

“This bacon is so good. A lady’s man. But no blushes.

No sputtering. No cute, breathy voice she uses when she talks to you. Yet, she tells me you're avoiding her."

Hunter's words tested Erik's self-control, but he kept his expression blank. The idea he was the only one that caused those reactions in her made it difficult not to go into the kitchen and...talk to her. He wouldn't do anything about his attraction though. He was trying to be honorable, and it made him want to break things. "Yes, I am."

"Why?"

"Because I'm trying to do what's right for her."

"Yeah, sure. Makes sense. So, I'll be shadowing her in the next couple of days." Hunter poured himself more coffee.

"What? Why?"

"Because I want to cook for a girl."

"Is winking not working for you anymore?"

"I just want to diversify my talents."

He wanted to tell Hunter no. The idea of another guy, even his own brother, spending time with Melanie made something possessive in him stir with outrage. "It'll distract her from her duties."

"Is this about salt again?"

Erik glared at his brother. "Maybe she doesn't want to."

"She said she'd be happy to."

"Maybe she feels coerced."

"Ask her."

"Fine," Erik muttered, feeling harassed. "Melanie," he called out.

She rushed out, her blue eyes filled with concern. "Is everything all right with the food?"

"Oh, it's not about the food. The food is still amazing," he said. He was satisfied to see her cheeks flush again.

"What can I do for you?" she asked, her voice breathy.

God, the things he wanted to answer that question with. He cleared his throat. "I was explaining to Hunter that it wasn't fair of him to ask you a favor since you probably felt you had to agree, or your job would be at risk."

Melanie shook her head, her silky, black hair whipping back and forth. "Oh, no, I don't mind at all. I didn't feel like I had to say yes, I wanted to. I love teaching people how to cook. I told Hunter about that, too."

Erik gritted his teeth but stretched his lips into a convincing smile. "I see. Well, I guess I worried for nothing."

She bit her lip. "I mean unless you're not comfortable with me teaching him how to cook. I understand if you would prefer I didn't. It's totally fine."

He crossed his arms, and his fingers dug into his elbows. "Nope, it's fine with me."

"Great. Then you can start shadowing me whenever, Hunter."

"Perfect. The sooner the better." He grabbed a piece of sausage.

"You know, you should eat some fruit or something besides meat," Melanie said, frowning.

"Men eat meat," Hunter said. He flexed his arms behind his head, and she laughed.

Erik scowled at Hunter, but his brother wasn't paying attention, he was too busy smiling at Melanie. "Now that this is settled, do you mind getting back to work, Ms. Clark?"

He regretted his clipped tone when her face fell, but he couldn't stand his brother flirting with her. He racked his brain to figure out how to bring back her smile, but before he could open his mouth to apologize, she spoke. "Yes, sir," she said, and then turned on her heel and left.

"Smooth. Now I understand how you get so many women into bed," Hunter said, whistling low.

"Maybe you shouldn't have been flirting with my employee."

"I wasn't flirting. You know, I had a hunch she might think you don't like her, but now I'm pretty much certain."

"Why would she think that?"

"Avoidance tips a normal person off that you don't like them. Couple that with your tone...what would make her think you like her?"

Erik stared at his brother, and something in his look must've read as a warning because Hunter threw up his hands. "I'm just telling you how it looks."

Erik fought his frustration. He should've just given in to temptation and fucked her. She would have no concerns about his lust, and he'd be satisfied. He wouldn't have to wake up every morning needing to work out for an hour and a half and deal with a skin-stinging cold shower. He would be able to enjoy being in his own dining room that now faintly smelled like a mixture of citrus and some sort of flower. But no, he'd done the right thing, she was hurt anyway, and he was left dreaming of a kiss that had happened almost a week ago. Well, no more bullshit. He was going to get her out of his head. Starting tomorrow, he'd go running, let the early morning jog pick up his spirits, get down to business in the afternoon, and hit the bars in the evening. He'd find a sophisticated woman with curves and forget all about his tiny, innocent chef.

7

Melanie

Melanie turned over in her bed, stretching under her sun yellow comforter, and smacked her alarm so that the darn thing stopped beeping in her ear. She was tempted to curl up in a ball and hide under the covers all day. Nothing had happened, she wasn't sick or injured, and yet she felt like crap, all because her employer snapped at her. Pathetic. She sighed and yanked down her comforter. No more moping. She was twenty-three years old, had a decent job, a good family, and great friends. Her self-esteem didn't need to be wrapped up in some jerk's behavior.

She got out of bed and went to her dresser to grab some running clothes. She picked black shorts, a black sports bra, and a tie-dye jersey. Stripping out of her purple, silk nightshirt and shorts, she threw on her exercise clothes. She laced up her sneakers, slipped out of her room, and closed the door. Her room wasn't close to anything except the kitchen, but the house was so quiet at six in the morning that she was afraid the noise would travel. The hallways always seemed bigger in the morning. Her steps echoed as she walked to the back door. She opened the glass door and stepped outside, feeling better than when she'd woken up.

The sun shined down on her face, and warmth enveloped her. She rolled her neck and took a deep breath, noticing that spring perfumed the air. The back door opened to the pool deck, and a path around to the front of the house was to the right. She walked quickly down the path, and by the time she made it to the driveway, she was running.

She counted her breathing and listened to the sounds her feet made hitting the pavement. Birds chirped from the palo verde and mesquite trees she passed along the edge of the road. Her hair flew back as she ran, and she let the adrenaline cleanse her of the frustrations from the previous days. In the back of her mind, she realized she forgot her water and phone in her haste that morning, but she didn't intend to be gone long.

The path to the desert broke from the road and she took it. It wasn't the best decision to take that route at the speed she was going. She didn't have to practice trail running and hadn't brought water or a phone. It was probably a dumb choice. She was feeling reckless though. The sun felt great on her skin, and she felt strong, her legs straining toward their full stride.

She followed the trail, her footing uneven as she

jogged over gravel and pebbles. Her feet danced over larger rocks, and she kept her quick pace as the trail steepened and the turns sharpened. The outside of the trail became branches and cacti hanging on the edge of the mountain walls and the inside of the trail was lined with flat boulders reaching above her shoulder. Each step caused a surge of adrenaline, and within minutes she was smiling. She wanted to go faster, to push herself, to see what her body could do.

She sprinted, leaping from rock to rock, feeling the unstable ones slip as she lifted her feet. One rock slipped too soon, and she looked down at the ground to catch her balance. A pile of sharp rocks protruded from the trail, and her lagging foot caught on one. She flew forward. A scream ripped from her throat, and she braced her hands in front of her, skidding across the ground.

Throbbing pain and intense burning shot through her body. Her heart pounded in her chest, and she began to shake. Tears flooded her face as she laid there, her face to the gravel. She moaned, the stinging intensifying as she turned over. New pain clawed at her arms and legs, but she managed to get on her back. She forced herself into a sitting position against a boulder and looked down to assess the damage. "Oh God, oh God, oh God."

Both legs from her knees down were covered in blood. At first, she couldn't make out where the cuts were. Red lined her shins and ankles, the liquid turning pink as it seeped into her shoes. The sight of blood made her shudder harder. She lifted her hands to shift each leg and searing pain screamed through her left wrist. She looked down at a piece of jumping cholla cactus embedded in her wrist. "Goddammit!" she yelled through her tears.

She looked around for a stick or branch and found a small one within reach of her right hand. She stretched for it and grabbed it. The stick seemed sturdy enough, so she lifted her left wrist and wedged the piece of wood between the cactus and her flesh. She turned her wrist away from her body and flicked the stick hard so that the cholla popped off. Dots of blood beaded on her skin, but she ignored them and looked back down at her legs.

She took three deep breaths and surveyed her body to determine how bad the damage was. There were no strange twists, and there were no bones protruding. She looked for the gashes. Her right knee was covered in a giant raspberry, skin scraped away from her knee. The outside of her ankle looked the same. She'd landed hard on the right, which explained the pulsing pain in the right side of her hip. She peeled down her shorts a couple inches and saw blood on her hip too. Cuts and scrapes covered her left leg, but it didn't throb the way her right leg did.

Melanie looked skyward to calm herself. That's what she got for running in the desert with no phone or water. She couldn't believe she'd been so stupid. She was lucky though. If something had been broken, she wouldn't have been able to walk back on her own. As it was, it would be a long, painful trek back to Erik's house. She decided to take a minute before she forced her aching body to stand. Taking slow, even breaths, she shut her eyes, waiting for the adrenaline to leave her system.

Birds called to one another, and gravel shifted nearby. "I swear to God, if that is a mountain lion, I'm going to be so mad," she muttered to herself.

"Melanie!"

Her eyes flew open, and a shadowed form stood over her, blocking her view of the sun. She blinked as Erik's face came into view. He held a water bottle over his forehead, and his eyes were clouded with concern, the hard contours of his face looked even sharper than usual. Sweat dampened his blond hair. He wore shorts and sneakers, and he wasn't wearing a shirt. God help her, she was sitting on the ground bleeding, and all she could do was stare at his chest. He was tan and broad, blond hair sprinkled enticingly over his pecs and down to a happy trail she wanted to follow with her eyes, but that cut off at his shorts. His muscles were tight as he braced himself above her. His abs just weren't fair. She wanted to run her fingers over the grooves between each set to see how defined and hard they were.

He leaned down and braced his hands on his knees. She could make out a light sheen of sweat covering his chest as he got closer. "Shit. I think you must've hit your head. Melanie." He snapped his fingers in front of her face.

She'd been drooling over his chest so long, he thought she had a brain injury. Fantastic. "I didn't hit my head."

"It's a wonder. It seems that's the only thing you didn't hit. What the hell happened?"

"What does it look like happened? I fell." She straightened her shorts and winced as her left wrist hit her thigh.

Erik

Erik clenched his fists but couldn't keep from shaking

as he looked down at Melanie covered in blood. He hadn't been this terrified in a long time. Looking down the trail to see her leaning on the rock, not moving...he'd almost lost it. He was so relieved she was alive. Until he looked around and found she had no water, no phone, no anything. His teeth clicked together hard.

"So, you fell?"

"Yes. I was running, and I tripped," she said.

"And you were running without any water, or a phone, or anything? Did it ever occur to you how dangerous that was?" The muscles in his back knotted. Tear tracks on her face glinted in the sun, and he just wanted to draw her into his body and hold her, but he couldn't believe she'd done something so stupid. She could've been stuck out here if he hadn't come along.

"Do you have a phone?" She crossed her arms and winced.

"No, but I do have water. What would you have done if I hadn't come along?"

"I would have walked home. Can you give me the fifth degree later, boss? I'm the one hurt here. I don't need to be yelled at like I'm some misbehaving kid."

Erik blinked at her. This woman was infuriating. She could've been badly injured because of her choices, and she thought he was the one in the wrong here. Her lips started trembling and he frowned, feeling guilty for harassing her. What was it about this woman that made his emotions switch mid-thought? He crouched down beside her. "Hey, it's okay. Everything's going to be okay. I'm sorry."

Tears dripped down her dirty cheeks and fell to her tie-dye jersey. "No, I'm sorry."

He cocked his head to the side and wiped a thumb over her cheek. Her skin was so soft. He gave in and let his hand linger on her face. Her breathing became shallow. "Why are you sorry? You're the one that's hurt."

She looked down at her lap. "Because now you're here, and you think you have to help me. I know you hate being near me and don't like me."

Erik's eyes widened. Not like her? Every time he was near her, he thought about how much closer he wanted to get. He couldn't believe Hunter was right. "What would make you think that?"

She pursed her lips and seemed to contemplate answering, but then she shook her head.

"You can tell me," he said.

"After we kissed you made it clear you didn't want it to happen again. You've been avoiding me. Don't try to deny it. You send me messages through Mary."

Maybe leaving her with those perceptions would've been best. Then he wouldn't have to worry about doing the right thing or worry about their employer-employee relationship because she wouldn't want anything to do with a man who didn't like her. He couldn't let her think that though. He wanted her too damn much, and he hated to think of her hurting. He dragged a knuckle along her jawbone and tilted her chin up with his fingers. His gaze captured hers. "You're right, I have been avoiding you."

Her eyes clouded, and she looked away.

"Look at me, Melanie. I've been avoiding you because you're an employee of mine, and I'm trying to do the right thing here. I'm trying not to take advantage of my innocent chef."

Her blue eyes widened. "You're saying that—"

"That whenever I see you, I think about fucking you against whatever surface you're standing near. Be it pushing you up against a wall, or bending you over the dining room table," he said, his voice a low growl.

Her pupils dilated with desire, and her tongue darted out to wet her lips. "Okay."

Erik clenched his jaw. "Okay?" God, this tiny woman made his life difficult. "Melanie, I'm not a very nice guy. I don't do relationships. I'm not interested in that kind of emotional attachment. What I do with women isn't all flowers and romance. I expect them to fuck, no holds barred, and when I say we're done, we're done." He watched her face for a reaction. He'd been more explicit than he should've been, but he couldn't decide if he was trying to entice her or scare her away. Damn, he was weak.

She didn't say anything, and he found himself disappointed. "Let's get you cleaned up, and then I'll help you get back to the house."

She nodded, and he unwrapped the bandana from around his water bottle and poured some water on it. "I can do it." She reached for the bandana.

He nudged her arm away. "I don't mind." He picked up her left wrist and swabbed the bandana over the pebbled dots of blood. They diminished in size, and then he looked down at her legs.

"I'm going to clean up the biggest cuts. I don't have enough material to wipe away everything." He grimaced at the small square bandana. He had intended to use the cloth around his head if the morning got too hot. It wasn't good for much else.

He looked at Melanie. Determination shone in her

squared jaw. She gripped the bottom of her tie-dye shirt and lifted it over her head. "You can use this," she said, her voice shaking.

She handed him the shirt and looked away. He looked at her cleavage peeking over her black sports bra, and then down at her small, muscular waist. "Thanks."

He cleaned her left leg first, going from scrape to scrape, slowing his hands whenever she cringed. He switched to her right leg and poured water on her knee, dabbing around where the skin was scratched off. Her leg twitched. "You fell on your right side."

"Yes."

"How's your hip?"

"It hurts a bit."

"I'm going to help you stand up, and then I'll check the rest of your leg and your hip."

She nodded and started to brace her hands on the boulder behind her. Before she could get a grip on it, he wrapped his right arm around her waist and held her ribcage with his left hand. He lifted her up, shifting her weight against his body. Her heartbeat quickened against his stomach. Her arms gripped his shoulders. Her body was hot against his. "Can you stand?"

She nodded and let go of him. He kept his grip on her ribcage but released his other hand. "Show me your hip."

Melanie blinked and shook her head.

"I want to check how bad it is."

She kept shaking her head. "No, it's fine."

"If you don't show me, I'm going to take your pants off myself." His eyes were hard, and he reached for the edge of her pants.

She jerked back. Her eyes widened for a second, and then she narrowed them. "Okay, fine. I'll show you, you, big bully."

He raised an eyebrow and waited. He had to bite his cheeks to keep from smiling at her failing name calling abilities.

She peeled down the running shorts to reveal a gash at the front of her hip. He bent over to get a closer look. The cut looked painful but not as bad as her knee. That close to her waist, he couldn't help but admire her smooth, pale skin. His breathing deepened as he noticed how her low pants revealed the dip between her hip and her lower belly. He put a hand on her side, trying to focus on her cuts. He poured water over the wound, and his gaze was drawn to the rivulets streaming down underneath her shorts.

"It doesn't look too terrible," he said, standing upright.

"I told you that." Her voice was laced with indignation.

"Well, you were so eager to take off your shirt..."

Her mouth dropped open, and she started sputtering.

He grinned. "Okay, let's get you home, and then we can get you some bandages."

He wound his arm around her shoulder to support some of her weight, but as they began to walk, she was still limping. It would take them over an hour at that pace. "I'm going to carry you."

"What?"

He stopped walking and braced her against a tall boulder. She stared at him as he turned around and crouched. "Get on my back."

"What? No. I can walk."

He looked over his shoulder at her.

"Fine," she said, huffing.

He crouched lower and she clambered on. Her arms snaked around his collarbone, and he held her thighs, trying not to think about her soft skin.

"Let me know if you get tired." She leaned into him, her body relaxing against him. Her curves and bare stomach pressed into him, and he held in a groan. She felt so good against him.

"You're tiny. Don't worry about it," he said, his voice hoarse.

He hoped he could walk fast. Every minute she was wrapped around him, he felt his self-control slipping.

8

Melanie

Melanie was relieved when they got to Erik's driveway. She enjoyed being on his back far too much. She needed to get away from him to figure out her thoughts on everything he'd said. Finding out about his attraction to her was both empowering and anxiety-inducing. The fact that this man found her enticing was exhilarating, but she wasn't a one-night-stand kind of girl.

"How bad is the pain?" he asked as he hauled her to the front door.

"It's a lot better." After being near him for some time, she would've thought his effect on her would wear off. The truth of the matter was that the heat of his skin against hers felt delicious.

He reached out from under her leg and opened the door. They walked, or rather, she rode, into the foyer where Mary mopped the floor.

"What happened?" she asked, mid-mop.

"I just had a little fall," Melanie said, digging her hands into Erik's shoulders. She glanced around the room hoping no one else was around. She didn't need concern from any more people. Her klutziness was as embarrassing as being carried around by her boss.

"Do you need help getting cleaned up?" Mary asked.

"Oh no, I'm fine. Don't trouble yourself," Melanie said.

"Don't worry, Mary, I'll help her," Erik said.

"Okay, good. Let me know if you need anything later."

Melanie nodded, and Erik carried her toward her bedroom. As they passed the kitchen and approached her door, she panicked. This was her only privacy. She wasn't sure she wanted him in her space. She couldn't remember if the room was messy or clean, or what she'd left lying out the last couple days. A bedroom revealed too much. "You can put me down now. I can take it from here."

"I don't think so. You need help."

"I'm fine. I promise."

He stopped in front of her room. His shoulders tightened under her grip. "You could barely walk. Stop being stubborn."

"I just don't want...people...in my room."

"Oh, for the love of—you realize that there couldn't be anything in there I haven't seen before, right?"

"How would you know?"

He tilted his head toward her, and she blushed. He sighed. “Fine. How about this? You go in by yourself, and then let me in when you put away whatever it is you’re concerned about so that I can help you.”

“Thank you,” she muttered.

He slowly lowered her, her body sliding against his. She wobbled once she landed on her feet and he turned and grabbed her, holding her up against his chest. She grasped his biceps and looked up at his face. His gaze was dark and clouded, and his Adam’s apple bobbed as he swallowed. His hands tightened on her waist for a few seconds, and then he let her go. “You better go,” he said, his voice hard.

She nodded and turned around, pulling her shaking body from his. The loss of warmth was disappointing. She opened her door a crack and slipped in.

“Just so you know, this makes me imagine things that are probably far worse than what’s actually in there,” he said as she shut the door.

“Don’t worry, there aren’t any dead bodies. Give me one minute.” He was probably right. She was only concerned about bras and panties. She looked around, tugged her delicates off the back of the door, and shoved them in her dresser drawer. She found her pink bra on the bed and put it away, and then, looking around, she realized there wasn’t anything else to be concerned about. Her legs started to wobble, and she was still in pain, so she sat on the edge of her bed.

“You can come in,” she called out.

Erik opened the door and stepped in. He didn’t glance around the room like she thought he would, he walked to where she sat on the bed and knelt in front of her, surveying her knees. "I'm going to get some first aid supplies and then we'll deal with this."

"I don't need help. You've helped enough already. I'm fine."

He braced his fists on his hips and stood. He hovered over her, and just watched her. Darn him and his patience. Exasperated, she blew out a big breath. "Fine."

He nodded and turned around to walk out of the room.

Then she put her foot in her mouth. She couldn't seem to help herself. "You're such a pain in the butt."

He stopped, but he didn't turn around. Melanie put a fist to her mouth. Crap, she couldn't believe she'd done that. She hoped he wouldn't fire her or be too upset. She just hadn't been thinking.

She waited and held her breath. He clenched his fists, but after a few seconds, he walked out, slamming the door behind him.

"Ugh," she moaned.

Erik

Erik stalked from her room seething. God, she was infuriating. All he did was help her, and she's the one that gets annoyed. She'd been reckless in her actions, and she'd been unappreciative after. She drove him nuts.

And there was no way he'd make it to the bar later that night. If he spent all morning doctoring Melanie, he wouldn't get his work done early enough in the day to justify going out. So much for clearing his head.

He walked to the hall closet from her room and

looked through the shelves to find the first aid kit. Someone's shadow fell over him as he rooted around in the closet, and he got ready to snap at Melanie for getting up when she was hurt. When he looked up, he saw Hunter instead.

"Hey, man," Hunter said.

His brother wore his usual jeans and a white T-shirt. He leaned against the wall, watching Erik dig through the closet.

"Hey," Erik said, leashing his temper. "What are you doing over here?"

"I didn't realize I needed a reason to come over. We work from here a lot. I'm here almost every single day."

Erik ran a hand through his blond hair. "Now is not a great time to talk." The closet was filled with cleaning supplies and old bedding. Mary had clearly organized this space but he didn't recognize the pattern. It was taking forever to search for the damn kit. Finally, he found the white box on the bottom shelf, wedged behind pillowcases. He yanked it out and straightened.

"No biggie. I'm here to shadow Melanie today anyway. I couldn't find her in the kitchen though. Where is she?" Hunter asked.

"She's in her room."

"I can wait."

"She won't be cooking today. She fell in the desert."

"How bad is it?"

"Nothing serious enough to keep her from mouthing off." Erik squeezed the first aid kit until his fingers were white.

Hunter smirked. "Well, good. Does she need any help?"

"I can handle it."

"All right. I'll be around if you need anything."

"Sure." Erik went back to Melanie's room.

He walked in without knocking, and she was sprawled out on the yellow comforter. She jerked up when he entered the room. "You don't knock."

Erik's nostrils flared and he walked toward her with a determined stride. She leaned farther back down the bed. At first, he thought he saw fear in her gaze, but she stuck her chin up in defiance. "You want to lecture me about etiquette?" he asked, his voice low and menacing.

"Umm..."

He leaned over her, his hands in fists braced on the bed around her hips. He caught her blue eyes with his deep brown ones and raised an eyebrow. "Well?"

Her forehead wrinkled in anger. She opened her mouth, and then a buzzing filled the room. She jumped and looked around. The noise came from her phone that sat a foot away from her on the bed. She grabbed it and looked down.

"Oh, shoot," she said.

"What is it?"

"It's my mother. She's called like five times this morning. I'm sorry, but I should answer this." She looked at him and paused for a second.

"Go ahead." He straightened and crossed his arms.

She looked between him and the phone. He stood there unmoving. She sighed and held the phone up to her ear. "Hi, Mother. Are you all right? No, I'm fine. I just was running, and I didn't have my—yeah, I tripped. It's no big deal. No. You don't need to—he's not. Son of a gun." She looked down at her phone.

"What happened?"

Melanie looked up at him sheepishly. "I'm sorry. She wants to make sure I'm okay. I have to meet her somewhere because she's trying to come here."

Erik frowned. "She can come here. You shouldn't be driving anywhere right now anyway. Is she always so concerned?"

"Sort of. She just...she worries about me running." She averted her gaze.

"You are such a terrible liar."

"Fine. She thinks you might be a serial killer. She thinks you pushed me."

Erik bit his cheeks and rubbed his temples. Her mother must be something else. "Well, we'll put her mind at ease when she gets here. Until then, let's get you cleaned up."

"I should warn you about my mother. She's a little odd."

Hmm. Shocking. He'd never had a house staff before, but he had a feeling that family members didn't come around to the boss's home. The longer Melanie worked for him, the more unorthodox her position seemed to be. Of course, since he'd already admitted to wanting to fuck her, he supposed he couldn't lecture her about professionalism.

Melanie

By the time the doorbell rang, Melanie's stomach was in so many knots she thought she might have to open herself up to get them untangled. She wasn't sure how Erik convinced her to let her mother come over. It was a terrible idea. She was pretty sure family members of staff weren't supposed to come knocking at their employers' doors. She knew little about being a live-in cook, but Mary hadn't brought her brother around.

The doorbell made her jump from her lounging position on the sofa in the living room. Hunter and Erik sat around her on the black couch. Hunter had the TV on, and Erik worked on his iPad. She was relieved that neither was interested in a lot of deep conversation. Coherence wouldn't have been her strong suit at that moment.

At least she'd had enough time to take a shower and put on something her mother might think was acceptable before the doorbell rang. She wore a teal sundress her mother bought her a couple years ago. Both Erik and Hunter gave her a funny look upon seeing her in it. Melanie shifted to stand to get the door, but Erik stood first.

"I can get it," she said.

"It's fine. You should be resting."

"I didn't even sprain anything."

Hunter looked at her. "I wouldn't bother arguing with him. Besides, from the way you've been wincing, the impact was bad enough that you should be off your feet for at least a day."

Erik left the room, and Melanie groaned. "One of them is going to need physical protection. I just can't figure out which."

"She that bad?" Hunter asked, turning off the TV.

"Yes."

They both quieted and listened for noises from the

foyer. The door opened with a slight creaking noise. "How do you do, young man?" her mother asked.

"Hello, ma'am, I'm Erik Graham. It's nice to meet you."

"Diane Clark. Now, be a dear, and tell me where I can find my daughter. If she's not at the door to greet her own mother, she's very injured."

"Yes, ma'am."

After a few seconds, Melanie heard steps coming down the hallway toward the living room. Hunter stood, but Melanie's knees buckled underneath her as she followed suit, so she sat up straight instead.

Her mother walked into the room in front of Erik. She held a leather clutch in front of her dress, and her dyed red hair hung in waves to her chin. When her eyes found her daughter, she clasped her cheek with her hand.

"You look awful." She turned around and glared at Erik. "I want you to know that there is GSP in my vehicle outside, and I have the cops on speed dial. If you try to harm us, don't think you'll get away with it."

"He didn't do anything. And it's GPS. GPS. We've talked about this. A GPS is a Global Positioning System, and yours does not have some kind of homing beacon on it when it's not even turned on."

"Oh, well, I had to be sure. You can't be too careful," Diane said.

Melanie thought she was going to throw up. Erik hadn't batted an eye at her mother's rant, but she could only imagine what he was thinking. He was probably trying to figure out if he could get away with firing her while her mother was in the room.

Hunter cleared his throat and looked expectantly at Melanie. Her forehead wrinkled in surprise. He wanted to be introduced to her? Fine, he could enjoy those moments of regret later. She smiled wide. "I'm sorry. Hunter, this is my mother, Diane. Mother, this is Hunter."

"Lovely to meet you, Hunter," she said, shaking his hand.

"Nice to meet you, Mrs. Clark."

Diane looked around the room, and her gaze settled on her daughter. "This seems unorthodox. Where is your chef's uniform?"

She thought about pointing to the obvious wounds on her legs, but that seemed irrelevant. "I don't have a chef's uniform."

"We're not overly formal here," Erik said from the entrance of the hallway.

"I see. How contemporary of you." Diane smoothed her dress.

"Diane, can I offer you something to drink?" Erik asked, smiling politely.

"I hope you are not offering alcohol, young man. Drinking is a sign of loose morals and poor character."

"We have a delicious iced tea that your daughter made."

Melanie was impressed by how well he sidestepped everything. She wondered where he learned the skill. It seemed useful. Maybe she could learn. She glanced at Hunter, wondering what he thought of the whole exchange. He mouthed, "Is she serious?"

She glanced at her mother to make sure she wasn't paying attention. Diane was focused on Erik. "That sounds fine. She makes it a little tart, but it'll have to do, I suppose."

Melanie nodded at Hunter. "Yes," she mouthed back.

"I think it's great. I'll bring us a carafe," Erik said.

"Melanie, dear, isn't that your job?"

"Oh, yes, I'm sorry. I'll go get it," she said, pushing off the couch.

Erik sent her a dark look and shook his head. "It's fine, Diane. She's injured. I don't mind getting it."

"Her wounds don't look that bad. I can't imagine that they prevent her from doing her work."

"Actually—"

Melanie was not going to be a silent monkey in the middle. Neither of them could dictate what she should do. At least Hunter was quiet. One of them understood she was an adult too. "My injuries make it difficult for me to serve us tea," she said, glaring at Erik.

His jaw tightened at her look, but she stared unblinkingly right back. Hunter looked between the two of them. "I have an even better idea. How about I give you a tour, Mrs. Clark, and we can have tea afterward?"

"That sounds fine." Hunter ushered Diane out the same way she walked in.

"Meet you in a few minutes then," Erik said.

Once Melanie was sure her mother wouldn't be able to hear her, she turned to Erik. "I don't need you to speak for me."

"I was trying to help."

"Why is it that your idea of helping always seems to involve you stepping in for me or telling me what to do?" She scowled and drummed her fingers on her thighs.

"Because you're too stubborn to listen to reason."

"Look, I don't know what kind of weak women you've been around in the past, but I will not be pushed around as an employee...or otherwise," she added as an afterthought. Their conversation from earlier lingered in her mind.

"Somehow, I don't think you're in any danger of that happening. Do I need to remind you that you left an interview because of salt?" he asked, raising an eyebrow.

The hilarity of it all hit Melanie. The grease fire that led her here, the stupid salt, and her current situation. Here she was, stuck on the couch because of a reckless run while her mother was wandering around her employer's house, probably trying to find evidence that Erik was a serial killer. She couldn't help herself, she started to giggle. "I'll admit now that it may have been over the top for me to leave because you asked for salt."

"So, you're saying you were wrong?" The barest smile tugged at the corners of his mouth.

She crossed her arms. "Don't push it."

His eyes burned bright, but he didn't say anything.

"Once again, I'm sorry about my mother."

"She's a little fanatic."

"Yes."

"Has she always been like that?"

"Yes."

"Why?"

She was surprised by the turn of the discussion. They were rather personal questions, and she was tempted to tell him to mind his own business, but he seemed genuinely confused by Diane's behavior, and interested, she decided to answer.

"I'm her cautionary morality tale." She smiled, but

the bitterness inside her turned it into a grimace. Her mother probably should've gotten over Melanie's birth a long time ago, but for some reason, she hadn't.

9

Erik

Erik sat down beside Melanie. After meeting her mother for five minutes, he had no idea how such a sweet person like her could've come from Diane. He didn't like where this conversation was going. The idea of Melanie hurting tugged at something protective in him. He wanted to wrap her in his arms.

"Cautionary morality tale?" he asked.

"She was pregnant with me before she married. Her entire family turned their backs on her. She doesn't let me forget it. After she married my dad, she became super religious. At least, that's what my dad told me once." Her voice was falsely cheery. She was usually so animated and happy. It was painful seeing her this way.

Then it occurred to him she might be religious too.

That would make him a bigger asshole if he'd come on to some religious virgin. Shit. He cleared his throat. Better to find out now. "Are you religious too?"

"Yes. Everything I do speaks to my religious integrity." Melanie rolled her eyes. "Not so much. I don't know what I believe. Not like her."

He breathed a sigh of relief.

She looked at him and cocked her head to the side in an unvoiced question.

How this conversation turned into one that made him uncomfortable, he wasn't sure. He shrugged. "I would've felt bad if..." He trailed off, not sure how to finish.

"If I had been saving my belt buckle expertise for marriage?"

He grinned. "Cute. So, how does that work then? With your mother being such a fanatic?"

She shrugged, her lips thin. "She knows little about my personal life."

"I see."

"It doesn't matter. Everyone's parents are a little whacky. My mother loves me, she just has limitations. Not even big ones. It's not like she used to hit me or made me hate myself. She's just kind of weird. It's entertaining, except for the part where she decides to come over to my boss' house. Sorry."

"It's fine. I run a casual household."

"Apparently. Should we go rescue Hunter?"

"Let him enjoy a few more minutes of your mother. He does well with middle-aged women." Erik grinned to himself, thinking about his brother talking about him with Stacie. Hunter deserved payback. Erik relaxed into the couch.

"So, what were you working on earlier? A new app?"

"A summer program for foster kids."

"No, seriously," she said and laughed.

Erik raised an eyebrow. He wasn't sure if he was more offended she didn't believe him or amused. He was no saint, but they did philanthropic work every once in a while.

She clapped a hand over her mouth. "Oh my gosh, you're serious."

"Yes, I am. I met with the activities director for the program a few days ago." He wasn't sure why he felt the need to elaborate. For some reason, her low opinion grated on him.

"That's great. How did you get into that cause?"

For a second, Erik was tempted to be honest. He wanted her to know him, to recognize him as a full, well-rounded person. Few people knew that part of him though, and not everyone he was honest with stuck with him. She made it far too tempting to share though. "My PR person recommended it to me." The lie was harder than he thought it would be.

He watched her to see how she would react. She nodded. He was frustrated by how fast she bought it. What was wrong with him? She hadn't even done anything, and she was under his skin.

"That's great. It's always nice to give back."

Melanie

The couple of days after her mother's visit were calm.

Erik tried to convince her to take more than one day off, but Melanie felt silly. She was only in pain for the first afternoon, so the next day she refused his offer. Besides, she didn't like resting. She liked moving, cooking, doing. Inactivity stressed her out.

She'd been concerned Hunter and Erik would be upset after her mother left, but both seemed unfazed. The next day Hunter even began to shadow her in the kitchen over lunch and kept at it through dinner. Breakfast had been out of the question because he'd refused to get up that early on his day off. Erik stopped trying to avoid her, but he had been professional to the point of stiff. Every time he saw Hunter with her, he became even stiffer. She wondered if he disapproved of his brother's behavior with the staff.

Settling into the job started to seem like a real possibility. She even decided to put an ad online for her apartment. Erik was still on her mind all the time, and he messed with her equilibrium whenever he was around, but at least the attraction was mutual.

She thought she would have to make a choice about what they'd discussed in the desert, that maybe he would proposition her, but it didn't come up. If she was being honest with herself, she was disappointed that he hadn't. But every time she thought about what he'd said, about what he wanted, her palms started to sweat. She'd never experienced lust like this for any other man. She'd loved her ex. How could she not? They'd been together for six years. She hadn't felt attraction like this before though. She was conflicted. No, conflicted was an understatement. Every time she saw Erik, she thought of kissing him, and then she remembered what he wanted from women. Was she prepared for that kind of arrangement, the kind with just sex, no feelings? She had no idea how to do that, and if she ended up having feelings for him, she would only get hurt. But good Lord, he was sexy. She needed to decide soon though because every time she saw him, she wanted to jump him.

For now, she needed to put Erik out of her mind this evening because she was supposed to help Hunter bake brownies from scratch. She took out the ingredients after dinner and waited for him to finish eating. She loaded the dishwasher, and then Hunter walked into the kitchen.

“Your chicken marsala is great. You know, I’m pretty sure I’ve gained weight since you started here,” he said, patting his flat stomach.

Melanie rolled her eyes. “You shouldn’t say that when you’re in such good shape. It comes off as bragging.”

“You think I’m in good shape?” There was a twinkle in his brown eyes.

She smacked him with the towel she’d been holding. “I’m not inflating your ego.”

He blocked and jumped back. “Nice try.”

She dropped the towel and shook her head. “I printed out the recipe. I want you to look it over, and we’ll get started.”

“All right.” He walked to the recipe on the counter and read it.

“Can I ask you a question?”

“Sure,” he said.

“Why didn’t you ask your chef to help you learn how to cook?” She’d been wondering for a while. Not that she thought Hunter had some nefarious purpose for wanting her to teach him, but she did find it odd that he was at Erik's place all the time.

"I don't have a chef."

"What? Why not?" she asked. Hunter seemed much more interested in Erik's staff than Erik was.

"Because I live in a studio apartment. Finished." He put the paper on the counter.

Outrage filled Melanie. She couldn't believe Erik would buy a mansion and leave his brother to live in a studio by himself. It was sick to take advantage of his own flesh and blood in business like that. She knew he was ruthless, but this was ridiculous.

Hunter laughed. "You should see your face—you're like an open book. You look furious. I know what you're thinking, but Erik and I take home equal pay. I decided to buy a warehouse instead of a house. I don't like a lot of space to sleep in."

"A warehouse?"

"Yeah, it's sweet. It's got a basketball court, a loft workspace, a creative room, and some other great stuff."

"That sounds pretty cool." She got out the measuring cups they would need.

"It is. You'll have to see it sometime. So, what do we do first?" Hunter clapped his hands together.

"Eager student, great. So, you're going to mix the dry ingredients in one bowl, and the wet ingredients in another."

He nodded, and she thought this would be an easy process. She figured he just wanted her around to watch for mistakes. Boy, was she wrong. He stuck the cup into the flour sack and lifted a heaping, overfilled scoop. Without getting a knife to even out the top, he carried the cup to the dry ingredient bowl.

"Stop. You need an even cup." She rushed to take it out of his hand.

She showed him how to use the back of a knife to make the cup flat and showed him how to make sure liquids were measured correctly. Measuring out the ingredients took triple the amount of time it should have, but Hunter looked satisfied with himself when they got to the next step: mixing. He stirred both bowls and then poured the wet ingredients into the dry ones. Then he mixed some more.

"This isn't too bad," Hunter said, stirring. He had flour on his nose.

"Nope, not at all." Melanie grinned.

The kitchen door opened as she set the glass baking dish on the counter. She looked up to watch Erik saunter in. "Do you need anything?" she asked.

"I'm just checking on how it's going. These are going to be my brownies after all," he said to Hunter.

"Don't worry. I didn't let him ruin them."

"Hey. 'Ruin them'? I've been doing great." Hunter poured the chocolaty liquid into the dish.

"I'll believe that when I taste them. By the way, you have flour on your nose," Erik said to Hunter.

Hunter set the dish on the counter and turned to Melanie. "How long have I had flour on my face?"

"I have no idea. I never even noticed," she said, her eyes watering as she held in laughter. "Although I may have a picture of it on my phone."

"I'll be stealing your phone later. I'm gonna go clean up," Hunter said, walking out and leaving Erik and Melanie alone in the kitchen.

She could feel Erik standing beside her, watching her. She turned toward the almost empty bowl, his dominating presence making her very aware they were alone. She scraped a finger against the side of the bowl and licked the chocolate off. "Do you want some?" She offered him the bowl with her clean hand.

He didn't say anything, and she scraped her finger across the other side of the bowl. The silence continued, and chocolate still on her finger, she finally looked at his face. His searing gaze fastened on her. Her own eyes widened, and her mouth parted at the intensity of his look. She could feel his desire reaching out to something feminine inside of her, and heat pooled in her lower belly. He took her wrist in his hand. She froze as he brought her finger to his mouth and sucked the chocolate off. The sensation of his mouth on her made her gasp aloud. His tongue wrapped around her finger. As he drew it out of his mouth, he nipped her fingertip, and electricity shot through her.

Internal conflict be damned. If the opportunity to sleep with him arose, no matter how he wanted their arrangement, she would go for it.

Erik

Erik couldn't sleep. His clock passed 12 a.m., 12:42 a.m., and 1:14, a.m., but still he couldn't sleep. He flipped onto his back and tugged up his dark green sheets. Then two minutes later, he decided the temperature was too hot, and he pushed his sheets back down to bare his chest and waist. He couldn't sleep because of his little chef and her damn brownie batter. Not even a cold shower helped after licking chocolate from her finger. All he could think about was drizzling chocolate over the rest of her body and licking it off inch by inch. Normally he wasn't this into food, but Melanie made everything around her sexy. Now his number one fantasy involved her, and some X-rated dessert.

He covered his eyes with his arm and groaned. Sleep wasn't coming any time soon. He rolled out of bed and decided to stretch his legs. Remembering he didn't live alone anymore, he grabbed a pair of gray pajama pants and pulled them on. Certain everyone would be asleep, he walked with light steps out of his room and shut the door behind him. He wasn't sure where he intended to go, but he wasn't surprised when he ended up outside Melanie's door. Not that he would do anything, but he couldn't seem to help taunting himself.

He sighed and walked toward the kitchen, deciding that maybe he was hungry. His steps were slow, the hallways were dark, and his eyes took time to adjust. When he got to the kitchen, a crack of light was coming out from underneath the door. He walked in and wondered who in his employ ate late night snacks.

When he stepped through the door, he saw Melanie's small, heart-shaped behind sticking up in the air from her position bent down with her head half in the fridge. She wore tiny, purple silk shorts that didn't cover the entirety of her ass. He could make out the crease where her thighs met her cheeks. Her matching silk shirt looked equally tiny as it revealed a few inches of skin on her back. He backed into the counter and groaned.

Melanie squealed and jumped, turning around

midair. "You scared the bejeezus out of me." Her chest heaved as she gasped. The purple, silk shirt she wore had spaghetti straps and dipped low between her breasts.

He swallowed and looked her over from head to foot. He was staring, and he didn't care. She looked luscious, a swath of her stomach exposed, her thighs almost bare, and her breasts small, but perky. He wanted to devour her.

The open fridge's bulb lit her body and face with its dim glow. His gaze raised to her wide eyes, and he could make out their sky-blue color even in the dark.

"I didn't realize anyone else was awake." She crossed her arms over her chest.

"This is what you wear to sleep?" Erik asked, his voice strained.

Her stare lowered to his body and caught on his chest. "No, I usually sleep naked. I just figured I should wear pajamas here, you know, in case I had to get up in the middle of the night." Her voice sounded dreamy as if she hadn't been aware of what she'd said.

"Jesus, Melanie, do you ever think before you speak?" He gripped the counter behind him so hard his fingers hurt.

"What?" Her gaze snapped to his face, and her cheeks turned pink. "Oh, yeah. You're a little distracting."

"I'm distracting?" He ran a hand through his hair. "Do you have any idea how hard you're making this? I walk in and your ass is in the air covered by a scrap of silk so tight on you that I can see the curve of your..." He checked himself and cleared his throat. "Do you have any idea what you're doing to my self-control?"

She shook her head and licked her lips. His cock

jerked in his pants.

"Bad things. You're doing bad things to my self-control."

She didn't stop staring. Her arms dropped to her sides. She just didn't get it. He stalked toward her, and she shifted her stance but didn't step away. After closing the fridge, he braced his hands on the counter around her. Her light blue eyes turned dark with longing and her lips parted. He stood over her, leaving a few inches of space between them. "Your pajama set is leaving very little to the imagination, Melanie. I'm trying to do the right thing here, and you're making it difficult. You have no idea how badly I want to take you right now," he said, his voice low and dangerous.

She shivered and nodded. "Okay."

"'Okay'?" he asked, dumbstruck.

She nodded again. "Yes. You can 'take me.'"

He blinked in surprise. "Are you sure? We're not talking about romance or a relationship. We're not talking about making love. We're talking about me taking you, me having you tonight."

"One night," she whispered.

"One night."

"Okay," she said again.

He was starting to appreciate that one word. "Thank God." He closed the distance between them and took her mouth with his, devouring her and coaxing her lips open. She moaned and clutched his chest. He ran his hands up her shoulders, and threaded them through her hair, controlling her head to give himself better access. Her body melted against his and her nipples pebbled against his chest. He released her hair and fingered the hem of her shirt.

As he lifted her shirt, she shifted away. “Wait, what about the door?”

He tore himself from her, walked to the kitchen door, and locked it. Then he turned around to face Melanie. She leaned against the counter, her mussed hair framing her face, her silky shirt wrinkled, and her shorts hanging low on her lean waist. He had to see her body.

10

Melanie

Melanie stood against the counter hoping her knees wouldn't give out. She was dying to drag Erik across the room to bring him back. She wanted to feel his hands tangling in her hair, his body on hers, but he stood by the door watching her. Erik's masculine features looked harsher in the shadowed kitchen. The lights were still off, but her eyes adjusted well enough. She could even make out the light hair that trailed over his defined pecs, six-pack, and downward in a V to disappear beneath his low hanging, gray pants. Her mouth went dry looking at him.

"Take off your shirt," he said, his voice demanding.

A shiver of nerves ran up her spine. She had never stripped for someone before. Under the guise of 'passion,' she and her previous boyfriend had fumbled to remove one another's clothing, but she had never done anything like this before. Not when that someone stood simply watching. Just the idea of it made her feel vulnerable. But his tone was so masculine, so commanding, that something inside her hummed with desire in response. She found herself reaching for the hem of her shirt without realizing she'd made a choice.

She stripped off the purple camisole in one fluid motion and dropped the garment on the floor. The cooling air of the AC made her bare, sensitized skin tingle.

Erik still didn't go to her. He watched her, his eyes black, his jaw hard, and the evidence of his arousal pressed against his pants. Knowing he was this excited watching her undress was thrilling.

"Take off your shorts," he said.

She looked away, her skin hot, but once again, her body reacted to his words before she could think about it. She tucked her thumbs into her pajamas and pushed them down until they hit the floor, and then she stepped out of them.

She looked up and his gaze held hers for a minute. Then he looked over form, lingering to stare at her breasts, catching on the small thatch of black between her legs, and finally down her legs. His gaze was possessive, burning.

The vulnerability was too much; she wanted him near her, touching her. She couldn't say the words though–she didn't trust her vocal chords to work.

"You are so damn sexy." His voice was a seductive growl. He stalked toward her and stopped less than a foot from her.

Her manners got the better of her. "Thank you," she said even though she had trouble breathing.

He smiled, his teeth flashing white against his tan skin. The look was feral. "You're quite welcome."

He grabbed her hips, his fingers digging into the top of her bottom, his thumbs wrapping around her pelvis, and he hauled her flush against him. She gasped at the contact of her pebbled nipples against his chest. She tilted her head up and he kissed her again, first with soft brushes of his lips, and then harder, his lips unrelenting. His erection nudged against her belly and desire flowed through her. She whimpered, desperately wanting him to slake the throbbing between her legs.

He slid his right hand over her waist until his hand was level with the side of her breast. The anticipation of him touching her made her stir against him, but his other hand held her hips still. He continued to kiss her as he slid his right hand under her breast, cupping her, holding the weight of her in the palm of his hand. He stroked the underside of her breast, avoiding her nipple until she gasped against his mouth.

She tore her head back and whimpered again. "Oh please, please touch me." She didn't care that she was begging. Anything to get him to touch her.

He rubbed a thumb over the sensitive tip of her breast, and her knees buckled. His grasp on her hip tightened as he held her up. He nipped her earlobe. "You're so responsive." His breath was hot against her.

She wasn't sure if she was supposed to say something back, but her mind was almost empty of coherent thought. All she could think about were the sensations running through her body as he caressed her. She was going to explode, she needed release.

"I've been meaning to ask you a question. It's something only a chef would have the answer to," he whispered against her ear.

He nipped at her neck, and she shook her head. Did he want to ask her a question about cooking? Now? Was she supposed to respond to him in some way?

He rubbed his knuckles over the side of her breast. "What food would taste best licked off your breasts?"

Oh Lord.

Erik

Melanie stilled after Erik asked the question. She blinked, clearly trying to think of a way to respond. After opening and closing her mouth, Erik thought she might have given up. Then she spoke. "I think..." He rocked against her and she stopped talking on a whimper.

The effect he had on her was intoxicating to watch. Her inability to complete a sentence while they were hooking up filled him with vain smugness. He chuckled. "Is it more to personal taste?"

She leaned her head back, her eyes dark and foggy. "Whipped cream with chocolate sauce as an accent. Chocolate is too sticky on its own."

Erik's cock jumped in response to her words. He grinned at the obvious challenge in her voice. Normally, he would've wanted to pick, he would've enjoyed if she were too turned on to speak, but her spunkiness thrilled him. He looked forward to challenging her back. He spun her by her hips to face the direction of the fridge, a couple of feet away, and she squealed. "Why don't you go get them for me."

She peeked at him over her shoulder. "Happy to."

She sauntered to the fridge. Her hips swayed with each step. She'd never walked like that in front of him before. She was teasing him. He couldn't take his eyes off her ass. From beside the fridge, she glanced over her shoulder and stared at him until he looked up, a shy smile playing at her lips.

She opened the door and bent her knees to reach the lower shelves.

"Stop. Bend over to get it. I want to see you."

She froze, and he wondered if he'd pushed his little chef too far. She may not have been a virgin, but she wasn't experienced either. He didn't intend to back down though. He crossed his arms and waited.

After a few seconds, she bent over, the back of her thighs tightening. Clanging sounds came from inside the fridge, but he couldn't take his eyes off the sight of her. Her long legs stretched longer from her position, her soft lips peeking out from between her thighs, and her smooth back was flat as a board.

She set a bottle of chocolate sauce on the counter and then she bent back over in the fridge. He walked to her, stopping when his pants brushed across the back of her thighs and her cheeks. Her body tensed against him.

"Find the whipped cream yet?" he asked. He drew the back of his fingers up the inside of her right thigh, reveling in her smooth skin, but drew them away just before he reached her center.

She moaned and thrust her hips back against him,

catching his shaft against her ass. His nostrils flared, and he fought his impulse to rip his pants off and fuck her against the fridge. He wanted to go slower than that; he wanted to enjoy the night. He had plans for the whipped cream.

“Found it,” she murmured, straightening.

“Finally. Grab the chocolate too.”

She grabbed the chocolate and turned toward him. He hooked his arms under her knees and her back, and then lifted her. She squealed, and he nuzzled her neck. “I promise I won’t drop you.”

He walked to the kitchen door, and she clutched his neck with her arms, the chocolate, and whipped cream still in her hands. “What are you doing? I’m naked.”

“Trust me, I’m aware.”

“Erik.”

“No one’s up, and I’ll lock the dining room door.”

“We’re going to the dining room?”

“We’re going to need a table.”

She wiggled against him as he carried her through the door. He laid her on the dining room table, her legs dangling off at her knees. She set the ingredients on the table and leaned up on her elbows, watching him as he walked to the door and turned the lock. “You realize how messy this is going to be.”

“Don’t worry, I don’t intend to use much. Mostly, I want to taste you.” She was beautiful, lying out on the table, her breasts pert as she braced herself on her elbows, her stomach smooth, and her legs slightly parted. He stepped between her thighs and spread her knees to see all of her.

❦

Melanie

Anticipation hummed beneath the surface of her skin. She felt so open to his view, lying wantonly on the table, her legs spread to his dark, hungry gaze. He stood above her, his face covered in shadows from the low lighting of the room. The only light was a glowing sconce hanging on the back wall.

Her heart pounded in her chest, curious about what he planned to do. She had thought she might be nervous or self-conscious, but she was just impatient waiting for whatever sensations he would give her next. The lust in his gaze made her anything but self-conscious.

She felt brazen, free in her sexuality. "When do I get to see you?"

He groaned and bent over her, bracing his left hand on the table by her shoulder. He slid his forefinger down her throat, between her breasts, and stopped just above her center. She froze, waiting for his touch to continue where his hand's direction promised, but he withdrew. She moaned in frustration.

"When I'm done eating."

He picked up the can of whipped cream and shook it. He straightened, took the red cap off the can, and then he looked down at her body. For a few seconds, he did nothing but look at her. The anticipation was driving her crazy. "Need a map?" she asked.

He chuckled. "Impatient?"

She narrowed her eyes, but before she could think of anything to say, he grabbed her right hip with a tight grip. "Hold still, or it'll go everywhere."

He held the can over her navel and pressed the nozzle

so that the fluffy, white confection spilled out. The initial contact was cold and smooth and made her shiver. He traced a line with the whipped cream down from her navel, over her lower belly, and stopped to set a dollop on her mound. She shivered at the cooling sensation on such an intimate place.

His gaze cut to her face, the fire in his look cutting to her core. “Don’t move.”

She swallowed, wanting to do as he said and argue at the same time. It was easy for him to tell her not to move. He didn’t have whipped cream chilling his navel and other sensitive areas. Well, she couldn’t say anything even if she wanted to. Her mouth had gone dry from the realization that he would be licking this off.

He picked up the chocolate sauce bottle by her shoulder and her eyes widened. He leaned over her and brushed a strand of her hair over her ear. “You didn’t think I would stop after one line of whipped cream, did you?”

She shook her head, and he straightened. “Lay down all the way,” he said, his voice low.

Her core burned at his tone. She slid her hands down and lay on her back, the hard table biting into her shoulders. From her view on the table, she could see only the upper half of his body. But oh boy, what a fantastic view that was.

His hand went back to her waist again, and he brushed his thumb over the divot between her hip and her stomach. “Now, be still.”

She braced herself, but nothing could have prepared her for the erotic sight of Erik standing over her, shirtless, an enraptured gaze on his face as he drizzled chocolate over her breasts. She gasped at the cold of the refrigerated chocolate.

He made a tsking noise. “Next time I’ll tie you down if you can’t be still.”

Her stomach lurched in response to his words. An image of her lying on the table, her hands above her head and tied, entered her mind. The thought sent an electric jolt through her, something she didn’t expect. Being tied up wasn’t a fetish she thought she was interested in, but the idea of Erik controlling her and pleasuring her was entirely too erotic. She wondered if he was kidding.

He bent over her, avoided touching her body, and kissed her hard, making her his. Desire rolled through her, and she tugged him closer. He grabbed her wrists with both hands and pushed them down on the table. She twisted and turned beneath him, longing to touch him.

“You’ll get me dirty,” he said, a twinkle in his dark eyes.

She looked at him indignantly. “And whose fault is that?”

“Mine.”

He lowered his head and nipped at her collarbone while still pinning her hands. Then he moved his head downward. Starting at the bottom of her rib cage, he licked all the way up to one nipple and then swirled his tongue around her. Her back arched off the table, her skin burning. Finally, he released her wrists. He did the same to the other side of her ribcage, but this time when he reached the stiffened peak, he tugged. Lust shot straight through her, and her core grew slick and swollen. Neediness drove through her.

"Please, please, Erik," she begged.

He flicked his tongue at her navel, lapping up the whipped cream. "Please, what?"

She could feel him grinning against her stomach, and she wanted to smack him. He enjoyed teasing her far too much. It wasn't fair that she was losing control and he was affected so little. She stubbornly kept her mouth shut and looked down at him. He looked at her face, his eyes smoldering, and his breathing heavy. Maybe she was wrong about him being unaffected.

He watched her, his eyes feral and possessive, the look filling her with heat, as he licked downward, his tongue skating over the curves of her belly and down to the depths of her femininity. He lapped once between her lower lips, and her back bowed off the table.

"Oh, God."

"You're so hot and wet for me. I love the way you taste."

The things his words did to her...His thumb dragged between her folds once, and her body quivered beneath his touch. He spread her outer lips with his thumbs and thrust his tongue inside her. She throbbed against him, need building and building. She was on the edge, sensations whirling around her as he pleasured her with his tongue. Finally, when she thought she couldn't take his ministrations any longer, he wrapped his lips around her clit and tugged. Her body tightened and then shattered, convulsing around his fingers as she came in a rush of sensation.

❧

Erik

Melanie came apart below him. She still breathed heavily, but her face looked serene and content. Something primitive in Erik purred at her satisfaction despite the painful erection still straining against his pants.

She looked up at him, the deep blue color of her eyes pure, and the gaze guileless. She was beautiful. He sucked the taste of her from his fingers as he watched her. “You are so sweet.”

She licked her lips. “I’m all sticky.”

He raised an eyebrow, surprised by her brazenness, but pleased.

She cleared her throat. “I mean from the chocolate and whipped cream.”

He grinned. “I’ll get a washcloth, and then we’ll go to my bedroom.”

She nodded and lay back down on the table. He looked at her once more, searing the image of her sprawled and satisfied on his kitchen table into his memory, and then he walked to the kitchen.

He grabbed her nightclothes off the floor, and then searched for something to clean her up. He found the clean hand towels under the sink and grabbed an orange one from the top of the stack. He turned the faucet on and drenched the cloth once the water was warm. Wrapping the towel in his fists, he squeezed out the remaining water and carried it back to Melanie.

When he returned, he wasn’t surprised to see she hadn’t shifted from her spot on the table since he’d left the dining room. She looked at him and reached for the washcloth. "I can do it."

He held the hand towel away from her. "Let me."

She let her head fall back onto the table. He started at her nape, running the towel down, between her breasts to her navel. At first, she lay still, but as he covered her breasts with the cooling cloth, she squirmed under him. He dragged the material down between her legs and ran his towel-covered fingers through her folds. She inhaled sharply in response.

He looked at her face, her eyes burning with hunger for him again, her lips plush and swollen...he couldn't wait to be inside this woman. He took a deep breath to control himself. His condoms were in his bedroom. He had to wait longer.

"I want you," she said, her voice shaky.

Erik exploded in movement, tossing the hand towel, grabbing her hips, and lifting Melanie into his arms. She squealed, but before she could say anything, he hauled her out of the kitchen and headed to his bedroom through the pitch-black hallways of the house.

"Erik."

When he got to his room, he flung the door open and carried her inside, shutting and locking the door behind him. The room was filled with oak furniture and a king size bed covered in a dark green comforter. He set her down beside the bed, and she hit him on the shoulder.

He stepped back. That actually hurt. She brought her hand up to hit him again, but he grabbed her wrist mid-swing. She did the same with her left hand, and he grabbed that hand too. "What?" he asked, bewildered.

"You carried me naked through the house. There are other people here," she said, scowling. She tugged at her arms, but he wouldn't let go. He transferred both her wrists to one hand, and she growled in frustration.

"No one is up, so no one would've seen."

"Give me back my arms."

"Are you going to try to hit me again?"

She smiled, her eyebrows halfway up her forehead. "No."

"Yeah, right." He looked down at her, a little surprised by her annoyance.

She tugged her arms, and her cleavage was pushed together. God, she turned him on even when she frustrated him, even when she wasn't trying. She looked up at him, and he surveyed her curves. Blushing, she looked away. "You can't just carry people around naked."

"I'm sorry."

Her mouth dropped open, and half a smile formed on his lips. "Oh, okay."

He nodded but held on to her wrists. She was far too enticing this way.

"Can I have my hands back now?" she asked.

He shook his head and grinned. He liked her this way too much. His grip tightened slightly. He jerked her hands above her, and she gasped as he pulled her against the hard contours of his body.

Her breathing became shallow as he nuzzled her throat and inhaled. Her scent was intoxicating: citrusy, earthy, and sweet. He laced a hand through her hair and brought her mouth to his. She met his fierce passion with her own, her tongue battling his for dominance.

He caressed her shoulder, her side, her hip, and then he brought his hand between them to cup her intimately. She stilled at the touch, her head falling back in passion.

"God, I want you so bad."

Her eyes flitted open. "Take me."

Melanie

Melanie couldn't believe how brazen she was being, but she was hot and needy, her body sliding against his. His eyes widened, his nostrils flaring at her pronouncement, and then he smiled slowly. Dang, he was sexy. His gaze promised all kinds of carnal pleasure.

With one hand still holding hers, he leaned her down until she felt the soft comforter underneath her. Her breathing caught in anticipation as he stared at her, devouring her body with his gaze. He stepped between her legs and slid one long finger inside her. She moaned at the feeling of him caressing her from the inside.

"Ready for me?" he asked.

"I want to see you."

"You're about to, baby."

She left her arms above her after he released them, enjoying the sensation of being exposed beneath him. He tugged his pants over his hips and tossed them aside in one quick motion, and when he stood...good Lord. He was glorious. Tan muscles swept up the entire length of his form and—oh geez was he big. His cock jutted out from a thatch of dark blond at a length she had never seen before.

She licked her lips in anticipation. Never taking his eyes off her, he grabbed a foil packet out of the top drawer of his nightstand. He ripped the package open and slid the condom on. He was hot with his dick held in his hand, his eyes black, and his jaw clenched in determination.

He bent over her, and she could feel him poised at her entrance. She whimpered, her body arching off the bed. He laced his fingers through hers and plunged, his cock stretching her, filling her, pinioning her against the bed.

He swore an oath and began to pound into her, his body grinding against her clit. She lifted her hips to meet him stroke for stroke, and pressure built within her. Again, and again he thrust, his hands holding hers onto the bed. Pleasure swelled inside her and she came, calling out his name and shuddering against him. As her body tightened around him, he stiffened above and finished with her.

His weight warmed her as she stopped quivering. After a minute, he kissed her forehead and then rolled off her. The loss of him made her shiver. She turned over onto her side as he disposed of the condom in a small wastebasket.

The orgasm held her in a haze, but it began to clear. She was in her boss's bed. She had just fucked her boss in his bed. She had orgasmed in his kitchen. This could get very, very awkward.

She scooted to the headboard to sit, and he walked over and sat beside her.

"Hey there." He brushed a strand of her hair behind her ear.

She made herself look at Erik and told herself not to freak out. They had decided on one night, and she was darn well going to enjoy it. "Hey, boss," she said, grinning. She knew it was a silly, post-sex smile, but she couldn't help it.

His eyes darkened. "I like when you call me 'boss' in the bedroom. It implies you'll do what I say."

She swallowed, and her face heated. "Don't push your luck."

"Melanie, after today, I intend to never stop pushing my luck." He pounced on top of her, trapping her legs between his thighs.

Her heart tripped over itself in her chest at his sudden action. For some reason, his words caused a purr of satisfaction to vibrate through her. Her last coherent thought was "This can't be good" before his mouth was on hers, stirring passion within her once more.

11

Melanie

Melanie woke up in a foreign bed, glancing between the unfamiliar deep green sheets and the shadowed man beside her. The previous hours rushed back. Her skin warmed at the memories of her and Erik. Everything floated through her mind in graphic images and thinking of her uninhibited behavior was both empowering and embarrassing. She was glad he was not awake beside her to see her simultaneous self-satisfied smile and pink cheeks.

Erik's arm draped over her naked waist, and the covers were crumpled across her hips and barely covered his behind. His face was slack and innocent in sleep. She was tempted to peek at his butt because she hadn't gotten a good view despite all the positions they'd been tangled in a couple of hours before. She didn't want to wake him by tugging on the sheets though.

Light crept in around curtains on one wall of the room, but it still seemed early. She looked around for a clock and found one on the nightstand beside Erik. Careful not to shift too much, afraid she might wake him, she braced herself on her elbows and strained her neck. It was 5:40 a.m. She had only been asleep for over an hour.

She looked again at Erik's sleeping face, and she knew what she had to do. The easiest way to handle this situation would be for her to slip out before he woke up, and then they could act as if it had never happened. Her heart clenched at the thought of pretending but leaving was the right thing to do. She would remember the night with relish, and she was sure he would play a heavy role in her fantasies for a while, but reality chased the sunrise. They had agreed on one night, and she didn't want to make things weird between them. She lived there for goodness sake.

She would go back to her room, take a long shower, and then start cooking as if nothing had changed. Yeah, that was possible. Who was she kidding? Everything felt different, but she was a grown woman. She could do this.

She lifted his heavy arm and slid out of bed. One of his shirts peeked out of a dresser drawer and she threw it on. Before changing her mind, she glanced back and then left. The tile was cold against her feet as she went to her room, and a strange emptiness filled her. No regrets, she told herself. There was nothing to regret. She'd had her fun, and now it was time to get back to work.

❧

Erik

Erik woke up alone. The revelation should have made him relieved, but it didn't. She had snuck out in the middle of the night, God knows at what time, without him waking up. Disappointment coursed through him as he looked at the side of the bed she'd been sleeping on. Everything would be easier because she'd left already. She had given him an easy out, and yet there he was, feeling disappointed. Images of the night before flashed through his head, and he could feel his cock hardening. He wanted her again.

This was supposed to be easy. Lusting, fantasizing, it all should have gone away after he'd fucked her. Instead, he thought about her more, and all he wanted to do was carry her back into his room and fuck her again. He needed to get his libido under control. It was better this way.

He looked at his clock and groaned when he saw that it was eight in the morning. He had overslept. What was this tiny chef doing to him? He stumbled out of bed and headed straight for the shower. Cold, cold water was in order.

After the shower, he felt a lot calmer and more collected. Melanie was being mature by slipping out. He had been concerned she was so innocent that she wouldn't be able to separate feelings from sex, but apparently, that wasn't a problem. He wondered how many one-night stands she'd had. The thought made him pause. For all he knew, she could've had dozens. Maybe she was barely affected by him. Maybe she fucked him and got him out of her mind.

He ripped boxers and a navy-blue shirt from a drawer in his dresser. He wanted to punch something. Who cared if she'd had dozens of one-night-stands? He wasn't looking for anything long-term. He didn't do relationships. He didn't intend to get close to someone. It was not jealousy that made him grind his teeth.

Fuck. He massaged his temples and put on his clothes. The sooner he saw her after having sex, the better. He had to put this behind him. This would not end well if he couldn't control himself.

He tied his shoes and then headed to the dining room for a very late breakfast. When he entered the room, he was reminded of Melanie naked and covered in chocolate on the table. Those images were not going away anytime soon. Not that he wanted them to.

A half-empty cup of orange juice, a bowl of grapes, and a paper sat on the table. It looked as if someone's breakfast had been cleared away. Melanie's giggling and Hunter's muffled voice drifted in from the kitchen. What the hell could his brother say that was that entertaining?

He walked to the kitchen and poked his head in. Ignoring his charming brother, he looked straight at his chef. She wore stiff, tight jeans and a curve-hugging, yellow button-down, a button shy of being chaste. Her cleavage was pushed up, and her legs looked impossibly long in her jeans. Red bloomed up her neck when she caught sight of him. He bit back a grin. She still wanted him.

"I'm ready for breakfast now," he said.

"Coming right up."

"Oversleep?" Hunter asked, stirring thick batter in a silver bowl.

Erik ignored him and walked out. He wanted to throw his brother out of the room and away from Melanie. He sat at the table and thoughts about Hunter and Melanie bombarded him. He wasn't sure why he cared what the kid did. Hunter wasn't interested in a romantic relationship with her, at least he didn't seem to be, but he spent so much time making her laugh.

Hunter walked in while he was stewing in the dining room. "Problem?"

"Do you have to flirt with her while she's working?"

"I'm not flirting. I'm talking. It's strange. She's like a girl that's a friend."

Erik rolled his eyes. His brother could be such a pig. "Hasn't she been able to teach you one meal yet, or are you really that dense?"

"Touchy. You realize this is only the third time I've done this."

Erik shrugged his stiff shoulders. He hadn't realized that.

"Right. Well as much fun as this is, I'm going to go back in and learn how to cook pancakes."

Erik's eyebrows flew up his forehead. Holy shit, he had missed something. "You're going to cook a girl breakfast?"

"Only for dinner."

Of course. Hunter turned around and walked back into the kitchen. Erik picked up the newspaper to clear his head. He opened it and started to read the first page, but he didn't get more than a line into the story. Something about the local sheriff and dogs, but the sentences were going over his head. Melanie's giggling grew louder, and Hunter talked animatedly. Their arrangement was souring his mood. Every few seconds, images of Melanie naked would distract him. Screw this, maybe he wasn't done yet. Who was he to deny himself pleasure? He'd been the one to decide on one night, and maybe now he'd changed his mind.

He turned to the newspaper once more as Melanie walked into the room with a plate full of pancakes. They smelled great. His mouth watered. He had a full appetite after the previous night's' activities. He looked up at her as she approached, his gaze holding hers. "They look delicious. Almost as delicious as you," he said, dropping his voice.

The effect was immediate; she blushed scarlet and licked her lips. She opened her mouth to say something, but the kitchen door opened again. Hunter walked in behind her.

"Did he try them yet?" Hunter asked.

Panic lit Melanie's eyes. "Not yet."

His brother had the worst timing. He glared at Hunter, but his brother smiled back. "Will you please grab me coffee, Hunter? I have something to discuss with the chef."

"I can get the coffee." Melanie dropped the plate on the table and jerked away.

"That's okay. I'd like to talk to you." Erik suppressed a smile. Jumpy, wasn't she?

Hunter looked between the two of them and then nodded. "I'll be right back."

"Take your time."

Hunter walked out, and Melanie fidgeted with her sleeves. Erik motioned to a chair next to him, and she glanced down the hall before she sat.

“What can I do for you, boss?” she asked, putting stress on the word ‘boss.’

“You can tell me why you left without saying anything while I was still asleep,” Erik said over his steepled fingers.

Melanie

Melanie had to grip her seat to keep from jumping at the question. It never occurred to her he would bring up what happened. She assumed he would be pleased she hadn’t lingered or made things awkward. Apparently, she was very, very wrong. “I thought it would make things easier. Since we agreed on one night.”

Erik’s gaze clouded. Was she missing something here? He didn’t like that answer, but she wasn’t sure why. It took a lot of effort to drag herself out of bed, but she thought she’d been strong and done the right thing. Now here he was, looking all tempting with his navy-blue shirt molded to his muscular form, and his darn lusty looks. It wasn’t fair.

“Maybe I want more than one night.” His tone made her insides feel like liquid. He watched her, his gaze intense as it slid over her body, catching on her nape and breasts. She clenched her thighs at the heat flowing through her.

She wanted to say yes, but she had to think. This was her boss, and he wasn’t talking about a relationship. He was talking about having sex again. “I have to think about it,” she said. The answer cost her a lot. She wanted to thread her fingers in his hair and kiss him then and there.

He reached across the table and brushed a strand of her hair behind her ear. "I know you enjoyed yourself last night."

Cocky jerk. Although, he was right. Her cheeks burned. "I didn't say I didn't, but...can we talk about it after I finish cooking for the day?" She glanced toward the kitchen realizing Hunter would probably walk in at any second.

"If I want you, I will be able to convince you." He dragged a thumb across her lower lip, and desire shot straight through her.

She closed her eyes for a second and inhaled. "I know, but I'm not used to arrangements like these. I need to think." Her voice was small.

Erik muttered an oath. "Meet me in my office after dinner?"

"All right." She couldn't deny her attraction to him. She wanted him again, and he was too intriguing for his own good. What if she didn't know how to separate her emotions from sex? What if she ended up with feelings for him, and then he decided he was done with her? She could already feel how drawn she was to him, and he wasn't the relationship type. She knew something about being with someone who wasn't ready for the long haul. Forcing someone to make a commitment led to loneliness.

Hunter walked back into the dining room carrying a white mug of coffee. Melanie was grateful for the distraction. She smoothed her shirt, trying to remember Hunter had no idea what they'd been talking about.

"Anything else I can get you, sir? I could iron your

pants. I could get you fresh goat milk from the nearest farm," Hunter said, setting the mug on the table.

Erik picked up the cup. "No, but we need to finish organizing the lunches for the camp. Maybe we can discuss it on the way to the office. Also, have you and Jennifer decided on team splits?"

Hunter's twinkling eyes darkened. "No."

"Act like an adult and deal with it."

Melanie wondered what Erik and Hunter were annoyed about, but she decided she didn't want to stick around to hear the details. She needed to get back to work, and then she needed to decide what to do about Erik. Maybe she'd call Sheila. Who was she kidding? She'd call Sheila right after cleanup.

"I should get back to work," she said, standing before they could continue their discussion. She looked up at Erik, his eyes, full of promises of pleasure, captured hers, and he nodded. How was a look so darn persuasive?

She walked to the kitchen, hoping a little space would help with her ability to think. Why did he have such a powerful hold over her?

She looked around the counters. Splatters of pancake batter and grease marks from meat were all over. Teaching Hunter to cook was going to give her way more work to do. She started scrubbing, trying not to think about how she'd been naked and standing against the counters in this very kitchen the night before. She hummed to herself and couldn't hear the conversation that was going on in the dining room.

It took her half an hour until the dishwasher was loaded and the granite countertops were sparkling, but she was happy to focus on something other than her internal conflict. As soon as she was done cleaning, thoughts of Erik flew at her at full force. She left the kitchen and walked to her bedroom. Once she got there, she locked the door and called Sheila.

"Hey, how are you?" Sheila answered on the first ring. Things must be slow at the office today.

"I'm pretty good. How are you?"

"That's it? You're pretty good? You're working at Mr. Hot Boss's home and it's been pretty good. Does he have weird food habits or something?"

Melanie rolled her eyes. She had said two words, and yet it was apparent to her friend something was up. Might as well go for the full confession. "It's nothing like that. I slept with him."

"Oh my God. Really? Look at you. I didn't even know you had it in you. Was he good? I bet it was good."

For a minute, Melanie regretted telling Sheila anything, but now that she had, she went for broke. "It was. Very good. But I don't know what do about it."

"What do you mean? You don't have to do anything 'about it.'"

"He wants to do it again."

"And?"

"That's all he wants. Sex."

"Ah, I see."

"Yep." She didn't bother to elaborate. They'd been friends for a long time. Sheila knew Melanie hadn't been a free spirit when it came to sex. She'd slept with only the one boyfriend despite Sheila's encouragement to get back out there after the breakup. Now she'd had a one-night stand.

"What do you want?" God love Sheila, she was so

pragmatic.

"I want him, I'm just afraid of getting hurt. I think I might be starting to like him."

"So, make some ground rules. But don't be afraid to enjoy yourself."

"Ground rules?" She hadn't thought about that. Maybe she could come up with a couple during the afternoon. She was young; she deserved to have some fun. If she didn't try new stuff now, when would she? Eighty and wrinkled didn't make for great one-night stand. She also knew this might not end well. "Will you keep looking for jobs?"

"Even though you're going to give in to your carnal desires?" Sheila asked, her tone playful.

"That's why. Don't get me wrong, I want him, but I don't want to be stuck here if this ends badly."

"You're so responsible. It's such a shame."

"Yeah, it's a horrible personality trait. Anyway, just because this job has gone well doesn't change my life goals. I want to be a head chef at a restaurant. I'm not going to give up my dream because I'm boinking my boss."

"Boinking? Who says that shit? How old are you?"

"Very funny. How are *you?*" Melanie was ready for someone else to be the focus of this conversation.

"Don't think I don't know what you're doing, but it just so happens that there's shit to talk about. My sister is coming to town tonight."

"Who is she bringing with her?" Sheila's older sister, Angie, always brought a shit-show girlfriend with her. She could not stand to be alone. Every time the girl visited home, she wreaked emotional havoc for her sister for a few weeks and then left. Some days Melanie wished she could tell her friend not to let Angie bring her girlfriends, but Sheila had a soft spot for her older sister. Her parents had kicked Angie out when they found out she was lesbian. Sheila felt like she owed it to her to be supportive.

"That's what's odd. She's not seeing anyone," Sheila said.

Melanie's eyebrows rose. What was happening in the world? "Think something is going on?"

"I guess I'll find out tonight."

"Let me know if you'd like a buffer while she's in town."

"I'm not pulling you away from Mr. Hot Boss."

Melanie groaned. There went her distraction. Her stomach flipped as she thought about the coming evening. Thank goodness she'd be able to focus on cooking for a while first.

12

Erik

Erik spent a good portion of his day at his Phoenix office meeting with designers and programmers for their logo app concept. He loved working with the dedicated creatives he had hired, but today he'd been distracted. Melanie was making him wait for an answer about whether they would continue their tryst, and he didn't enjoy waiting. He could seduce her, he'd seen how she reacted to him, but she wanted time to think, and he was trying to do the right thing. Damn the right thing. He never worried about doing the right thing for anyone but Hunter and himself, and recently, for Stacie. He was used to women who just wanted to have fun, who didn't get their feelings hurt. He hadn't had to worry about them. Melanie was different. He might've had his own interests in mind, but that didn't mean he wanted to hurt her. If he was smart, he'd go back to avoiding her; he'd tell her she was right to be wary. The problem was that he couldn't stop thinking about licking whipped cream off her body.

Despite his preoccupation, the day had been productive. Hunter took the lead on the meetings, and they'd picked a color pallete and a logo concept. They'd also begun to work on new ideas for other apps. Erik's mind was still on the previous evening though, and he couldn't focus on them. He was glad his personal assistant, Derek, took notes.

Thankfully the day was over, and Hunter was driving them back to Erik's to drop him off. The car seemed to be going slow despite the fact that Hunter had a terrible speeding habit.

"You seem distracted," Hunter said, turning down the loud rap he'd been listening to.

"I'm thinking about the meetings we went to this afternoon," Erik said.

"I'm glad you are now because you weren't before." Hunter smirked.

Had it been that obvious? Erik looked out the window, reigning in his annoyance, and watched the highway curve and the splashes of color on the cars they passed. "I was paying attention. There was a lot to take in," he said, lying.

"Sure, of course. So, do you like the color scheme we picked today?"

Erik rubbed his jaw. Fuck. "Yeah, it's great."

"I remember we decided on a neon pink, but I can't seem to remember the other two colors, they slipped my mind. What were they?"

He didn't even remember pink. They could've flashed him photos of flying orangutans for their icon and he wouldn't have remembered. "Fine. I wasn't paying attention. Happy?"

His brother's smile widened, and he turned off the highway. "Very. Want to admit what you were thinking about?"

"Admit?"

"Oh, come on, we both know. Why not just say it? Go ahead."

Erik would admit nothing. A girl, some chef, should not have distracted him from an important business meeting. It was embarrassing. He would be damned if that's where their conversation ended up. "Did you ever call Jennifer?"

Hunter nodded once, and the teasing smile slipped from his face.

"Did you apologize?"

Hunter nodded again and didn't say anything.

It was Erik's turn to be amused. Something about this woman drove his brother nuts, and Erik loved every minute of it. He hoped they didn't lose Jennifer because of Hunter's behavior. She was tough though; he couldn't imagine that happening. "How did it go?"

"Not well." He flexed his hands on the steering wheel.

Erik looked at his brother, surprised. He couldn't imagine Jennifer not taking an apology well. She was the consummate professional. "Why not?"

Hunter shifted in his seat as they drove through Erik's neighborhood. "I ended up calling her a ball-busting shrew."

Erik's mouth dropped open. "That's your idea of an apology?"

"I didn't mean to. It just slipped out. I was apologizing, and everything seemed fine." He turned the car and sidled up next to John, the man operating the gate, and unrolled the window.

John waved, and the wrought iron gate opened.

Erik shook his head. He couldn't understand how his brother could behave this way. Hunter always handled difficult people well. "How did you go from 'everything seemed fine' to 'ball-busting shrew'? Because that seems like a pretty big jump to me."

Hunter's hands turned white on the steering wheel. "I don't know. We got to talking about coaching and techniques, and suddenly she called me a sexist pig."

They pulled up to the top of the driveway, Erik's large windows and oak doors coming into view. "Oh, Jesus, Hunter, what did you say?"

"I don't know. Something about being a good coach or co-ed teams. I don't know what set her off. She just freaked out."

"And a 'shrew'? How did you come up with that? Are you reading Shakespeare now?"

Hunter turned off the ignition, and red rose to his tan cheeks. "I'm not used to insulting women. I didn't want to cuss."

"I can't believe you're letting her affect you like this. She's completely under your skin." Erik unbuckled his seatbelt.

Hunter let out a bark of laughter but there was no humor in it. "You're going to criticize me for this? That's rich. Melanie is so far into your head she's coming out both ears."

"I don't even know what that means."

"Every time I talk to her, and you decide it's a little too flirty, you go all macho man and act like you're going to punch me. And then today at work it was like you were on a different planet."

Erik seethed in anger. He wanted to throw something, and part of the reason why was because Hunter was right. She distracted him, but he couldn't help himself. Every time he thought of her, he pictured her lithe, sexy body molding against him and he lost focus on whatever he was doing. It needed to stop, and after he squared an arrangement away with his little chef, he'd be back to his old self. He would just work her out of his system; fuck her until he stopped reacting like a horny teenager. It was that simple.

Melanie

The eggplant was baking, the table was set for two in case Hunter ate with him, and the side dishes had been prepped hours ago. Melanie had a whole five minutes to herself before she would need to check the eggplant. She used two of her five minutes to debate whether or not she should change into something more seductive, and then she spent one minute after to berate herself for wasting her time to think about clothes during her five minutes of *me* time. To make up for it, she mapped a run on her cell phone for later in her two minutes left.

The timer beeped on the microwave, and she grabbed the red fire-retardant oven mitt off the counter by the stove to open the oven door. The eggplant looked great. The cheese was golden, and the sauce sizzling. A few more minutes and everything would be set. Assuming Erik didn't come home late, the meal was timed perfectly.

She placed the oven mitt back on the counter and clicked her nails on the granite. She was uncertain about how this evening would go. She had her mental list of ground rules, and she was ready to try to enjoy herself. If she could tell her neck muscles to stop tightening into a brick, she might believe she was excited. The tension she held in her shoulders was impossible to shake off. She wasn't a virgin, nor was she some uptight, prissy girl with a stick up her ass, and yet she thought she might start shaking at any moment. What was it about this guy that made her react this way?

The front door slammed with a heavy thud, and she almost jumped out of her black boots. Erik was home. She bit the inside of her cheek, listening for the sounds of him moving through the house. Of course, she couldn't hear anything at first, the house was huge, but she listened anyway, waiting. Finally, she heard the dining room door open and close, followed by his muffled footsteps. She braced herself against the counter, wondering if he would wait in the dining room or come into the kitchen. She kind of hoped he would wait in the dining room because she was a coward and wanted to use their professional situation as a buffer. But she wasn't that lucky.

The kitchen door opened, and Erik walked in. He looked...furious. Jeez, what had happened to him? Melanie wished she had room to take a step back. His eyes were dark and dangerous, his lips thin, and his jaw hard. Even his stance was intimidating. He stood with his legs shoulder width apart, his hands clenched into fists at his sides, and his back rigid. His gaze captured hers and turned stormy. She wished she knew what he was thinking.

Her body reacted at his scrutiny, her heart rate increasing, her skin tingling. The anger in his eyes faded into a look of feral desire. His mood shift was palpable, and she wasn't sure this was any safer.

"Hi." She cringed at the breathy tone of her voice.

His body relaxed, and a slow smile spread across his lips. He stalked toward her, and she thought about moving, but she couldn't tear her gaze away. She felt like prey and more than anything she wanted to be captured.

He stopped when he stood towering over her, the heat from his body traveling the distance between them. He combed his fingers through the back of her hair and tugged the strands. She was forced to look at him. The slight pain sent sizzling electricity through her.

He leaned close, and she could feel his breath on the shell of her ear. "I've been thinking about wrapping my fingers in your hair all day." His voice was like silk.

"Oh?" was all she could manage. Her breath seemed to have left her lungs.

"Want to know what else I've been thinking about?" he asked, his voice low and sexy.

She found herself saying, "Yes," before she'd given it any thought.

He trailed his tongue across her jawline and nipped. "Good. Let me give you a demonstration."

His mouth captured her bottom lip, and he tugged with his teeth. She opened her mouth, feeling the sting of his teeth surge down to her toes. He growled in appreciation and deepened the kiss. With his fingers in her hair, she felt helpless under his exploration. Her body burned and need built under the surface of her skin.

He released her hair with one hand but held her tight in the other, and then unclasped the highest button of her shirt. With the one undone, he would be able to see her teal, lacy bra. He looked down, his nostrils flaring at the sight of her cleavage.

She smirked in pride at her ability to arouse him, but then he tugged her bra cups down, exposing her breasts in the kitchen. She gasped as he cupped her, and his palm skimmed over her nipple. Her back arched of its own accord into his hand despite the tugging in her scalp. Before she could ask for more, the timer on the microwave beeped.

She shook her head to clear the lust filled haze, but Erik didn't let go. He continued to tease her, moving his finger in a circle around her areola, ignoring the timer. "The...the eggplant is ready."

He released her, taking a step back. She looked down and righted her bra and shirt. Her gaze caught on his length, straining against the seam of his jeans. She swallowed, remembering how he felt inside her. She glanced up and his pupils were still dilated, his breathing shallow.

She looked around for the oven mitt and slipped it on when she found it. She removed the ceramic dish from the oven as if she hadn't been on the verge of screwing her boss in the kitchen again. They hadn't even gone over ground rules yet, and she'd been all over him. She needed to get it together.

Erik hadn't moved since she put on the oven mitt, but she worked around his presence. She put the heavy dish on a cooling rack on the counter. Finally, hoping her breathing was no longer so ragged that she couldn't speak, she turned back to him. "Dinner is ready to eat, and then we should talk."

"Talk?"

"You know, about continuing this..." She motioned awkwardly between them. Why did she have to be the one to say something? He was the one who wanted to continue. Well, the one who said it first anyway. Then again, he also seemed fine without any ground rules. He probably had lovers all the time with whom he didn't have to figure out boundaries. She bet they threw themselves all over him...she rolled her neck. The idea of him with other women spurred anger and a sharp pain in her gut she didn't want to think about.

"We need to talk about it? You seemed pretty convinced thirty seconds ago."

Melanie's cheeks burned, but she held her ground. "There need to be some ground rules," she said, crossing her fingers that he wouldn't laugh or tell her no.

He nodded. "Good idea."

She let out a breath of relief. "Okay. So, I'll bring out your food, and then we can talk."

He shook his head, and her heart sank. Shoot.

"I don't want to eat. We should have our little discussion now."

She blinked at him. In theory, she was ready to have a mature discussion about their fling, but it seemed beyond embarrassing. "Okay," she said, her voice small.

"But can we discuss it in your office?"

"Why?"

"Because being in here with you after yesterday is a little distracting."

Erik

Melanie's pale, smooth cheeks, turned pink and Erik couldn't help the slow grin that stole over his face. He enjoyed the fact that him being in the kitchen with her flustered her. After all, she was to blame for his distracted behavior at work. It was only fair he got to turn the tables on her. But he also wanted to assuage whatever concerns she had about continuing their affair so that he could bury himself deep inside her again as soon as possible.

"That's fine." He took her hand. He was looking forward to turning his office into another place that flustered her.

He ushered her through the kitchen and the dining room, and they walked down the hall that led to the other side of his house, near his bedroom. They passed through the great room, where the two spiral staircases sat, and down the hallway toward his rooms.

"If the food gets cold though, I don't want to be blamed," she muttered.

He opened the door of his office and released her hand. "Melanie, even if your food gets cold, it'll still taste great."

She grinned at him, her face open and guileless. A surge of warmth rushed through him at her smile. Her smile lit up the room, and whenever he was the cause, he almost smiled himself. He shook his head. This was about sex, their arrangement needed to be about sex. He couldn't do a relationship. He had learned young, repeatedly, not to trust people, that they would only screw you over and hurt you. He couldn't be vulnerable right now. He was all Hunter had in the way of family, and work and the foster kid camp were too important to be distracted from.

He ran the pad of his thumb over her lip, watching her blue eyes darken and her breathing change. That was better. This was his territory. "Why don't you take a seat?"

She nodded and sat in one of the armchairs in front of the large, oak desk. He walked around to the other side and sat across from her. Melanie scooted to the edge of her seat. He was struck by how obviously she'd never done anything like this. She was probably a relationship kind of girl, through and through. She needed to understand what she was getting into. "How about I start?" he asked.

"All right." She tucked her short, black hair behind her ear.

"There is no commitment." He steepled his fingers together.

"No romantic feelings. If one of us develops feelings, it's over," she said.

He thought he would have to say that. Considering that this had never been an issue for him in the past, he wasn't concerned. He was concerned Melanie would want a deeper relationship and that he wouldn't be able to give her more. Him developing feelings wasn't an issue. "Agreed."

She straightened in her seat, her face serious. "Also, no physical relationships with other people while we're doing this."

Erik narrowed his eyes. This went without saying for him. He wasn't a player; he just didn't want a long-term relationship. He wondered if this needed to be said because of her. Was she bringing this up because she had thought about someone else? An image of Melanie kissing some other man popped up unbidden into his head. Fuck that.

"Agreed," he said through his tightened jaw.

"There's one last thing," she said and paused.

He raised an eyebrow, impatient. He wanted to reach across the desk and claim her. He wanted to lay his mind at ease about any other men by ravaging her until she couldn't think of anyone else.

"I don't want there to be any lies between us. I know we're not in any sort of relationship, and I know we don't owe one another anything, but this is the first time I've done anything like this. I wouldn't want to do this with anyone I couldn't respect, or who didn't respect me."

"And to you, respect means honesty." He could understand that. His relationship with Hunter was built upon a foundation of respect and honesty.

She nodded. She looked small and innocent sitting at the edge of her seat. He may not be able to give her anything like romance, but at the very least, she should know he respected her. She was so strong and beautiful.

"I won't lie to you, Melanie. I do respect you. You are kind, driven, and smart." His gaze locked on hers.

She looked up at him through her black eyelashes.

"Thanks. I respect you, too."

His lips quirked up. "I'm glad. Now, is there anything else on your list of ground rules? Because I'm on the verge of hauling you across this desk to have my way with you."

"Um, that's it."

"Good," He smiled, and, in a blur of sudden action, he shoved the contents of his half-empty workspace to the edge and reached across it, gripping Melanie's shoulders and lifting her up. He pulled her until her hips were pinned against the wood, and her upper body bent over, meeting him halfway across the desk. Then he kissed her hard, sharing the passion he'd been controlling since he'd brought her to his office.

He stepped closer but was thwarted by a drawer. Looking forward to breaking in his office in an innovative way, he slowed his kiss. After a moment, he leaned back, and lust flowed through him as he took in Melanie's appearance. She was bent over, her arms braced on the desk, giving him a provocative view of her heaving cleavage, and her eyes were hooded with desire.

"Stay like that."

13

Melanie

Erik's low command echoed in Melanie's head. Everything intellectual in her rebelled as she stood self-consciously at the desk, but everything primal and base held her fast as she bent over, and Erik walked around her. Her skin hummed in anticipation as she waited to feel what he would do next. He didn't make her wait long.

He stood behind her, his upper thighs a wall of firm pressure against her behind, his hands resting on her shoulders and then running down her body until they captured her hips. He rocked against her as he held her in place, so she could feel his jean-clad, hard length against her butt. "Feel what you do to me?"

She sucked in a breath, wishing there were fewer

layers of clothes between them. He reached around to the buttons on her shirt and undid them one at a time until her shirt fell open. He slid his hands over her lacy bra, and her nipples stiffened against the slight padding. She curled into him, needing to feel the contact of his flesh on hers, his fingers touching her without any obstruction.

He flicked the front clasp open, running his hands over her when her breasts were free. "I want you topless."

He pulled her straight up, and then he slid her shirtsleeves and bra straps down her arms. She turned at the waist. She wanted to explore his body with her hands, but he caught her shoulders and kept her facing away.

A rustling sounded behind her, and she saw him tug his shirt over his head as she glanced over her shoulder. His mouthwatering body was made of planes and planes of hard muscle. He leaned down, pressing the wall of his chest against her back and she shuddered at his hard, unyielding body.

"I want to fuck you bent over my desk." He bit down her shoulder.

Her throat went dry at his words. Pressure built between her legs, and she rubbed her thighs together. "Brace your hands on the desk again," he said, his voice a persuasive purr.

She bent and held onto the desk, waiting, licking her lips in anticipation. He ran his hands all over her, possessing her, setting each inch of her skin on fire. She gripped the desk hard, the wood biting her palms.

He tugged softly on her nipples, and wetness pooled between her thighs. Sliding his hands down her stomach, he unbuttoned her pants and slid the zipper down. He moved so damn slow. Melanie grew desperate. A keening noise came from the back of her throat. "I want you."

"Soon, baby." He tugged her jeans and her thong to her knees in one quick flick.

The sensation of cool air against her hot, needy skin made her shudder. For a moment, Erik's hands disappeared from her body, but she could feel his gaze on her most intimate part of herself. She squirmed and heard Erik's sharp intake of breath.

After what felt like hours, his palm cupped the sensitive petals of her sex. Her knees buckled as he gave her a gentle squeeze. He ran his finger between her lips down to her entrance. He circled it with his fingers, and she thrust against him. "Please," she said and whimpered.

"Is this what you want?" He sunk two fingers inside her. He rocked his hand back and forth and found her clit with his thumb, stroking her in a maddening rhythm. Her body tightened as she ground against his hand, helpless to her body's fervor, but then his hand disappeared.

She cried out at the loss. "Erik. I was so close."

"I want to be inside you when you come."

She looked over her shoulder to watch him unbutton and unzip his own jeans. He took a condom out of his pocket and shoved his pants down his legs to free his shaft. She shuddered, looking at its size and remembering how he had felt inside her the night before: so big and hard. He tore the wrapper open and slid the condom on. Then the head of his member was at her entrance.

"Are you ready for me?"

She moaned as he pushed his hot, smooth rod against her slick folds, but avoided her entrance.

"Yes." She rocked her ass against him. "Please."

Erik threaded his hand in her hair and tugged while he drove inside her in one forceful thrust. The shock of the pleasure and pain at the crown of her head and the fullness of him inside her sent her over the edge. Her body tightened from the tips of her toes to her womb, and she shuddered as waves of pleasure rocked over her.

Erik

Erik grit his teeth trying to keep from coming as she cried out and clenched around him, her body quivering in pleasure. Christ, she was sexy, her tight inner muscles milking him, her long neck exposed, and her head thrown back as he held her silky hair in his fist.

He began to thrust as her body slackened beneath his, but he wasn't done with her yet. He slid his hand up her stomach and rib cage until he caught one of her small, peach nipples between his fingers. She arched her back as he caressed her, and he thrust harder.

Her hands turned white as they gripped the desk, and he could feel her breasts swaying against the palm of his hand. He rammed into her, losing control as her ass slapped against him in time with his strokes. He lost his ability to think, only knowing instinctively that he wanted to mark this woman, possess her. He leaned down, slid his tongue up the side of her long neck, and then nibbled her ear. She gyrated against him, her body making silent pleas for him to make her come again. He cupped her mound. She gasped, and he slid a finger over the bud of her sex and thrust hard.

"Erik," she cried out. Her legs stiffened and this time he came with her. He shuddered against her neck as pleasure took him.

For a minute, neither one of them spoke. His legs weakened under him, and he took a deep, shaky breath. The things this woman did to him. He released her hair and leaned his hands on the desk around her. He kissed the side of her neck, and then pulled out.

Erik removed the condom and drew up his pants while Melanie straightened.

"Well, that was..." she said, trailing off, uncertain about what to say post-sex.

He didn't want her to feel awkward or embarrassed. The sex had been mind-blowing, and she was incredible. He gripped her arm and turned her around. She stumbled, her jeans still around her knees, but he held her up. Her eyes were half-closed, her skin was flushed, and her hair wild. She was gorgeous. A rumble of approval at her satiated state ran through him. "It was amazing," he said.

She looked up at him, a shadow of uncertainty in her eyes. He couldn't help the smile that took over his lips. "You're going to hurt my ego. Didn't you enjoy yourself?" he said, teasing.

"Your ego couldn't be dented with a crowbar."

Erik raised an eyebrow. "Since you're not responding to my questions about sex, should I take that as a negative? Do I need to bend you over again, and work harder?"

Melanie's skin turned a deeper shade of red. Cute.

She shook her head. "No, it was...wonderful. Incredible. I hadn't realized it could be so good. I mean I've had sex before I just—" She stopped talking, and averted her gaze, "I don't think you need to exaggerate. I know you do this a lot."

How could she think it wasn't as good for him? He lifted her chin with his knuckles, so she was forced to look up at him. "I told you I would be honest with you. It was amazing. You are amazing."

"Thanks," she mumbled.

"You're welcome. Now, how about we get dressed and go eat? I want to make sure we get some sustenance before round two." He picked up his shirt and put it on.

She put on her pants and buttoned them. "Round two?"

"You didn't think I was done with you yet, did you?"

"Um, maybe?"

He shook his head.

She crossed her arms over her breasts, and she looked around the room. Once she spotted her shirt and bra, she grabbed them and threw them on. "Dinner now?"

Erik nodded but before they took a step toward the door, knocking echoed inside the room. Melanie clapped a hand over her mouth and stared horrified at Erik. "I'm sure they didn't hear anything," he whispered to her. "Who is it?"

"It's Stacie." His aunt's voice was muffled from behind the door.

"One minute. I'm with the staff," he said.

Melanie looked around, her blue eyes wild. "How long do you think she's been out there? Do you think she heard? Who is Stacie?" she whispered.

"Relax, sweetheart. She wouldn't listen outside the door. She'll think we had a meeting. Just sit and try to act normal." He motioned to a seat and started to walk to the door once Melanie straightened her clothes and sat. He stopped after a step. "Oh, and maybe straighten your hair a bit."

She patted the sides of her head. She groaned and ran her hands through the black strands.

"Ready?" he asked.

She nodded and sat as still as a statue. Erik shook his head. Yeah, because that looked normal. Damn, she was adorable. He opened the door to his aunt.

"Hi, dear," she said. Her short, blonde hair curled around her ears, and her smooth skin wrinkled as she smiled. "Don't tell me you forgot about our meeting this evening?"

He squeezed the door handle. He had forgotten. All he had thought about in the past two days was Melanie. "I did, I'm sorry."

She looked up at him in concern, and then looked toward Melanie who was still seated. "Are you too busy to have our meeting?" Stacie motioned to the two of them.

"I'm sorry. Where are my manners? This is Melanie, the chef. Melanie, this is Stacie—"

Melanie stood and walked to his aunt, a big smile on her face. "Is this your mother? You two look so much alike."

Erik shifted, uncertain what to say and the silence stretched between them. Shit. Of course, Melanie didn't know about his past. Only someone as innocent as she wouldn't bother to Google her employer's history. He was tempted to say something about that kind of irresponsible behavior, but he didn't want her to know about his past. She didn't need to hear some sob story about an orphan, and he didn't need to open up that way. Even if he might want to. For a second, he let himself wonder what her reaction might be: pity, sympathy, annoyance? Or maybe she'd leave him? He shut down that direction of thinking. He didn't want to discuss his past with anyone.

Stacie looked between the two of them, and Erik hoped she wouldn't say anything incriminating. She opened her mouth and closed it.

"Did I stick my foot in my mouth? I'm sorry. I didn't mean to..." she trailed off.

"You didn't say anything wrong. This is my aunt. She's helping me set up the summer program," Erik said into the developing silence.

"So truly a family affair, huh? That's great." Melanie shook hands with her.

Stacie smiled again. "It's good to meet you. Hunter goes on and on about your cooking. I hope I get a chance to sample it sometime soon."

"Does he really? That's sweet." Melanie beamed. Her wide smile almost made Erik not want to hit Hunter for discussing his life with Stacie.

"I don't want to interrupt your staff meetings. Maybe we can pick another day to meet?" Stacie asked.

"Oh, we were just finishing," Melanie said.

"Excellent." Stacie turned toward the door.

"I'm the boss," he mouthed to his chef.

She cringed. "Sorry," she mouthed back.

He stepped next to her. "I'll be sure to find a way to keep you from forgetting," he whispered against her ear.

Melanie swallowed and stepped away.

"You may get a chance to taste Melanie's food sooner than you might've thought. I haven't eaten dinner yet. Would you like to join me?" he asked Stacie.

"That would be great."

"I'll go heat up the food," Melanie said and scurried from the room.

Melanie

Office sex followed by an impromptu meeting with the man's aunt. Fantastic. Her luck could not have been worse. She'd be forever wondering if the woman heard something. Oh well, at least Stacie wasn't his mother. That would have been so much worse.

Once she got to the kitchen, she turned back on the oven. It was one thing to serve Erik microwaved eggplant, but she wasn't serving that to his aunt. Stacie looked so elegant and formal. She probably hated microwaved cheese.

Melanie would serve them salad first, and then warn them that dinner might be a while. She took out her homemade vinaigrette from the fridge and spritzed the salad. After tossing the lettuce with the tongs a few times, she leaned against the counter and waited until there were voices in the other room. Once she did, she carried the blue salad bowl into the dining room. She was pretty sure the bowl might be coming across as a shield the way she held it out in front of her, but she didn't care. This was more awkward than when she started the grease fire.

Erik sat at his usual spot, the head of the table, and his aunt sat to his left. Melanie barely noticed Stacie as she walked in though; Erik always dominated the room. He emanated a casual confidence and tightly leashed energy. He looked up at her approach, his gaze catching on hers. The fire in his eyes warmed her insides. The looks he gave could turn any woman to goo. It wasn't fair.

With his aunt sitting right next to him, did he have to look at her like that? Didn't he have an off switch? She took tore her gaze away from Erik to speak to Stacie. "I thought I would serve the salad now. The eggplant will need to be reheated, and it might take a few minutes. I was planning on serving it at six."

Stacie looked at her watch. "Your staff meeting must've taken quite some time."

The bowl slipped in Melanie's fingers. She tightened her grip, and then set the bowl on the table by Erik.

"I needed to meet with them all. Performance reviews," he said smoothly.

Stacie's eyebrows rose in surprise, and then she turned to Melanie. "No worries, dear. I like a little time between my salad and the main course."

"Great." Melanie left the room as fast as possible without running. She didn't have a stoic face, and she didn't want to give anything away. If Stacie referenced their 'meeting' one more time, she might vomit.

Once she got back to the kitchen, embarrassment still hot in her stomach, her focus was only half on the food. She had to prep the fresh grilled veggies and check the pasta. The oven beeped as it finished preheating, and she stuck the eggplant back in the oven. The dish was still warm, so she hoped it wouldn't take long.

The pasta and veggie situation was desperate because both had been done over an hour ago. She took out a pot and boiled water. Time for a couple of cheap tricks. She decided to re-grill the veggies for a couple of minutes on Erik's amazing indoor grill, but she didn't want to boil new pasta. She dumped the pasta into a metal container and then dipped it in the boiling water. After a minute or so, the pasta was hot once more.

She stirred the noodles and transferred them to a serving dish, and then focused on the vegetables. Or tried to. As she grilled, she thought about Erik's promise of round two. She needed to focus on her own life. She hadn't been running in several days. Granted, falling had interrupted her exercise regimen, but the injuries were healing quickly. She needed to start searching for a job herself. Sheila wasn't the end-all for the job hunt. Sure, Sheila had the inside scoop on a lot, but there were things like wanted ads in the newspaper that she could look at. At least, those might still exist. But there she was, roasting veggies, and thinking about sex.

She sighed and took the vegetables off the grill, placing them on a serving dish that matched the salad bowl. She wondered where Erik had got this stuff. He didn't seem like the type to care about picking dishes. Maybe a girl he'd slept with had picked dishes. Maybe his aunt had chosen them. Yeah, she much preferred that explanation.

Shoot. What did it matter how he'd got his dishes? He owed her nothing. She needed to remember that.

She shook off her musings and grabbed the oven mitt. Opening the oven, the scent of melted cheese and basil permeated the air around her. She inhaled, and a sense of calm washed over her. A finished meal always made her feel better. She placed the eggplant on the cooling rack and prepared to serve dinner.

14

Erik

Dinner with his aunt was quiet. Erik had been so hungry that as he ate his first two servings of eggplant, he couldn't contribute anything to the conversation beyond grunting. Melanie had given him quite an appetite. He didn't intend to stop at two servings, the food was addictive, but after finishing his second round, he focused on business.

"I'd like us to consider my dinner social idea," Stacie said, wiping her mouth with a white napkin.

"I think it's doable, but we'll need more staff," Erik said.

"I know it means a lot more money up front, but I think we can cover it with the fundraising banquet."

Erik waved a hand. "I'm not concerned about that.

This is the one cause our company supports. We have enough to cover a dinner social for the kids."

Stacie gripped Erik's hand. "You're such a good man."

He shrugged. "It's nothing."

Stacie opened her mouth to say more, but then she closed it again and smiled, removing her hand from his.

"We'll have to find someone to deal with the particulars of this event," Erik said.

"You'll also need someone to create a menu."

Shit. She said that way too innocently. "A catering company could do that."

"Yes. But if you have someone that can help you figure out some basics you might want, it might be easier to deal with a catering company."

"I'm sure kids will like burgers and hotdogs."

Stacie ignored him and snapped her fingers. "You know, I bet Melanie could help you," she said as if it was a revelation.

Erik almost groaned aloud. "I think burgers would make everyone happy."

"I like her."

"Yes, her cooking is great," he said, being intentionally obtuse.

Stacie looked at him, her eyes sharp. "Nice try. You can't date your employees."

"I know. And I don't intend to date anyone. I'm not looking for a relationship, Stacie. I'm quite happy on my own" He stabbed his veggies with his fork. The prongs clicked on the plate, and he supposed he was being a little aggressive. She showed too much interest in his personal life. He was grateful to have found her, but there were certain things he didn't want to discuss. His personal life was his personal life.

Stacie ignored him again. "Firing her wouldn't help your chances. Maybe you could help her find her dream job. I'm sure you'll think of something."

"Stacie, I appreciate your interest, but this isn't your business."

"Touched a nerve, have I? Excellent. Well, don't be stupid. If you lose her because you're stubborn, you'll regret it." She went back to eating her vegetables.

Erik wanted to hit his head on the table. She refused to listen. "There's nothing to lose."

"If you say so, dear." She scooted her chair back from the table and stood. "If you'll excuse me, I'll be back in a bit."

Stacie walked out, and Melanie walked in to clear the dishes. "Are you all done?"

"Yes, thank you," Erik said sharply. He could hear the anger in his voice, but he couldn't stop it. A guilt-ridden, well-meaning aunt, an obnoxious brother, and a distracting, sexy chef had altered everything in his controlled and regulated life. A few weeks ago, the company had been productive and profitable. They'd finished project after project with efficiency and had successful results. He'd lived in a small place with Hunter that they managed by themselves. His relationships were brief flings with women that had as many boundaries as he. Now, he was living in a house managed by other people, multiple parties were interested in his personal life, and he couldn't get a girl out of his head. At least business was still going well.

"You ok?" Melanie took his dishes.

"Just stressed. Round two will help," he said, trying to ignore his inner turmoil.

"Looking forward to it. I have to start the dishes."

"The dishes can wait."

She backed into the door and pushed it open. "Easy for you to say. You don't have to scrub them after the food sets."

He stood up and followed her. "I'll help you after."

She snorted and put the dishes in the sink. "Yeah, right."

While she turned on the water, he stalked up behind her and placed his hands on the counter around her hips. He leaned into her, enjoying the warmth of her body. Nuzzling her neck, he felt her melt against him. "Are you sure I can't change your mind?"

She groaned and turned off the water. "The dishes can wait."

He smiled and dipped his head to kiss her. That's what he liked to hear.

Melanie

They fell into an easy pattern with their fling. Melanie cooked throughout the day while Erik was at his office. She stole off in the mornings to jog and read in the afternoons when she had time. In the evenings after he came home, they locked themselves in his room, hooking up for half the night. Sometimes he wouldn't even wait to eat, taking her to his bedroom to have his way with her, and then they'd go back downstairs for a late supper.

By the end of the week, Melanie was sleepy but more satisfied than she could ever remember being. After the second night, he told her that she didn't need to sneak off to her own room after they were finished. His expression seemed guarded when he told her. The invitation had spread warmth through her chest, so she turned him down. She was having too much fun, enjoying his company—more than she should. Sleeping with him would lead to feelings past attraction and beyond friendship, she was sure of it. She thought she might like him already, but she had to draw the line somewhere. Waking up tangled in his arms was an intimacy she couldn't handle.

On Saturday, she found herself a little surprised that he wasn't done with her yet. She'd been afraid he'd grow bored. But that morning before he left for work he'd asked for steak and told her that he was looking forward to their night together, his dark eyes stirring desire within her.

That night she wore a tight black shirt and high-heeled red boots. She pulled the steak off the grill after six. Erik came to see her as she was plating the food. He stood in the doorway, his broad form imposing, a slow grin spread across his face. "Looks delicious."

She blushed at the ambiguous comment. "Food first?"

"I could be convinced otherwise." His stomach rumbled, belying his words.

"Food first," she said, sniggering at him.

A buzzing filled the kitchen. Melanie looked around and saw her phone vibrating on the counter where she'd left it before mashing potatoes. The screen lit up, and she had a text from Sheila.

"I know I said I wouldn't bother you this week, but Angie is shit-faced. If you're not indulging in some man meat, can you come hang out?"

Melanie's eyebrows rose. Angie wasn't the only one drunk. Ugh, 'man meat.' Looked like she'd have to postpone her evening with Erik.

Erik

Melanie's expression clouded. Erik had big plans tonight. After a week, he still found his appetite to be insatiable. It unnerved him a little, but he ignored the sensation. They were having fun; there was no harm in that. There was no work tomorrow, so he planned on a marathon after dinner. But from the look on her face, he wondered if he was going to be thwarted.

"Is everything ok?" he asked.

"Actually, I got a text from Sheila. I need to go see her." She stepped back from the table.

"What's going on?"

Melanie looked away and opened her mouth, but before she said anything Erik cut in. "Don't even try to lie. No lies, remember? Besides you're terrible at it."

She grimaced. "Fine. Sheila's sister is in town and she's a troublemaker. And they're both drunk. Last time Angie hung out with us, she got handcuffed after flashing a cop. Granted, they didn't take her in, but the female cop didn't enjoy the show."

"This doesn't sound like something you should be involved in." Why she would walk into a situation where this incendiary woman was drunk was beyond his understanding.

Her eyes narrowed. "Excuse me?"

Erik shrugged. "You really think you can help them?"

"It's not about that. She's my friend and she's having a hard time, so I'm going to go give her moral support."

How could she not realize what a bad idea it was to go hang out with a drunk troublemaker? The girl had got arrested. Yet Melanie was pissed at him. "How can you keep them out of trouble? What can you do if she gets arrested again?"

"I'm going to her house. It's not a big deal. And this is not up for discussion. I can go out with my friends if I want to. My shift is about to be over so it's none of your business."

Erik stood, irritation buzzing through him. He wasn't even sure why he cared. Of course, hanging out with friends shouldn't have been a big deal, but he couldn't ignore his concerns. What if they got out of control? What if someone got arrested again? He took a deep breath. This was getting ridiculous. What the hell was wrong with him? "Will you be drinking?"

"No, not that it's any of your business, but no. I don't drink on work nights. Now, if you'll excuse me. I need to clean up and head out." She walked into the kitchen, and he followed her.

"You have my phone number?" he asked.

She put the dishes in the sink. "Um, yes. Why?"

"Will you promise me one thing?"

"That depends, will you quit acting like such a ginormous caveman if I do?"

She was so difficult. She announced she was going

to go hang out with people that get arrested, but he was the irrational one. And how did she come up with her insults? He bet Hunter and she collaborated on the worst insults ever. He raised an eyebrow. "A ginormous caveman?"

Melanie bit her lip. "The big part seemed like an important piece of the insult."

One minute he was pissed off, and the next minute, when she bit her lip, he felt like he hadn't got any in weeks. He took a step toward her. "After this week? Should I be flattered?"

She licked her lips and took a step back, bumping into the counter. "That's not what I meant."

He braced his hands around her. He wanted to kiss her, but then he remembered how this discussion had started. "As much as I'd like to do other things, I still need you to promise me something."

Melanie crossed her arms. "All right. What is it?"

"If you have a problem or need a ride, or anything happens, will you call me?" He swept her hair behind her ear.

Melanie sucked in air. "What you're doing isn't fair."

"I'm not above playing dirty." He stroked her cheek with his thumb.

"Okay, fine, you win. But don't get your panties in a twist when I call you because I feel like it at two o'clock in the morning."

"I think you'll find I would have a very different reaction if you called. In fact, please do call me at two in the morning so I can come remove yours," he said, his voice low.

"I'll think about it," she mumbled, her eyes darkening.

He grinned and kissed her lightly, not wanting to lose control. A difficult feat since just the skim of her lips sent electricity jolting through him. As he watched her leave, he hoped that at least she would remember she could call him if she needed to.

Melanie

By the time Melanie got in her Jeep and started driving, an hour had passed since she'd got the text from Sheila. She called her before she left, but they hadn't had a productive conversation. Mostly, Melanie had heard a lot of rambling and shouting from the other end of the line. However, she had gotten the gist of Sheila's monologue. The sisters were still at Sheila's house in Chandler because Sheila's car was in the shop. Also, they were too drunk to drive.

Melanie drove fast, but she didn't make it to Sheila's apartment until nine-thirty. She rolled into the parking lot of the beige apartment complex, looking for a spot and dodging drunken young people in bro tanks.

After a few minutes, Melanie pulled in a spot being vacated by a middle-aged couple in an SUV. She unbuckled her seatbelt, grabbed her purse, and hopped out of the car. Sheila's Unit sat on the second floor near the parking lot. She didn't have far to go. She walked down the curving sidewalks surrounded by trimmed hedges that looked gray under the glare of the outdoor lighting, and then she took the stairs two at a time to unit 246.

She had a key to Sheila's place, so she didn't bother

knocking. She opened the door and was hit with the stench of cheap booze and pizza. Shouts could be heard from down the hall. It was great to hear that they were past giggles and on to bitching. Melanie shut the door behind her. She passed the bedazzled mirror in the foyer, walked down the hall filled with pictures of friends and family, and turned into the living room.

The bright space was lit by ceiling lights and multiple, colored Christmas-style bulbs that hung over the never-used fireplace. Sheila sat with her legs curled under her on her plush, green sofa. She wore jeans and spandex, all black, and had a tumbler tilted in her hand.

Angie sat cross-legged on the floor against a cream-colored wall by the small television. She wore low-cut faded jeans and a crop shirt that showed off her trim stomach. Her short hair was styled in a multi-length hairdo that Melanie couldn't dream of pulling off. Also, true to form, Angie had a bottle of whiskey in her hand.

They both stopped shouting at each other when they saw Melanie approach.

"God, finally." Sheila groaned.

"I hear you're fucking your boss," Angie said.

Melanie cut her gaze to Sheila. Really? Her friend shrugged but had the decency to look apologetic.

"Is this what you've been doing all night, gossiping about my love life?" She dropped her small, black purse on the coffee table in front of the couch.

"Your fuck life, you mean." Angie took a swig of her half-empty bottle. Melanie hoped that the missing alcohol hadn't all been consumed this evening.

"No. We've been talking about what my sister is going to do with herself since she lost her very married sugar mamma," Sheila said.

Before Melanie could respond, Angie jumped in again. "If I had known you weren't such a goody-goody, I would have jumped in your pants long ago."

Melanie couldn't help but grin. The girl was ridiculous, full of flattery and cool, but wouldn't try to hook up with Melanie in a million years. She had been the badass, fucked up, older sister. She may have enjoyed getting her younger sisters into trouble, but Melanie knew she was far from any of Angie's fantasies.

"Maybe we should work on getting you sober." Melanie walked over to her and reached for the bottle.

"No way." She jerked the sloshing alcohol back.

"Don't you want to hear how Angie lost her blonde bimbo?" Sheila taunted.

"Maybe you shouldn't be drinking anymore either," Melanie said. Sheila was even drunker than Melanie had thought. Angie being drunk was a given, but Sheila tried to keep a level head around her sister. Clearly, she was past that point tonight.

"No, no, it's funny. The woman's husband found out. But wait, that's not why. He thought it was hot, and he asked for a threesome. Only after Angie said 'no' did the husband get all pissed off. Said she was defiling their marriage, right? Right? You sure know how to pick 'em, Ang."

"Versus the men you sleep around with who don't even have the cash to buy you a drink? I can picture the morning after. 'So, um, I wanted to leave in the middle of the night, but my car is out of gas. Do you think you can lend me a twenty?' Much better," Angie said, mimicking a man's deeper voice.

"Fuck you, you hipster bitch," Sheila shouted and smacked the couch, sending droplets of wine flying.

"Fuck you, you entitled whore."

Melanie held her breath. Two ways this could go... and they started giggling. Fantastic. It was a toss-up when they started hurling insults. Sometimes they ended up wrestling. Of course, when the arguing started this early, it could always escalate to something more violent.

"Okay, I came all the way to see you guys. How about we lay off the liquor and hang out? We could watch a scary movie." Melanie said, trying to make her voice sound enthusiastic. She had a theory that if one talked to drunk people like they were children, they could be tricked into thinking the most boring stuff was fun.

"Oh, yeah, we should," Sheila said, clapping her hands. Worked on one.

"I want to go out," Angie said. And the theory failed on the other. It was always about fifty-fifty.

"We're not going out," Melanie said.

"Do you remember that hot waitress that worked at your last job? At the Hivin' Diner or whatever?"

"The Jivin' Diner," Melanie corrected without a thought.

"Yeah, whatever. Does she still work there? The blonde with the big tits?" Angie asked.

"I have no idea."

"We should go there."

"I don't want to go there. Fake Elvis is still probably on shift. Besides, we're not going out. We'll get thrown out of wherever we go because of how drunk you guys are." Melanie crossed her arms, getting ready to battle it out.

"But–"

"No 'buts.'" She felt like a mom. It was the worst.

"Fine. I have to pee." Angie got up, wobbled past the couch, and left the room.

"She's such a pain in the ass," Sheila said.

Melanie's eyebrows rose. "Just her?"

Sheila started giggling. "I was supposed to have one shot, but the whole thing with the married woman...I couldn't help myself. It's so fucked up."

Melanie sighed and sat on the couch next to her friend. The situation was depressing. Angie was young and vibrant, but she made God-awful decisions. They sat in silence for a few minutes.

"Do you think she's ok?" Melanie asked.

"Probably, but maybe you should go check, just in case."

"Me?"

"Yes, you."

"Fine." She got off the couch and walked down a short hallway to the bathroom. When she got there, the bathroom door was open, and there was no one inside. She ran to Sheila's bedroom to find it empty. Shoot.

15

Melanie

Melanie and Sheila rode in the back of a taxi heading toward The Jivin' Diner. Five minutes after Melanie checked the bathroom, they pieced together what happened. They'd hoped Angie had stepped outside to smoke, but when Melanie walked outside, Angie wasn't there, and neither was her Jeep.

The girl must have grabbed the keys off the couch and drove off. Sheila called her sister, but the call went to voicemail. They decided The Jivin' Diner was as good as any a place to check first since Angie had seemed interested in going, so they'd called a cab.

Erik's offer stood out in the back of Melanie's mind as they rode to the restaurant, but she figured she would suffer enough humiliation by the end of the night. She didn't need to compound it by Erik finding out. She'd been the victim of the least sneaky car thief ever. All because of a blonde with big breasts.

Sheila giggled the entire ride to the diner. She thought her sister was hilarious. Melanie wanted to shake Sheila, but she figured the hangover her friend would have tomorrow would be suitable justice.

She hoped Angie could drive okay. She also hoped she wouldn't go anywhere but the diner. The irony was not lost on her.

They pulled up to the restaurant, its neon red sign glowing brightly in the night sky. A couple families trickled out, but for the most part, the parking lot was filled with teenagers who were coming and going. They had late night grub, and teenagers were always hungry. Melanie scanned the parking lot for her Jeep.

"I don't see it."

"I do. It's over there, near the trash," Sheila said. She pointed in the direction of the far side of the building that could barely be seen from their position in the parking lot. Melanie squinted and could make out the back of the Jeep around the corner.

"Oh, thank goodness." She paid the driver, and they both got out of the car. "I'm going to maim your sister."

Sheila stumbled across the sidewalk, trying to keep up with Melanie. They walked into the restaurant, and Melanie took a deep, fortifying breath. This was going to be painful. She hadn't given a two-week notice. Her ex-boss thought the fire was her fault, and she didn't want to see any kind of Elvis. Old, blue, dumb, or with wings; she wasn't in the mood.

The doors opened to a cashier's booth with

merchandise displayed beneath the glass counter. She had no idea who would want to buy a shirt with Jivin' Diner across the top and a weird illustration of people dancing below it, but people did. The spandex-clad hostess stood next to it, blocking the view of the massive dining room. Melanie didn't recognize the woman. They went through a lot of hostesses here. No one liked the boss.

"Hi, I'm looking for a woman with short hair, a couple of tattoos—"

"Was she drunk?" the hostess cut in.

"Yeah, she is," Sheila said.

"She's in a booth by the window chatting up Zoey." The hostess jerked a thumb behind her.

"Thanks," Melanie said. They walked through the dining room. There were booths, tables, and a bar, and the seats were covered in red vinyl. Waitresses ran from table to table with platters full of greasy food in the busy restaurant. The noises of chatter competed with Elvis's voice, which blared from the overhanging speakers. Good Lord, she hated this place.

She spotted Angie in the far corner, her arm tossed over the side of the booth, and her head cocked as she grinned at the blonde waitress holding a pitcher of water. Melanie grabbed Sheila's arm and tugged her along to the table. Ignoring the waitress, Melanie turned to Angie. "What the heck were you thinking?"

"Excuse me, I'm in the middle of a conversation with Zoey here," Angie said, winking at the woman. She seemed to be drunker than Melanie had realized. She leered up at Zoey's ample cleavage hanging over the red spandex top, rather than at the woman's face.

"Well end it. You took my freaking car." Melanie seethed. To be honest, the car-stealing part wasn't what bothered her most. She hated when Angie drove drunk.

Zoey looked between Angie and Melanie and took a step back. "Um, I'll put your order in."

Melanie slid into the booth and hauled Sheila in with her as the waitress walked away.

"Do you realize that you just said 'freaking' and 'heck' after someone stole your car? It's like you're a child," Angie said.

"I'm polite."

Sheila giggled again. "Don't you remember her parents? Her mother would've belted her if she ever cussed."

Melanie rolled her eyes. Her mother may have hated cussing, but she hated violence more. "I never got belted."

"I can't imagine someone who has sex but doesn't say 'hell.'" Angie shrugged.

"Why are you so interested in my sex life?" Melanie said, exasperated.

"It's so...hard to fathom. I figured you and your ex broke up because you were saving yourself for marriage."

She shook her head dumbfounded. Saving herself? Yeah, right. She'd lost her virginity to Dave when she was sixteen. She hated talking about him though. She was about to tell Angie this when Sheila spoke up instead.

"Angie, Dave broke up with Melanie because he wasn't ready to settle down for the rest of his life," Sheila said.

Yep, it still stung when Melanie thought about it, or when people talked about it. It had been naive to think they would be together forever, but they were a couple for six years. They'd been planning their future together when Dave decided that he wanted to transfer to another college, somewhere far away. He said he needed to see the world, and he wasn't ready to settle down. She could understand that, she really could. But going from seeing each other daily for six years, to never talking to one another again because he needed to "commit to the breakup," still hurt.

"Some people need time alone to discover who they are before they can decide who they want to be with," Angie said, nodding.

"Why is she so coherent when she's this drunk?" Melanie asked Sheila.

"Because she takes all of mine," Sheila said, and then burst out laughing.

"Was that supposed to be a joke? I don't even know what that means," Angie said.

"Okay, you know what, all this doesn't matter. You guys need to be safe at home. You're too drunk, and I don't want to be here. C'mon, we're going." Melanie started shoving Sheila out of the booth.

"Wait, we can't go, I ordered food," Angie said.

"Oh, no, I need food. We can't go. Food is excellent. I love food," Sheila said, her eyes puppy-dog wide.

"For the love of—"

"I got you wings and iced tea," Angie said, wiggling her eyebrows.

Melanie felt weak for even considering staying, but maybe the food would sober them up. "Extra spicy?"

"Extra spicy."

"Fine. We'll eat and then we'll go." Melanie leaned

back in her seat. She needed to work on her patience. She had a feeling this was going to be a long night.

"There's Elvis. Elvis, Elvis, come sing for us," Angie waved a hand at Bob.

A very, very long night.

Erik

Erik was worried about Melanie. He couldn't believe it. He felt worried about someone other than Hunter. Once Stacie left, he couldn't stop wondering whether Melanie was walking into some kind of trouble. This was ridiculous because she was an adult and was going to a friend's apartment. Besides the fact that he shouldn't have been worried at all because her choices were none of his business. Yet, in his bedroom, he paced back and forth, wondering if the so-called troublemaker would lead his chef into a dangerous situation.

Worry wasn't a feeling that he was unaccustomed to. When he was younger, he always worried about Hunter. Every time his brother left for the shitty high school that advertised the fact that they had foolproof metal detectors, and every time Erik knew he'd have to work late, and that Hunter was somewhere out on the street, Erik worried. It had been a long time since he'd felt this kind of concern for someone though. The worry put a hole in his skin over his chest, a path in for something to hit him where he was most vulnerable. He hated the feeling.

He started pacing to the hallway. He was sure that Mary had long since gone to bed. He was so agitated that he needed a longer walking path. His bare feet slapped the tile floor, giving him comfort in the pattern. He considered calling Melanie, just to check in, but then his logical side mocked him. For what? He wasn't her boyfriend. He had no hold over her. She didn't owe him anything. The thoughts made him feel hollow. He wanted her, and not only for a few nights. He wanted to be with her, to be able to call her if he wanted to, to hear her voice. How had he got attached to her so fast? She was intoxicating. He couldn't get enough.

Could he do more than a fling? Could he be open enough to date someone? To be with Melanie? The idea of opening up about his past to anyone made him cringe. Maybe she didn't need to know everything though. Maybe they could take the relationship slow. Maybe if he could be there for her, it would be enough, and she would never need to know about his childhood.

Melanie

The first couple of times Elvis sang at their table, things went smoothly enough. Melanie slid farther into the booth when Elvis swung a wandering, leathery hand in her direction, and she managed to keep her mouth shut when Angie asked for another song. Overall, everything was under control. She ignored all annoyances once Zoey carried food in their direction.

The waitress brought wings, onion rings, mozzarella sticks, and a couple drinks. She served sodas to Angie and Sheila, and an iced tea to Melanie.

"Anything else I can get you?" she asked Angie,

smiling wide.

"You know, I hate to be a pain, but whenever my friend here eats hot wings, she drinks two iced teas. She loves spicy, but she can't handle the pain for long." Angie winked at Zoey.

"Coming right up." Zoey turned and threw her hair over her shoulder. Her sashay away made her gait about a foot and a half wider than it needed to be. It was a good thing they spread out the tables, or she would've bumped a patron in the head with her behind.

Melanie looked at Angie surprised by her thoughtfulness. She knew she was a fan of consistency, but it was impressive that her old friend remembered her eating habits. Angie turned to look at Melanie and cocked her head to the side. "Am I wrong?"

"No, I'm surprised you remember." Maybe she needed to choose a new favorite food.

"That's all you had at every single sleepover Sheila had. The same thing for twelve years."

Sheila burst out laughing as if her sister said the funniest thing she'd ever heard. "It's so true."

Melanie looked at Sheila but didn't say anything. Who cared if she had the same favorite food from twelve years before? She knew what she liked. She ignored the two sisters as they ate and threw onion rings at one another and focused on her own food.

The moment one wing touched her tongue, her mouth felt like it was on fire. Heat licked up the sides of her cheeks, but it wasn't quite good enough. She grabbed the Tabasco sauce and poured. Ignoring the pointless blue cheese dressing, she dug in once more and ate with gusto. Hot sauce made everything taste better.

Even shitty diner wings. She tuned her friends out and inhaled the food, enjoying the death of her taste buds.

After a few, she drank her first iced tea. She couldn't taste anything, just felt the cool liquid sooth her flaming cheeks and tongue. By the time she finished it, she detected a lemony bite. The drink was more delicious than it used to be. Maybe they'd decided to go with Lipton. She sat the empty glass on the table and got a brain freeze. Too cold too fast.

She scarfed down the rest of her wings, her mouth burning and eyes watering. Her lips started to buzz from the heat. Zoey brought her second iced tea just in time. She finished the last wing in the basket as the waitress returned. Sheila and Angie had moved on to the mozzarella sticks, using them as miniature swords to attack one another. Zoey set the new iced tea behind the empty glass, and Melanie drank.

Angie stopped fighting, watching her. Sheila didn't realize her sister had stopped and smacked Angie across the cheek with a cheese stick. "Gotchya."

Melanie winced, bracing for Angie's fit, but the girl stared at her as she drank her second tea. God, it tasted good. Her taste buds finally started to work. It was definitely new tea...it tasted different. But why was Angie still staring at her like that?

"You might want to slow down."

Then the new taste hit her. It was alcohol. They'd put alcohol in her tea. She slammed the empty, second glass on the table. "Fuck!"

Angie and Sheila's mouths both fell open.

Melanie began to feel spacey, her mind swirling, her tongue numbing. "You gave me alcohol."

Sheila looked at her sister, clapping a hand over her mouth. "You spiked her drinks."

Angie took a sip of her own drink. "I asked Zoey if she had anything. I thought you needed to mellow out."

Melanie wanted to yell about trust, how messed up the situation was, and what a horrible person Angie was, but her head felt heavy, and everything in the room was moving faster and faster. "I have to pee."

Sheila frowned and took Melanie to the bathroom. Melanie wasn't a lightweight, but she didn't chug. She was a slow wine drinker and enjoyed matching bouquets with food. The tea wasn't wine, and she sure as hell hadn't drunk slowly. Her walk to the bathroom was unsteady, but once she used the facility and threw water on her face, she felt a little better. There wasn't much to do now, she'd have to ride out the intoxication and hope she didn't do anything stupid. She would yell at Angie once she was coherent. She might never eat hot wings again, but that was a different matter.

Sheila helped wipe the water off Melanie's face, and then they walked back to the booth. Zoey was sitting next to Angie, and they were making out while Angie still had mozzarella stick crumbs on her cheek. Lovely. Sheila slid into the booth and yanked Melanie down with her. She hit the cushion hard and bounced. She bounced again on purpose and started giggling. Those vinyl chairs were funny.

"You okay, Melanie?" Sheila asked, sliding her drink away from the edge of the table.

"Yes. I'm good. Good. Good, like great, only less good."

Sheila tugged on her sister's arm from across the

table. Angie tore her face away from Zoey's. "What?"

"Do you see what you did?" Sheila hissed.

"They should combine mozzarella sticks and onion rings. I should do that. I'm a chef. I'd make so much money." Melanie picked up one of each and put the breaded cheese on top of the breaded onion.

"Oh, Christ," Sheila said.

"What? Look, she's revolutionizing greasy diner food," Angie said.

"Really? Really?" Sheila asked.

"Hey, Elvis is coming around again. Elvis. Elvis. Come sing," Angie said.

Melanie looked at the approaching Elvis and glowered. "I don't like him. He's an ass."

"Lower voice," Sheila whispered.

Elvis sauntered up to the table and braced his hands on his hips. His tight suit wrapped every lump and wrinkle in a layer of white. His tan skin looked orange under the diner's bright lighting, and his smile was as sleazy as ever.

"What can I do for you, ladies?" he asked, staring at Melanie.

"You can go jump off a—"

"Jump into a faster number. You know slang. We want to hear a quick one," Sheila yelled.

Melanie scowled at Sheila while Elvis smiled, oblivious to her annoyance. "I would be happy to oblige, babe."

He sang "Hound Dog" as he had thirty minutes ago, and Melanie scooted closer to Sheila. The guy smelled like grease and cigarettes. Angie and Zoey swayed to the music, and Melanie clung to the vestiges of her good humor despite him. It was just music after all. He wasn't great, but he tried to be entertaining. She smiled to be polite, but Elvis decided she was warming up to him. He reached down to put his hands God knows where, and Melanie punched him in the balls as he sang "dog." The G disappeared in a high-pitched squeal as he slumped to the ground. A few patrons nearby noticed, but the lure of conversation drew everyone back into their own business.

Old Elvis's wig started to slip as he fell sideways, and Melanie grabbed it and sat on the piece so that he wouldn't know where it disappeared to. Served him right. He would lose his wig privileges that night. She turned back to the table and all three girls stared at her. Zoey looked horrified, Sheila looked disgusted, and Angie looked a little impressed.

"What? I was aiming for his stomach, but someone got me drunk, and I can't aim my fist real well."

16

Erik

Erik's phone rang on his bedside table as he pulled out his iPad to get caught up on some emails before trying to go to bed. He was still too preoccupied with thoughts of Melanie to sleep. He grabbed his phone and looked at the screen. Melanie's name lit up the phone. He jerked upright in bed, glanced at the clock, which said it was ten until midnight, and wondered whether she had decided to call him just because after all, or because something was wrong. His lips twisted into a scowl. There was no way she would call just because. He slid his finger across the screen.

"Hello," he said.

"Hi, Erik," she said in a singsong voice. What the hell?

"Is everything all right?" He was more than a little concerned about her tone. Was this how she sounded drunk?

"Everything is stupid. Bob was a jerk, and the manager is a jerk, but I don't even care. It's just that we need a ride," she said and giggled. Oh yeah, she was drunk.

Damn it. He hoped she okay. He held his voice even. "Where are you?"

"At The Jivin' Diner."

"The place you used to work? With the Elvis that hits on you? That Bob? You've got to be kidding me."

"Aw, you remembered what I said. You can be so sweet, you know that?" She giggled again.

"Yeah, real sweet. How drunk are you?"

"Very. But I didn't mean to."

"What do you mean?"

"I ate hot wings, and then Sheila's sister handed me an iced tea. But it wasn't a regular iced tea. She gave me an alcoholic iced tea and didn't tell me. I chugged the entire thing. Didn't even taste it. And before I noticed, she did it again."

Her friend's sister, her trouble-making, once arrested friend's sister, had spiked her fucking drink. Fuck. "Are you okay?"

"I'm fine."

There was yelling over the line. Someone called, "You could have called a cab."

"Oh, I can call a cab, bye."

"No, no. Don't hang up," Erik said, his hands curling into fists.

"I'm still here."

"Don't call a taxi. I'll be right over."

"My Jeep is here too."

Erik rubbed his forehead, thinking of a solution. Hunter should still be awake. "I'll bring someone to drive your car."

"Okie dokie," Melanie said, and the line went dead.

He looked at his phone in disbelief. Was she really a bigger pain drunk? How was that even possible? He called Hunter and then left to pick him up.

The drive to the diner, once he had Hunter in the car, took forever. His GPS gave directions, but it was taking a lot of effort to concentrate. He hoped she was all right.

"So, do you know what happened?"

"Not exactly. I know that she's drunk." Erik gripped the steering wheel so hard his knuckles were white.

"You know, if she called asking for a ride, and she's with people, she's probably fine. I don't even know what you're worried about. It's just drinking. It's not like she's out doing meth out of a light bulb," Hunter said.

Bob and alcohol jumped to mind. So did the fact her sister's friend spiked her drink and got her drunk. Seemed like there was a fair amount to be concerned about. Erik grunted in response.

After a few more minutes, they drove into the almost empty parking lot of the diner. The restaurant's windows were dark, and he couldn't see anyone inside. The place was closed. He saw Melanie and three others near her blue Jeep. Melanie sat in the back of the car with her legs sticking out, one girl sat on the curb next to the car, and the other two danced in circles, but the more muscular of them seemed to be wearing some sort of wig. What the hell?

"Um, what are they doing?" Hunter asked.

"Hell, if I know." Erik shook his head.

All four women looked up at his vehicle's approach. He pulled up to the spot next to the Jeep. Recognition dawned on Melanie's face, and she jumped out of the car, yanking the wig off the other girl's head, and ran to his car. He stepped out, and she swayed back and forth in front of him, beaming the whole time.

"Hey, sexy," she said. She was so drunk.

"Hi, Melanie," he said slowly.

"Look what I got." She shook the wig at him.

"Is that a wig?" Hunter walked around the car.

"Yes. It's Bob's wig. I stole it."

Erik looked her up and down, checking for any obvious signs of damage, and sighed in relief when he couldn't find anything wrong with her. Before he could stop himself, he snatched her into a hug, crushing the wig between them. It felt so good to have her in his arms again. Remembering where he was, he released her just as fast. She started stumbling, and he held her up by her arms.

"Who's Bob?" Hunter asked.

"Elvis," Melanie said, handing the wig to Hunter. She turned to Erik. "We should get out of here and do things."

Hunter looked from Erik to Melanie and grinned. He was enjoying this way too much. "What kinds of things?"

"The kinds of things that one doesn't share with other people. Sexy things. Things that involve a bed and—" Melanie started.

Erik cut her off. "Okay, sweetheart, I think he gets the point."

Hunter chuckled. “I like her like this.”

Erik shot him a death glare.

The three other women walked up. The blonde and the short-haired woman were holding hands, the other glared daggers at the short-haired one. They all looked shit-faced.

“Damn. I get it, Melanie. I don’t like dick but if I did...” the short-haired woman said, looking at Erik.

Erik crossed his arms over his chest but didn’t say anything. He glanced at Melanie, but she avoided his gaze.

“What about the other? He looks yummy,” the blonde said.

Short hair pulled the blonde back by her arm and threw the girl over her shoulder. “No, just I got you convinced to try me on for size. You can’t have him.” She ran a few feet away.

Melanie giggled and then turned to the last woman standing there. “Sheila, this is Erik and Hunter. Erik and Hunter, this is Sheila. The one doing the carrying is her sister, Angie, and the one being carried is a waitress here, Zoey.”

Hunter shook hands and smiled. Erik managed the shaking hands part.

“I hope you’re not the one who spiked Melanie’s drink,” Erik said.

“Erik,” Melanie yelled in outrage.

Sheila glared at her sister. “No, that would be my dumb-ass sister. I didn’t want to get stuck here. Besides, I wouldn’t fuck with my friend that way.”

“Your sister did that? That’s screwed up,” Erik said.

Hunter let out a low whistle.

"You guys, it's not like she broke my nose or killed my cat. Sheesh. It was a mistake," Melanie said.

All three looked at her.

"What?" She swayed on her feet.

Erik shook his head, frustrated. He would bet a whole lot of money she would be pissed off tomorrow. For now, he needed to get her home before she did something she might regret in the morning. He couldn't imagine she wanted everyone knowing the details about their sex life. Although he was hoping that after tomorrow they would be telling people that there was more than sex between them. One night away from her, and he had to be more involved than a lover. He had to make her his. Even if only for the sake of his sanity.

Melanie

Melanie woke up to a headache the size of which she hadn't experienced since the morning after she'd turned twenty-one, and she felt like throwing up. Not that she was nauseous from any sort of hangover. No, she was beyond embarrassed. There wasn't any slow realization about what she'd done the night before—she woke up and remembered everything. The memories backhanded her the way her mother had always told her God would if he saw her choice in underwear.

Melanie groaned as she thought back to the evening. She had been one huge cliché and a gigantic idiot. Now, she felt like a headachy idiot.

Her poor behavior hadn't ended at the restaurant. No, it had extended to the car ride home, and she even tried to seduce Erik once they got to the house. The seduction had involved a dance that she thought was sexy, but in retrospect involved a lot of almost falling. If she could only sleep forever. At least Erik hadn't had sex with her; he hadn't made fun of her. He'd helped her into her own bed and kissed her goodnight.

She was going to kill Angie. If she could ever get up the courage to leave the bedroom, that girl was dead.

She looked at her bedside table and groaned. Perfect. It was after eight. She'd be lucky if she weren't fired because of all this. Erik had the foresight to put ibuprofen and water next to her clock, so she drank a few sips and took two pills before even contemplating getting out of bed. Then she would shower and run off to Mexico, where she'd never have to see Erik again. Could she sneak out the window and forgo a two-week notice?

She shook off the fantasies and took deep breaths to stay calm. Erik had been great last night. Maybe he'd understand. At the very least, she supposed she owed him some sort of explanation about what had happened. After all, he gave her a ride in the middle of the night. She could do this. She could face him without searching for a way to turn invisible.

After moping for a few more minutes, she got out of bed, naked because her seduction dance had been a striptease and headed to the shower to try to burn the headache out of her. Then she brushed her teeth for a long time. After, she searched for, and found, her favorite jeans and put on an orange blouse. To buy some time, she even put on some lip-gloss and eyeliner. When she couldn't stall any longer, she took a deep breath and walked out to find Erik and apologize.

She found him in the dining room, drinking coffee and eating scrambled eggs. There were a couple mugs, and an extra empty plate on the table. Her heart stopped. Someone else made breakfast? Another chef? Had he found a replacement so soon? This was it. She was canned. She'd be back at her apartment searching nonstop for a new job by the afternoon. Even as she thought about the fact that she was about to get booted, she couldn't help but notice Erik's gorgeous chocolate eyes, hard cheekbones, and firm jaw. He had good, strong shoulders and a broad chest she wanted to run her hands over.

"Good morning," Erik said, his voice tinged with amusement.

Because this needed to be more embarrassing, so she'd been caught staring at his chest. Fantastic. She looked up and held eye contact despite that her face felt like she'd been sitting too close to the fireplace.

"I guess I should start packing up," she said.

His eyes widened in alarm. "Pack up? Why?"

"Because you have a new chef. After last night and being late this morning, I don't blame you." Maybe this would be for the best. Leave before she became too invested. What a joke. The pain in her chest wasn't because of the kitchen appliances. Even though she would miss those too. She liked this man far too much. Now she was never going to see him again.

Erik looked confused but then looked down at his plate. "Melanie, how would I already have a new chef? I made these eggs. I'm not going to fire you."

"Good point," Melanie said. Her hangover must be making her slow. "You cook?"

He sent her a dark look. "Don't sound so surprised. They're just eggs."

"But you're really not firing me?" She could feel her heart pounding in her chest. She was terrified both if he said yes and if he said no. If he said she could stay, she would have to spend more time around him, and she didn't even want to think about how much more she could grow to care about him. The night before, when she'd called him, she knew she could've called a cab, but she'd pretended like she'd forgotten because she'd wanted to see him. How pathetic was that? And after he was so sweet last night...she was a goner.

"No, I'm not going to fire you. Although, I would like an explanation about last night." He motioned to a seat beside him. He served some eggs onto the extra plate and slid it toward the place in front of the chair.

"I suppose you deserve one." She sat next to him, and he pushed the plate closer to her. She looked at the food, uncertain.

"Please eat with me."

It felt weird to share breakfast with him. Late night snacks before round two were one thing, but this seemed more intimate than having sex. She knew it didn't make any sense, but everything they'd done had been so physical, it was odd to eat and talk with no impending sexual encounter planned. She took a bite of the eggs, and he poured her coffee.

"Do you like cream and sugar?" He set the coffee pot on the placemat beside him.

"Yes, please." His sweet demeanor made her nervous. "Are you sure you're not firing me?"

"I'm not firing you."

"It's—you're being so nice," she blurted out without thinking. If he wasn't going to fire her before...

Erik raised an eyebrow at her, and his eyes twinkled. "I hate to think that me being nice is such a surprise. Especially after last night. I thought I was very nice."

Melanie glared at him. "Yeah, you let me get all the way naked."

Erik poured cream in the mug of steaming coffee. "Nothing I haven't seen before."

"I suppose not." She willed her cheeks not to heat. No such luck.

"Besides, you were adamant I shouldn't try to stop you." He shoveled a couple teaspoons of sugar in her coffee.

"Any chance we can pretend that never happened, and you can try to forget about it?"

"Oh, no chance, I enjoyed it too much to try and forget it."

"You enjoyed me falling all over the place?" Melanie asked, annoyed.

He handed her the coffee mug and looked at her, his gaze intense. "No, but I enjoyed the part where you stripped naked for me."

She hid her face in the coffee mug and took a sip. Why was it so darn easy for him to frazzle her? Although, in his defense, she supposed this one was all her fault.

Erik

Erik surveyed Melanie over his coffee cup as she ate a few bites of scrambled eggs. There were purple circles under her eyes, but besides that, there wasn't any evidence of a hangover. She still looked beautiful, her blue eyes vibrant, her pale skin almost glowing as the light shined through the window onto her from the other side of the room. He wanted her so badly that he ached. He took a deep breath trying to remember he needed to do the decent thing here if he wanted her to himself. He was very impatient, and right now he wanted three things: the story about the previous night, Melanie naked and in his bed, and her to be his. Considering he couldn't do all three at the same time, he needed to work on prioritizing.

Melanie finished another bite of eggs and looked up at him, her eyes wide and earnest. "I didn't intend to drink last night. I wasn't lying to you when I told you I wasn't going to."

"I know."

"You know?"

"Yes. You said on the phone last night that Angie gave you alcohol without you knowing," he reminded her.

"Right. Because an adult that can't identify what she's drinking is so easy to believe. Stupid hot wings," she muttered.

Erik's lips twitched, but he clenched his teeth. He didn't want to laugh at her when she was so vulnerable. Plus, she could've gotten hurt. It's just that, well, she was adorable.

"Also, I didn't intend to go to the diner, but Angie took my car. Sheila and I had to go find her," Melanie said, her voice small.

Erik's blood surged through his ears. Melanie

accepted a drink from the walking disaster that stole her car. Unbelievable. He stared at her, and she tipped back an inch in her chair. Her eyes stayed locked on his and narrowed in defiance. "She took your car?" he asked, his voice dangerous.

Melanie nodded.

"And only after she took your car did you accept a drink from her?"

"Yes."

"Why would you do that?" Why was she so fucking trusting? This girl, Angie, clearly didn't give a shit about other peoples' well-being.

"Look, I've known her for over twelve years. She didn't intend to hurt me. She made a mistake. And the waitress gave the drink to me. The waitress. Besides, it's none of your darn business. I shouldn't have even called you last night."

Erik rolled his neck. She was so aggravating. Why did she have to challenge everything he said? Why couldn't she agree with him one time when she knew he was right? "I'm glad you called me."

She set her fork on the table. "I'm not. We're sex buddies. I shouldn't be relying on you for anything."

"Fuck buddies?"

"I wasn't going to say that." Melanie stuck out her chin.

"Well, you should. Rely on me, I mean. I want you to. I want your business to be my business."

Melanie's mouth fell open, and he ran a hand through his hair. He couldn't remember the last time he'd asked someone out. He wondered if he was coming on too strong, but also didn't care. He would make her his.

“All you want is sex.” She crossed her arms on the table.

“I’m not going to deny I want sex. But I also want you. I want us to date...exclusively.”

17

Melanie

Melanie gaped at him, and she didn't even care. Erik was asking her...out on a date? Or, wait, what? The man who had told her he didn't do long-term relationships changed his mind? He'd seemed pretty freaking sure before when he told her he wasn't interested in romance. Maybe she heard wrong.

"I'm sorry. Could you say that all again?"

Erik grimaced. "I don't want to watch you and keep my mouth shut. I want to be a part of your life. I want to date you."

His eyes looked so earnest, so hopeful, and it was, if she was being honest with herself, what she wanted to hear. She liked this man a lot, even when he drove her crazy or acted domineering, she enjoyed challenging him and talking to him. Even so, she wasn't sure she should say yes. He hadn't had a lot of relationships, he wasn't interested in relationships. If he changed his mind down the road, she'd be screwed. She liked him too much already. She knew better than to try to force a relationship where one person wasn't ready. Her history with Dave taught her that much. Erik would realize he'd felt pressured to do this and would end up hurting her. This was why she'd made ground rules, to keep from getting hurt. She knew pain would follow if she said yes. A tiny voice in the back of her mind told her a relationship wouldn't end in pain if they fell in love and had their happily ever after. Melanie told Ms. Fairytale-Princess-Optimist to shut it.

Melanie cocked her head to the side and scowled. What he had said about 'keeping his mouth shut' penetrated her thick skull. He was such a control freak, he wanted an excuse to be able to tell her what to do. Well, it was the twenty-first century, and that sure as heck wasn't going to happen. "Even if I said yes, you wouldn't be able to tell me what to do. I mean, I suppose you could try, but it wouldn't change my mind."

Erik tossed his head back and let out a bark of laughter. The sound was deep and rich and sent heat straight down to her—"Oh, sweetheart, I'm sure you'll argue with me as much, maybe even more. But I like you, more than I thought I would. And since I worry about you anyway, I'd like to have the right to call you when I want. I don't want to lose you after a week of... having sex."

Melanie looked at him, uncertain. "If I say yes then I want a recommendation letter before our date. Also, I intend to look for an alternative job."

Erik opened his mouth, but Melanie continued. "I'm not going to be the chef of the man I'm dating. It's weird. And yeah, the recommendation, I know, there should be trust and whatnot between us. But one of us has to be rational here, and it's not you since you said you don't date, but you just asked me out."

Erik scowled and drummed his fingers on the table

"Are you sulking?"

"I thought that by asking you out, I would get more of what I wanted, not less of it," he said, his voice a low growl.

"I explained that wasn't going to happen. I should get to work," she said, standing up.

Erik's arm snaked out and he grabbed her wrist. Before she could walk out of the room, he tugged on her and she fell into his lap. He put one arm around her waist, tugging her close so that they were chest to chest and her lips inches from his. The other hand combed through her hair. His hard thighs molded against her behind. Sizzling electricity rushed through her, and she found speaking difficult. She couldn't believe how much this man affected her. She couldn't believe this man wanted to date her.

"You never answered me," he said, his voice had a desperate edge.

"What are you talking about?" she asked wide-eyed, looking over his shoulder.

He tugged her hair. "Sly minx. Say yes."

She looked into his deep brown eyes and knew she would never forgive herself for saying anything else. "Yes."

"Tomorrow night?"

"Tomorrow night is fine with me."

Erik

Something animal and possessive inside Erik sighed in contentment as soon as she agreed. He felt lightheaded as if he'd been holding his breath the entire time they'd been talking. For a moment, he'd thought she might've said no, and the uncertainty had been disturbing. He would've kept trying, seduced her even, but the possibility of rejection hung heavy in the air around his head. He didn't want to lose her.

Now, he was far too distracted. Melanie sat on his lap, her luscious ass pillowing against his stiffening shaft. He could feel her breasts against his chest, and he wanted to remove the layers between them, but he had work to do this morning. Not that he couldn't enjoy himself first.

Her pulse fluttered in her throat as Erik dragged his thumb down the top of her neck and across her nape. Her lips parted in an invitation for his kiss, and he closed the distance between them, brushing his lips against hers.

He reached around her back and held her tighter against him as he deepened the kiss. Her gasp echoed into his mouth and she wriggled against the hardness protruding from his lap. He breathed it all in, enjoying the pliant feel of her body and her intoxicating taste. He wanted to brand her with the kiss. He wanted her to understand she was his and make her excited by the prospect.

He groaned against her lips, wanting to continue, but knowing Stacie and Hunter would be walking into his home any minute. He eased his head back, holding his passionate chef against him.

She looked into his eyes, her own hooded with desire, but the look was a little shy, a little innocent. "Do we have time to have sex?"

His cock leaped against his jeans. She did horrible things to his self-control. He shook his head. "I have to work today."

Melanie nodded, but her lips twisted in disappointment. She scooted away, but Erik held her fast against the hard planes of his body. She looked at him, waiting.

"Just waiting until my body agrees with my words." His lips quirked.

She rolled her eyes. "You need to get your libido under control."

Erik smirked at her. She thought his libido wasn't under control? He dragged his thumb over her bottom lip and then down her throat. Her eyes fluttered closed.

"My libido?" he asked, releasing her.

Her eyes snapped open. She glared at him and then glared down at her body. "Traitor."

Erik laughed, and she climbed off his lap. She took a step back and stretched her arms over her head. "How many am I making lunch for today?"

"Stacie and Hunter will be here. I'm betting Hunter will want to cook with you again."

Melanie frowned. "How many dishes is he trying to learn how to make? Is he dating a picky binge eater?"

Erik shook his head. "I have no idea. He won't tell

me anything. Maybe you can get the truth out of him."

"If he won't tell you, I doubt he'll tell me. You guys are so close, it's great. Sheila and Angie fight all the time, but you guys are sweet together."

He nodded and looked away. He didn't like the direction of this conversation since he wasn't ready to tell her the truth. Maybe it didn't make a lot of sense, but he didn't want her pity, he didn't want her to look at him through new eyes, and he couldn't bring himself to tell anyone the whole story. Talking about his past brought back all the memories of pain and rejection.

"It's funny how different you guys look for biological brothers. You must take after Stacie's side of the family."

"Yeah, I suppose so." The omission stabbed his chest, but he didn't say anything else.

Melanie

Melanie and Hunter worked in the kitchen. She decided on Tex-Mex, so they were cooking fajita fixings. She'd been marinating hangar steak since the day before and wanted an excuse to use it. Hunter was abnormally quiet as he turned yellow, red, and green peppers over on the grill. She wouldn't have minded, except she was trying to turn her mind off. She kept vacillating between believing that dating Erik was an abysmal idea, to thinking it was the best idea in the world. Every time she realized neither opinion helped, she would suffer a small panic attack about ending up on the street after getting fired and dumped on the same day. She had to find a different job.

"Okay, what's going on?" Melanie asked as she fluffed some Spanish rice.

Hunter stared at the multi-colored peppers. "What do you mean?"

"Either your dog died, or you hate cooking. Why do you need to learn so many meals? Are you trying to impress the entire food club at a local college? Because you do realize, if you're trying to make a specialty to impress women, you only need one. One-night stand equals one meal, maybe two," Melanie ranted, trying to fill the silence. It didn't work; it probably made Hunter suspicious.

Hunter's gaze snapped to her face. "What are you so nervous about?"

Crap, was she that obvious? "I'll answer yours if you'll answer mine."

He turned the peppers again. "Fine."

"Also, don't turn those so often." She covered the rice pot and leaned against the counter.

"You first," he said.

Melanie bit her lip. "Erik asked me to date him."

Hunter's eyes widened, and he put his hand over his heart in comical disbelief. His reaction was a little offensive, but he stopped rotating the peppers every eight seconds.

"Don't look so darn surprised."

"Sorry, it's just...he hasn't dated someone in a long time," Hunter said.

"Yeah, I've heard that. What's that about anyway?" She was about to roll her eyes, but her mom's voice rang out in her head. The devil will take your eyes if you keep doing that. She never believed the superstition, but the way her mother said it had given her the heebie-jeebies.

Hunter rubbed the back of his neck and then turned off the heat on the grill. The entire room smelled smoky and sweet. The pepper slices were marked with what looked like parallel, blackened prison bars. After a few silent seconds, he said, "Erik doesn't like opening up to people. He had a tough childhood, he doesn't want to make himself vulnerable."

Even though she hadn't met his parents, he appeared to have such a loving family. It was an odd thing to say. Who knew though, maybe his parents were awful people. She hoped he could get over his fear of opening up because if he couldn't, she would end up being the one that got hurt.

"All right. Your turn. How many women won't let you into their pants if you don't cook for them first?"

Hunter chuckled and shook his head. "You come up with the strangest theories. I swear, the inside of your head must be an odd place to be."

"It is, but don't change the subject."

"I'm not cooking for anyone I'm sleeping with or dating. I'm trying to figure out the perfect apology food." He scraped peppers off the grill with a fork.

"Use tongs. Apology food? What did you do?" A bunch of possibilities flew through her head, things that involved naked photos or handcuffs or a park.

He held up his hands. "It's nothing that bad. You know how we're working on that foster camp? The activities director and I don't get along."

"Is the activities director a woman?" Melanie pulled tortillas from the fridge.

He nodded.

A woman that this man couldn't charm the pants off of? How was that even possible? "And she doesn't like you? Marry her."

Hunter shot Melanie a death glare. "She drives me nuts. I don't want anything to do with her. But I'll be working with her over the summer. I'm coaching sports teams and helping her figure out programs."

"Go with cake. Nothing says you're sorry like cake. I'll make one tonight and give you the recipe."

"Thanks for the advice." He stood by the counter for a minute and rubbed the stubble on his cheeks. "Try to be patient with Erik. I know he can be an ass, but he's got a big heart. As dumb as that sounds, it's true."

Geez, what was it about Erik? He was a multi-millionaire CEO, with a body that gave her goosebumps, not a fluffy kitten stuck in a laundry sack. He was way more likely to turn around and break her heart than she was to ever hurt him.

18

Erik

By the time his workday ended, Erik was exhausted but felt pretty good about what he and his company had accomplished. The release date for the logo app was set for one month out, and Hunter was thrilled. The app was one of his earlier concepts, but it had taken some time to get the project underway. He didn't have the design skills for the project, so it had had to wait until they'd started a company and could hire creatives.

On top of their business successes, his summer program for foster kids was coming along as well. April fifth, a week after the logo app would be released, was the date of the fundraising banquet. The catering company and the country club were locked in for the event. Assuming Hunter and Jennifer didn't kill one another, everything should work out fine.

Stacie and Hunter left Erik's house about thirty minutes after enjoying a very animated dinner together. Everyone had been in a good mood, including his aunt who kept mock whispering how happy she was that Melanie worked for her nephew. Every time Melanie walked in with a dish, Stacie would go on and on about the delicious food. Erik was so impressed with how much everyone had accomplished, he wasn't even annoyed when Hunter let it slip to Stacie that Erik had asked his chef out on a date.

Melanie told Erik she intended to bake a cake after dinner, but Stacie and Hunter proclaimed themselves too full to eat another bite. Before they left, Melanie gave Hunter the recipe and a cake dish, and then she'd gone back into the kitchen to bake. Erik wondered if she was trying to hide from him. The idea made him smile. He wasn't done with her for the day. He wanted to see her and touch her, and he wanted to find out if she'd dealt with Angie and Sheila.

He walked into the kitchen and was met with the sight of Melanie stirring a chocolaty mixture in a cooking bowl with a beater. She had on an orange apron—which he thought must be her favorite color—and her hair was tucked behind her ears. Some flour smudged her right cheek and, of course, she was also singing. Horrible, horrible noises came from that girl's mouth when she sang, but she made the sexiest sounds when aroused. He would never understand it.

He leaned against the doorjamb and cleared his throat. He couldn't help himself, he loved doing this to her. She froze, mid-stir, and stopped singing. The beater whirred in the ensuing silence. Red rose to her cheeks but she didn't turn toward him.

"Hi there, little chef," Erik said, his voice only slightly louder than the beater.

She clicked off the beater, but still didn't turn around.

"Are you going to say hello, or turn around and acknowledge me in some way?" His voice was tinged with amusement.

"I'm debating all those options. How much flour can you see on my face from where you're standing?"

"Enough that I know you must have some on the other side of your face as well."

"And I don't suppose my singing was quieter than the beaters?" she asked, still not facing him.

"No."

"That's great." She turned toward him.

She had cocoa powder on her nose and flour in her hair. There was a white smear across her apron, but the rest of her clothes were clean.

She looked at him, and then looked skyward. "God must be entertained right now. How is it you're not laughing?"

Erik's lips turned in a wolfish smile. "I'm imagining you without anything on under that apron."

She nodded with a jerk of her head and swallowed. "Oh, good." She cleared her throat and looked back at the counter. She turned the beaters back on and went back to stirring.

He stalked toward her and stood against the counter, watching her. "So, how is it that you manage to keep yourself impeccably clean when you cook other foods without an apron, and yet as you bake a cake, you're covered in flour and cocoa powder?"

She sighed and glanced up at him. "I'm a dirty baker."

Well, he could only control himself so much. He chuckled.

"Not like *that.*" She turned off the beaters and put them on the counter. "I'm distracted. I'm making frosting, you know."

"Does that require a lot of attention?" he asked, raising an eyebrow.

She looked at him, her wide blue eyes open and guileless. They took his breath away. "No. You distract me."

"Good."

"Yeah, if you want your cake salty and not sweet."

"I'm not that distracting."

"No, no one is that distracting," she said, smiling. She put the frosting bowl on a counter farther away. Then she turned back to her raw ingredients and started measuring flour.

"Did you talk to Angie yet?" Erik asked.

"Not yet. I haven't decided what I want to do about it yet."

"What do you mean?" The whole thing was a no-brainer. She shouldn't see Angie again unless she was sober. That girl was a menace to everyone. If they had been in a crowded bar, and Melanie's drink was spiked, someone could've taken advantage of her. His blood boiled thinking about it.

"I'm not sure what I want to say when I see them in a couple days."

"You're going to see them in a couple of days?" He heard the anger in his voice but didn't hide it. She could not be serious.

Melanie

Melanie couldn't believe he was already getting on her back again about her friends. This was her life. They hadn't even been on one date yet, and he was meddling. She narrowed her eyes. "Yes, I am."

"Oh, good. That seems like an excellent idea," he said sarcastically. He walked toward her and leaned over her, his hands balled into fists at his sides.

Boy, did he look mad. She was tempted to take a step back, but she took a step forward instead. If she was going to pretend to be brave, she might as well go all the way. "I'm glad you agree. I'd hate for you to act bossy, domineering, and like a control freak for no reason."

A muscle in his jaw ticked. His eyes were dark and dangerous, and his muscles were tight, he looked coiled to strike. Yikes. Maybe "control freak" had gone too far. Melanie could feel her heart pounding in her chest, but the feeling wasn't all fear. She was exhilarated. Pissing this man off was a rush.

"Think she'll hit anyone with the car she steals from you this time?"

That was a low blow. "I'm not going to let her steal my darn car. I'll have my keys in my pocket, and I won't get my drinks from her."

Erik tossed his hands in the air. "You realize how this sounds, right? You are going to see a so-called friend in whose presence you have to hide your keys and check your food."

"I'm sure she could be trusted with most foods. Like chips. I could eat chips if she gave them to me. She only lied about pot brownies once." Melanie cringed. He'd never heard about that incident. Maybe he had a point, but she sure as hell wasn't going to admit it to him. He had an ego the size of Texas, and it did not need stroking. He was infuriating. She would not cave.

"Are you kidding me? Pot brownies? You shouldn't be hanging out with her." His nostrils flared.

"It's just pot."

"That she lied about."

"Even if you were right, I wouldn't agree with you. You're too stubborn, and a huge pain in the butt." She dumped a cup of flour into the silver bowl, and then slammed the measuring cup on the counter.

"I'm stubborn? You're the one being unreasonable. You're acting like a child."

"I'm so glad you said that." Before she thought better of it, she grabbed a handful of flour out of the sack and threw it up at his face.

Powder caught on the roots of his blond hair, across the tips of his eyelashes, and hung from his eyebrows. The white covered his cheeks and forehead and began to fall down to his shoulders. His eyes widened in shock. He looked like a dumbstruck ghost.

She couldn't help it, she covered her mouth and hunched over in a fit of giggles. "You look like a ghost."

The shock disappeared, and Erik pursed his lips, a devilish gleam appearing in his eyes. "Oh, it is so on."

She jumped back and squealed, but he grabbed the sack of flour before she could take a step. She threw her hands up over her head to protect herself, and he dumped the bag over her head. The powder fell on her arms, her head, down her forehead, and over her apron.

It was on. She ran to the other side of the kitchen and grabbed the stainless steel pull-out spray faucet. She turned and got ready to push the spray button, pointing it at Erik who walked toward her with the cocoa powder in hand.

"Don't even think about it," he said, the box of open powder braced at shoulder height.

She very much thought about it. Her heart thundered in her chest, and his deep voice sent heat through her. She had the upper hand on him. She would bet he knew it too. "You gonna stop me?"

He wound his arm back to chuck the cocoa, but before he could launch it, she pressed the button, and water shot forward. She got his face and sprayed down to his chest, soaking him. He dropped the cocoa powder, and she giggled maniacally. She eased her hand off the button. "Had enough yet?"

Erik was drenched. His navy shirt clung to his chest and biceps; rivulets of water ran down his face and his arms. His hair stuck to his forehead, and most of the flour was gone, except for a couple white smears across his cheeks and forehead. Water seeped down his jeans and dripped onto the floor. His eyes were black and laced with challenge.

Goodness, he was hot. The look he shot her sent goosebumps up her arms. He shook his head no, and she couldn't have been more thrilled by his response. She shrugged and hit the button again, spraying him with water once more. This time, it didn't stop him. He walked toward her, and she had time to screech once before his hands were around hers, turning the faucet toward her.

Alarmed, she yanked back, trying to take it away from him, aiming toward his face. She didn't have the strength. It took him about two seconds to direct the spray toward her face, and then down the rest of her, soaking her. He jerked the hose out of her hands, and knowing she lost the battle, she turned to run. Not fast enough. He sprayed her entire back as well before she had taken a full step.

She squealed. Her apron and clothes were drenched through. She moved to run around to the other side of the kitchen, but then the spray stopped. Her hair was plastered to her face, her clothes felt like they weighed ten pounds extra, and her skin was slick. She swept her heavy, short hair out of her eyes and took off her apron. It wasn't doing much anymore anyway. She set the apron on the messy counter and turned to face Erik.

He was still soaked, but he swung the spray faucet around like some kind of weapon, and his grin was predatory. She took a step back and wondered why something sexual always happened in the kitchen.

Erik

Every instinct in Erik told him to pounce. Her wet shirt clung to her curves, and her bright blue eyes darkened with desire. He wanted to peel her clothes off and have his way with her. Before he could take a step toward her, the kitchen door opened.

Mary stood in the doorway, her rubber gloves pulled up to her elbows, and her black hair coiled on her head, and she made the sign of the cross. "My God. What happened?"

"I dropped the flour." Melanie glanced around the room. Yeah, that didn't make any sort of sense for the rest of the mess. She was such a terrible liar.

"The faucet was leaking, and when I tried to tighten it, I loosened it by mistake," he said smoothly.

Melanie looked at Erik and scowled. "And I slipped in the water and dropped the ingredients I was carrying."

Erik cringed, and Melanie looked at everything but him.

"I see," Mary said, looking between the two of them.

He had no idea if she bought the explanation. He looked at Melanie whose face paled as she surveyed the room. She looked uncomfortable and skittish. If he didn't get Mary to buy the story and get out of the kitchen, he was going to lose his opportunity to enjoy his soaking wet chef. He was a terrible person, but he wanted her so bad.

"I'll go get a mop," Mary said.

"No, no," Erik said, "this was my fault, I'll clean it up. Don't let this keep you."

"Are you sure?"

"Positive. Also, Dan left for the day, right?" Melanie wet was giving him some good ideas concerning the swimming pool. Assuming the landscaper, Dan, wouldn't walk around the backyard at any minute.

Melanie looked at him, her head cocked in question, but he waited on Mary's answer.

"Yes, he left."

"Okay, good. Thank you, Mary."

She nodded and smiled at them. "Try not to slip anymore, Melanie. We don't want another set of bloody knees," she said and walked out.

Melanie turned to Erik as soon as the other woman was gone. "I guess I should go get a mop."

"Not yet." He ran to her and threw her over his shoulder.

"Erik put me down," she yelled.

He wrapped one arm around the back of her knees, holding her thighs to his chest, so she wouldn't be able to flail too much. He ran through the back door of the kitchen and down the hallway. "No," he said.

"Where are you taking me?" Each word was punctuated with a gasp as her sternum hit his hard shoulder.

He smacked her ass and she squealed. "You'll see."

He walked through the back door that led to the pool. She had him acting like a horny teenager, but he didn't give a damn. He couldn't remember the last time he'd had this much fun.

"Oh my," she said as her head faced the pool.

Turning back around, so he faced the pool, he walked toward it and couldn't help but grin.

"Don't even think about it, Erik. I mean it." She pounded on his back with her fists.

"You know that doesn't hurt enough to make me stop. Although it does make me want to throw you farther."

"Erik."

There was a sudden stinging pain in his right ass cheek. "Ow." He glanced over his shoulder. "Did you just bite me?"

She turned her head and glared up at him. "Maybe."

He rose an eyebrow down at her. "If you're not nice, I won't take your boots off first."

She fidgeted harder as he neared the pool's edge. Holding her legs in one hand, he pulled her pant legs up over her knees to access her boots and then unzipped one shoe after the other. They fell to the ground with dull thuds.

"I'm serious. You can't throw me into the pool. Don't you dare."

There would be hell to pay later, but he was enjoying himself too much to care. "Hold your breath, sweetheart," he said, and then he chucked her into the pool.

Melanie

Melanie crashed into the water butt first. Lukewarm water sluiced around her, and she held her breath as she dropped underwater. She sunk until she hit the bottom of the pool, and then propelled herself to the surface. Flinging her hair out of her eyes, she gasped for breath.

She wasn't sure how, and she wasn't sure how long it would take, but she would get Erik back for this. She wanted to yank him into the pool but figured he wasn't likely to go for the help-me-get-me-out trick. He'd probably laugh.

Of course, he was already laughing. She looked up, and he stood at the edge of the pool, hands braced on his hips, his head thrown back in laughter. He looked beyond smug, and it was infuriating. With the sun pouring down on him, he looked gorgeous. His eyes were shining, and his shirt clung to his chest.

Melanie glanced around the pool, hoping to find some sort of mechanism for revenge. There wasn't any.

There were a few lounge chairs, a spa, a couple tables with umbrellas, and a variety of well-groomed shrubbery and cacti surrounding the pool, but nothing useful. She kicked to keep herself above water. The pool was deep, but she had to admit the water felt pretty good. The sun had been beating down on the water long enough that it wasn't too cold. She sighed and dunked her head so that she could smooth her hair back. She was out of ideas.

"If you had a water gun I would own you." She combed her hair back with her fingers.

"Are you twelve?" he asked. He kicked out of his shoes and reached for the hem of his still wet, navy shirt.

Melanie's eyes widened in alarm. He wasn't going to get in there with her, was he? He tugged his shirt over his head, and she almost started to salivate. What did this guy do that made him look like he was carved out of some serious stone? He unbuttoned his jeans, and she licked her lips. He took forever dragging down his zipper. She wanted him naked, she wanted to see every inch of him...Could a view of his chest really make her thoughts take a one-eighty turn this way? Now she wanted him in the pool, desperately. What was wrong with her sex drive? It was working overtime.

Erik's hand paused once he'd pulled down the zipper on his pants. She glanced up, wondering what the hold-up was, and his eyes were boring into hers. Their dark lust seared her to her core. The things this man could do to her with a single look...it was unreal. She swallowed, and he shoved his pants off, revealing black boxer briefs that covered an impressive package, but he never took his eyes off hers. He peeled his socks off and then he crouched so that Melanie and he were closer to eye-level. He looked ready to attack, his leg muscles bulging, his impressive arms propped on his knees.

"Those clothes look kind of heavy."

Melanie shrugged, trying to act cavalier. "They're okay. I'm sure everyone around here is getting more than enough of an eyeful without me baring skin."

"This half of the pool can't be seen from any other houses or roads. That's why there's so much shrubbery around. For some privacy. That's why the Jacuzzi is on this side."

Jealousy rushed through her as she considered why the Jacuzzi would need to be hidden. She imagined him in there with other women. Sheesh, it was a good thing he asked her to date him because her reaction to the hidden Jacuzzi was a bad sign. She was pissed. "I'm sure your one-night stands appreciated that."

"Jealous?" He smirked. He was enjoying this far too much.

"No, I just don't want to catch anything while I'm swimming around in here." She leaned back to backstroke away. She lifted her arms over her head and her muscles burned. Darn it, the stupid sleeves were heavy. She swam a few feet and then stopped.

"Catch something?" he called after her.

"You know, from some STD ridden floozy you screwed." The words popped out of her mouth before she could stop herself. Wow, yeah, that didn't seem jealous at all. She cringed and turned around, so he wouldn't see her face.

"I haven't been here long. There haven't been any women in here."

"That's nice," she said, her back still to him. She was

so thrilled it was downright pathetic.

"If you don't take your clothes off now, I'm going to pull them off you myself."

His words sent shivers down her spine. She loved the challenge in his voice, but it was her turn to take control. She wanted to see how much she affected him, and she had the perfect idea of how to do that. "You'll have to catch me first. I can swim pretty darn well."

"In your soggy jeans?"

She shook her head. Her heart thundered in her chest, and as she played with the top button on her shirt, she watched his stare follow her fingers. She unbuttoned one button at a time and then let the shirt fall off her shoulders and into the pool, revealing a sheer, lace, peach-colored bra to his devouring gaze. Under his scrutiny heat coiled in her lower belly. She rubbed her thighs together and was no longer sure the wetness she felt was from the water.

Erik stood and looked like he was ready to jump in, but Melanie held up a hand. "I'm not finished yet."

A muscle ticked in his jaw. "I'm not a patient man."

The way he said that did terrible things to her insides. She wanted to give in, to let him come to her, but she wasn't done yet. She looked down at his body and her gaze caught on the large bulge in his black boxer briefs. Swallowing, she tried not to think about the way his cock felt so delicious inside her, and instead fumbled with the button on her jeans. After a second of a waterlogged struggle, she undid it and then tugged at the zipper. The tightness of the pants was an issue. If they got stuck she would never live it down.

The zipper wouldn't unzip all the way, but with

enough shimmying, she should be able to get them off anyway. She hooked her thumbs into her soaked jeans and tugged them down, swaying so that her hips gyrated under the water. After they were down to her knees, she ducked under the water and pulled her jeans all the way off. She broke the surface and balled up her pants.

"Now, I can swim away from you." She raised her arm and launched the jeans at him. So much for not finding something to get back at him with. She waited for the squelch of the pants hitting him in the stomach, but he grabbed them from the air.

Darn. That was badass.

A hint of a grin teased his lips, but his face was hard and determined. He dropped the pants and dove.

Erik

Erik opened his eyes underwater and gauged his surroundings. He could make out the lower half of Melanie's body several feet to his left. Her bare legs kicked in the water as she swam out of reach. Her sheer peach panties hugged her ass as she swam away, and he couldn't wait to tear them off and bury himself inside her.

He swam up to the surface and blinked into the sun. His face warmed, and he shook his hair, so the water wouldn't drip into his eyes. He couldn't ever remember messing around like this, ever being this relaxed. Ever since he was a teenager, he'd been looking out for Hunter, trying to give him a good life. Before that, he'd focused on survival as he jumped from foster home to foster home. But right then, everything felt perfect. He looked over at Melanie who smiled mischievously. This feeling, the feeling of being carefree, of warmth spreading through his chest, was because of her. God, that was terrifying.

"Too cold for you? You look like you've gone into shock. Do we need to get you inside, wrap you in a blanket, and put you in front of a fire?" Melanie teased, gliding past him so that she was closer to the house again.

He turned toward her and shook his head. His eyes were trained on her, waiting to see which way she would dart. Her gaze flickered around the pool. He was going to catch her, and she knew it. She wasn't the type to go down without a fight though.

She started to kick off the wall and to the right, but as he jumped that way, she dodged and dove deeper, gliding right under him. He swore and dove but it was too late, she was out of his grasp, coming up on the side of the wall closest to the Jacuzzi. Shit, she was a good swimmer. Not that her abilities would stop him. All it did was make their little game more interesting.

"It's like you're playing Marco Polo. You're so far away, I would think you've been swimming with your eyes closed." She lifted herself up onto the ledge and sat there, laughing at him. She was gorgeous. Her smooth, pale stomach and cleavage glistened with water, and he could make out the outline of her peach nipples under her thin lacy bra.

"Do you know what I'm going to do with you when I catch you?" he asked, his voice as rough as gravel. He glided toward her.

"What?" she asked, breathless.

"First, I'm going to drag those lacy cups down, so I can suck those nipples that have been hard and taunting me ever since you got in the pool. Then I'm going to peel off your panties, so I can feel how hot you are for me. Then I'm going to fuck you so hard you won't be able to move for a week without thinking about me."

Melanie made the faintest purring noise. He was getting closer to her. Close enough that he saw the way she pressed her thighs together and the way her skin flushed with need. She wanted him bad, maybe even as much as he wanted her.

He stalked closer. He approached an arm's length away, so she crouched on the pool's edge. She feigned right, but this time he waited. She dove over his head and his eyes widened in shock. Bold choice, but he was going to get her this time.

Her body flowed into the water, and she swam fast, but not quite fast enough. He turned in her direction and reached out to grab her leg. All he needed was a toe and he'd have her. His hand closed around her smooth calf and he tugged.

Splashing ensued as Melanie flailed around, trying to get away, but he held her leg tight. He tugged it toward him, so the rest of her body followed suit, her chest lining up against his as he yanked her leg past his side.

She gasped as their bodies connected, and a look of dismay crossed over her features. "I thought I'd last longer."

He brushed her wet hair behind her ear and leaned forward to nibble her earlobe. He heard her sharp intake of breath as he bit her. “I can be a very determined man, Melanie.”

He nudged his hard length against the apex of her thighs and she rocked against him. Even through their wet underclothes, he could feel her swollen need. He took a deep breath; he didn’t want to lose it already. He was looking forward to following through with his earlier ideas. He grinned at her. “It’s a good thing the water’s warm because I intend to enjoy you now that I’ve caught you.”

Melanie looked up at him coyly through her eyelashes. “Take your time.”

He was a goner.

19

Melanie

Melanie lathered the chlorine out of her hair for a good twenty minutes after enjoying her long swim with Erik. He had offered to shampoo her hair for her, but she had a feeling it would've led to more sex. She knew it after one look at Erik's not-so-innocent face. Not that more sex would have been a bad thing, as sore as she was, she didn't want to say no. However, she hadn't even started job hunting, and she'd had no time to herself whatsoever. If they were going to date in a more traditional manner, then they couldn't move at jet speed the way they were. She wouldn't lose herself to a man—no matter what he could do with his darn fingers.

When she'd been with her ex, she'd been like half a person. They'd done everything together. They had the same friends, the same hobbies, most of them were activities that he'd introduced her to. When he broke up with her, she felt incomplete. She felt like she had to discover who she was all over again. She didn't want that to happen again. No matter what happened with Erik, she would know who she was.

She explained this to him on her way to her bedroom. There'd been a lot of "I'm my own person" and "We need to get to know one another" and "I have hobbies besides sex." She thought he got it. He'd even said he wanted to go for a run with her. They'd put off more sex, more talking, more anything until the morning so that she could work on her own life.

She had one fun phone call to make, and one she wasn't looking forward to. After, she would work on finding a job. There were only so many times she could screw her boss until she felt like a total floozy. She was quickly reaching that number.

The shampoo suds slid down her shoulders and back as she rinsed out her hair. She soaped up the rest of herself with a pink loofa, and then rinsed, deciding she should get the boring phone call out of the way first. She finished and turned off the water. Steam dissipated, and the air chilled her bare skin. She pulled aside the sunflower covered shower curtain and grabbed a fluffy blue towel, wrapping the cloth around her before she stepped out.

The boring phone call would be short. She could even do it while she dried her hair. She flipped her head and grabbed a smaller blue towel off the rack, twisting it around her head. When she stood up straight, she shoved the twirled towel back, so it sat back on the top of her head in a neat twist. She glanced in the mirror above the sink. At least, a neat twist was the idea. The towel wrap sat loosely to one side, the ends flapping as she moved. It held in place though, so it didn't seem worth fixing.

She grabbed her phone off the counter and walked out to the bedroom bundled in fluff. Carpet squished under her toes, and she sat on the edge of her bed. She rolled her neck, and then she called her mother.

Diane answered on the second ring. "Clark residence, Diane speaking."

"Hello, Mother. It's Melanie."

"Oh, hi, dear. How are you?"

"I'm fine, thank y—"

"Is that employer of yours still doing your job for you? You should be careful. He may expect things of you in return that God doesn't even have a name for."

Melanie bit her tongue. She couldn't imagine her mother being thrilled about the things she'd done with him that did have a name. "My leg is much better, thanks. And I've been doing my own work."

"Don't start your sentences with the word 'and'. Doing so makes you sound like a hillbilly. We have never even met a hillbilly."

"Yes, Mother." Melanie bit her cheeks. A phone call should not be this difficult.

"Let's move on now. Howard and I have decided to throw an impromptu soirée in three weeks. I don't suppose by some miracle you'll have a date?"

Melanie's tongue froze in her mouth. Erik and she were dating, so she could have a date. But they hadn't been on a single date yet, and what if the evening fell flat? Of course, that didn't seem likely, especially since sex with him was out of this world. What if they didn't know how to socialize and weren't compatible in other ways though? What if he couldn't handle dating after all? If she told her mother yes, and then didn't show up with a man, her mother would have a field day. No way she was going to chance that.

"No, it'll only be me."

"I see. Please feel free to bring Sheila then. I don't want you getting bored with so many adults there."

Melanie shook her head in disbelief. "I am an adult."

"Oh, you know what I mean. People who are much older than you, people with...different interests."

Sure, "different interests," she bought that. Twenty-three years old and her mother was still concerned about Melanie embarrassing her in front of her friends. It wasn't worth getting into though. "Sheila's sister is in town, so I don't think I'll be able to drag her away from her family."

"Invite her sister as well."

"All right, I will."

"I have to go now, Bunco starts soon."

"See you soon."

"See you then, dear. Don't forget to watch your employer's habits. Just because he hasn't killed you yet doesn't mean he isn't a serial killer. He might be against killing his own employees. It's so hard to find good help these days. Bye, bye."

Thankfully, Diane hung up before Melanie could say another word. It was sick that the last part of that conversation sounded like a compliment about her job skills. Her mother made her nuts. She smacked her forehead with her phone before calling Sheila.

Sheila answered before Melanie could even hear the phone start ringing. "Hey, what's up?"

"You're invited to another family function. So is Angie." Melanie leaned back on her bed.

"Hold up, I have to go into the bedroom."

"Sure."

"Sorry, but Angie was nearby. So, your family wants to invite her?"

"Yeah, do you not want to invite her?"

"No, that would be great. She might be subdued. She got hurt while she was drinking yesterday."

"What? How bad?" Melanie's imagination ran wild. Alcohol and Angie...there was no shortage of things that could've happened.

"It's not life-threatening. She was drunk and decided to jump on a glass table. There was a whole lot of blood, and now she has a whole lot of stitches." Her voice sounded matter of fact, but Melanie knew better.

"How many stitches?" Sheila may have been calm, but she had a habit of making incidents like this one seem less significant than they were.

"A total of thirty-two in three or four different places. I can't remember it all."

"Oh God, that's awful. Is she doing all right?"

"She'll heal," Sheila said. Melanie could practically hear the shrug.

"How are you doing?"

Silence fell on the other side of the line. Melanie couldn't imagine how difficult dealing with Angie was.

"I'm fine," she finally said.

"What are you going to do?"

"She's on painkillers, so she's pretty mellow, but I don't know. I worry. Almost all the time, I'm worried about her."

Melanie had no idea what to say. She and Sheila were like sisters, and she was close to Angie too. Angie had a tough time with her family, but this was getting out of control. "I'm sorry."

"Yeah. It blows. Let's talk about something else. This shit is depressing."

"Got it. What do you want to talk about?" Melanie hoped Sheila didn't want to talk about Erik.

"I want vicarious sexy stories."

Melanie groaned. Of course she did.

Erik

It was early, well before six, but Erik jolted awake and got out of bed. He was used to getting up early to go jogging, and he was looking forward to jogging with Melanie, but he needed to hurry up and get out of bed. He had a feeling that if he wasn't ready and by the front door in twenty minutes, she'd leave without him. He wouldn't see her again until their date because she had the day off, and she intended to spend the time elsewhere. She said it was too weird to see each other all day before a first date. She said the whole thing was so backward already that at the very least he would have to pick her up from her old apartment.

He didn't mind that part. He wanted an opportunity to, as Stacie would put it, "woo" her. Christ, he'd never used the word *woo* in his entire life but woo was the closest fit for what he intended to do. He needed to convince her they should be together. While excellent, mind-blowing sex was a step in the right direction, he bet a woman like her didn't make her choices for romantic partners based on how often they could make her come. It was a pity. He was damn good at that. She'd probably like flowers and food or at least talking that didn't involve arguments or telling her what to do. He should be able to manage that...at least sometimes.

He groaned and took socks, boxers, and shorts out of his dresser. He thought about getting a shirt, but he loved Melanie's expression when she saw him shirtless. She was cute when she checked him out, especially when she thought he didn't notice.

He tugged on his shorts and laced up his running shoes. The clock on his bedside table read ten until six, but he needed to stretch before he ran. He grabbed his phone and a water bottle off his bedside table and headed to the foyer.

Melanie was stretching when he got there. She was bent over, facing away from him, touching her toes. Her black running shorts clung to her ass, and her fingers brushed over her tie-dye running shoes. Six in the morning and his cock twitched in his shorts at the sight of her.

He cleared his throat, and Melanie jerked up. She turned around, her eyes were half open, and her hair was disheveled. She picked at her red athletic shirt and yawned.

"I had you pegged as a morning person," he said.

"I normally am. Late night."

He lifted his leg behind him, bent his knee, and held

the toe of his shoe behind his back, stretching his quads. "We can postpone if you'd like."

"Oh no, I'm fine. I want to run." She surveyed him. Her gaze caught on his chest and stayed there.

Definitely worth not wearing a shirt to watch her eyes widen and darken as she stared. He put one foot down and lifted the other, knowing full well how the stretch would ripple across his abs. She watched his body with an enraptured gaze. As much as he was enjoying himself, he needed to stop her before his reaction made it difficult to run.

He cleared his throat and put his other leg on the floor. Her gaze jumped to meet his before darting away.

"I've been dying to give you a good morning kiss ever since I woke up, but at this point, I'm afraid that might prevent us from running," he said.

She narrowed her eyes. "I can control myself, thank you very much. But if you have no self-control, that's fine. I'd rather run anyway."

The challenge in her voice was so much fun. She could be as high and mighty as she wanted, pretend that she wasn't affected, but they both knew better. He stalked toward her, and she stepped back into the door.

He held her gaze as he braced his hands around her shoulders and leaned over her. She was trapped against the door. He could get used to her like this, her eyes a mix of alarm and desire, a conflicting play of emotions flashing over her face. He loved her riled up.

He bent his head and nipped her earlobe. Her shoulders spasmed. "I guess I can kiss you then," he whispered.

She nodded. She looked delectable waiting with her

lips parted. He wanted to devour her and this time, he allowed himself to, holding nothing back. He slanted his lips over hers, demanding and unyielding, and then leaned into her so that he could feel every inch of her curving back against him. Her sports bra and shirt left little to the imagination.

She was warm and soft. He sucked on her bottom lip and pressed the evidence of his own arousal against her. She ground against him, and her tongue swept inside his mouth, sending fire up his spine. He kept his hunger leashed, enjoying the way she started to lose control. He held his hands to the door and opened his mouth to her tongue's exploration.

Her hands slid over his tense abs and then to his back, her fingernails grazing him. She rocked against him and moaned. His hand slid down the door to tangle in her hair, and then he stopped himself. The run. They were going to go on a run. He eased back, pulling his lips from hers.

"We should start our run before it gets too hot," he said between shaky breaths.

She looked dazed and clutched his back. "What? Run?"

He couldn't help but grin. Yeah, she had so much self-control.

Melanie

That was great. She'd proven his point. Well, no reason to dwell. Best to get outside where she could breathe...and maybe lose him around a trail curve.

"You ready or do you need to stretch more?" she asked, pretending like nothing had happened.

"I'm good, but I wouldn't mind watching you bend over again if you need to stretch longer." His face looked serious, but his dark eyes twinkled.

She smoothed her shirt. "I think I've limbered up enough."

"Good." He reached around her to get the door. The latch clicked, and Melanie stepped away, so he could open the door. She ducked under his arm and walked outside, breathing in the warm, fresh air of spring.

The sun was rising over the horizon with swirls of orange and pink. Birds chirped, and a woodpecker tapped against a nearby tree. It was a fantastic morning for a jog.

"Ready?" she asked as Erik closed the door behind him.

He gave a sharp nod, and she took off, watching the cacti and dirt flow past her and listening to the way her shoes punctuated the sounds of the birds chirping as they smacked on the driveway pavement.

They said nothing for a few minutes. She wasn't sure if he liked to talk while he jogged. She could go either way, but she was curious about the man beside her. She'd had sex with him, argued with him, but she still knew so little about her employer...er, date?

The head of the trail path was a few meters away, and she turned toward it. Erik kept up easily beside her. "Trail jogging ok?" she asked, only a little out of breath.

"Sure. I have water and a phone."

Melanie rolled her eyes. It was a cheap shot. "Thank you, Mr. Boy Scout. You know, I don't think they give badges to people your age."

Erik's face hardened. "I'm assuming the only reason you don't have your phone with you right now is because I'm with you."

He could be such a pain in the behind. They hit gravel and were surrounded by trees and cacti as the trail curved. "Under the threat of another lecture, of course," she muttered to herself. His lips twitched, and she glared at him.

"Better be careful, or you'll get one about your attitude."

"Please tell me you don't lecture on dates." She picked up the pace. She was curious about how fast he could go, about how much he could handle. She wanted to outlast him. She had been jogging for years. She could do it; she would have to push him hard.

He lengthened his stride to fall in beside her. "No. Lecturing doesn't precede sex."

"You've already had sex with me." The path narrowed so she stepped in front of him.

"Good point. I suppose I'll be free to lecture if I wish then."

"If sex is no longer a priority." She snorted through heavy breaths. She was losing her counted breathing. The trail went uphill, and the pace burned her quads and calves. The man behind her was still acting like a darn machine. Well, she wasn't going to quit yet.

The son of a gun laughed. He didn't even sound winded. "Don't worry. I won't be lecturing. I'm too curious about you."

"Me?" she asked startled. She was curious about him—a CEO millionaire under thirty. He even did charity work. What on Earth was there to be curious about her? She was a twenty-three-year-old chef. Not that she doubted her self-worth or anything, but the most interesting thing she'd ever done was sleep outside in an alley in Canada once because she and Sheila had gotten so drunk, they forgot what hostel they were staying at. Besides that, she was pretty sure she had nothing on him in the way of interesting.

She hopped a couple of large rocks, and her knees wobbled in protest. She straightened her strides, and her legs relaxed a little. They'd climbed a bit of elevation quick, and she could feel it in her chest. Running could be so painful sometimes. The time between their comments grew as they jogged faster.

Erik was right behind her. "Yes, you. You're tenacious and have interesting life goals. You're loyal to your friends and funny."

Her heart flipped at the compliment. However, when she thought about it, the beginnings of a frown tipped the corners of her open, panting mouth. She was losing steam. "When do I say funny things?"

"All the time. Sometimes you don't say them intentionally, but they're funny all the same."

His voice sounded tight, and she hoped he was finally wearing himself out. She didn't want to give in first and ask for a break, but she wasn't sure she could go much farther. "I'm so glad you find me amusing."

"The rest of it was nice. Take the compliments."

Melanie rolled her eyes and prepared stop.

"Okay, that's it, I need a break." He grabbed her arm from behind her.

Holy cow, she'd done it. She'd outrun him. She

gulped air and turned around, ignoring her limbs' burning pleas to sit down. "All right, no problem," she said.

He took a sip from his water bottle and looked her up and down. Once he finished, he narrowed his eyes. "You were competing this whole time, weren't you?"

Melanie couldn't stop her smile. "Maybe a bit."

20

Erik

The day leading up to his date with Melanie felt like several rolled into one. Work moved at a snail's pace. To top his rough day off, he was nervous. It took him a while to recognize the feeling because it had been a long time since he was nervous about anything to do with a woman. Around lunchtime, he figured out the quick heart rate and the occasional dip in his stomach were a result of anticipation and anxiousness. What was it about her that made him act and feel like a teenager? He wondered if he'd ever figure it out.

He rubbed his temples and stood from behind his glass desk in his Scottsdale office. Hunter would be meeting him for lunch in a few minutes. He wanted to discuss the summer program, which meant he needed to get his head out of his ass. The date was seven hours away, so he shouldn't be thinking about the evening for at least another five. He ran a hand through his hair, and his office phone beeped.

Erik leaned over and pressed a button. "Yes, Derek?"

Derek's voice crackled through the speaker. "Hunter is here for your lunch appointment."

"Send him in."

"Yes, sir."

Hunter opened the office door and stepped in. He wore a black, button-down shirt, and his black hair curled over his ears. A feeling of pride stole over Erik. His brother had turned into quite the grown up, wearing ties, organizing events, becoming a confident man. He could remember Hunter's scrawny form enveloped in oversized hip-hop clothes from less than ten years ago. His transformation had been incredible to watch.

He was so glad they were family. Not biological family of course, but family all the same. The fact that Melanie thought that there was any way they were brothers by blood was almost funny. Or it would have been if he had done the right thing and corrected her. He couldn't do it though. He couldn't tell her about his past. Fuck.

"You ok?" Hunter asked, waving a hand in front of his face.

He snapped out of his internal debate. "Yeah, I'm fine."

"Nervous about your date?" Hunter taunted, his eyes gleaming.

Erik glared at his brother. "Do you want me to leave you here while I go get lunch?"

"That only worked when I couldn't drive."

"All right. Let's go." Erik grabbed his car keys off the desk.

They left the building and rode in Erik's blue Audi in silence. It took them a few minutes to get to the small, hole-in-the-wall Mexican restaurant, and Erik managed to find a prime parking spot right out front.

They walked into the restaurant and were met with the smell of fresh tortillas and grilled meat that made Erik's mouth water. The place was loud, dim, and jammed full of people of all ages sitting around tiny tables. A host stood at the front and waved stained menus at them. He directed the men toward the back of the restaurant. They followed him and sat at a table against the back wall by a small window.

Hunter always asked Erik why he came to places like these now that they had so much money. It was natural for him. He was accustomed to them, so why change his habits? Plus, this place's tacos were the best he'd ever had. Hunter, on the other hand, went only to places like these when Erik wanted to. Ever since they'd started making serious money, Hunter distanced himself from anything he'd done or had when they were poor. He'd moved onto bigger and better things, except for in his living space. His apartment was tiny. The place was luxurious but still tiny.

They sat, ordered drinks, and were left alone. "Where are you taking her?" Hunter asked.

"The Silver Bistro."

"Hmm. And here I thought you were so smitten that you would pull out the big guns. Like a trip to a vineyard in California, or at least front row seats at a concert after dinner."

"If you're taking a girl to a vineyard in another state for your first date, you might be overcompensating for something."

Hunter shrugged. "It's not a typical first date. She's your employee. She lives in the same house as you. Oh, and of course, you've been doing it."

Erik narrowed his eyes at his brother. He opened his mouth to respond, but an older, skinny waiter walked by and set glasses of iced tea on the table. "Do you need another minute with the menu?" he asked, cutting into their discussion.

"No, I'll have the chicken enchiladas," Hunter said.

"And you, sir?" the waiter asked.

"The same."

"I'll go put that in."

"Thank you," Erik said.

The man nodded and smiled, the lines around his mouth stretching to accommodate the expression. He turned around and walked off. Erik shifted in his seat and thought through the summer camp.

"So, we have about thirty-five hundred kids to contend with this summer," Erik said.

"Right. Which makes a single social event about impossible."

Erik took a sip of his iced tea and set it beside his plate. When Stacie had brought up her idea, he hadn't given any thought to the numbers. She'd seemed so thrilled, and he didn't like the idea of disappointing his aunt, but this was starting to seem unrealistic.

"What if we did a couple of opening events and split them according to age group? I think that would make more sense anyway," Erik said. It had occurred to him that seventeen-year-olds and six-year-olds don't socialize the same way.

"I agree. But I think the timing might be hard. What if we did a picnic event for those under fourteen and a mixer at the end of summer for the older kids? Maybe even a dance. Proms for high schools handle over a thousand kids in one venue sometimes. We could find a venue that does the same."

Erik gave his idea some thought. A dance function would offset some food costs as well. With the number of athletic facilities that they were going to need to rent, the cost of everything was going up. "I think that's a good idea. But we're still going to have split up the picnic events. We've got over two thousand kids that are under fourteen."

"So many kids," Hunter said, shaking his head.

"You're used to young people."

"Not that many."

"They won't stampede. Focus."

"All right, all right. Maybe we could do the split by area. You know, for the kids under fourteen. I feel like if we split this up by age, the kids might not be comfortable. This could ease them into the idea of activities within their age group, while they're still around people they've known for a while," Hunter said.

Hunter had a good point. Group homes had kids of all ages, so they'd be separating them if they organized the socials by age group. "Yeah, that sounds good. We'll break them up into five or six groups of a few hundred each and pick easy locations."

Hunter nodded, and the waiter returned with a platter full of food. He set chips and salsa in the middle of the table, and then put plates of chicken enchiladas in front of both of them. Erik looked at his plate, and his stomach rumbled. He was so hungry, and this looked delicious. Rice and beans sat to one side and the enchiladas sat on the other, covered with a thick layer of red sauce and a thin cheese layer. He picked up his silverware and started to cut a bite of an enchilada.

"Sounds like a good plan." Hunter put his napkin on his lap.

Erik took a bite of his food and the flavor of the cheese, chicken, and sauce exploded over his tongue. The food was fantastic. He took a few bites, and then looked up at Hunter. "I'm putting you and Jennifer in charge of hiring volunteers to coach and teach classes. Remember—"

Hunter cut him off. "Jennifer and me? I'm not sure that's such a good idea."

Erik couldn't mask his surprise. Hunter and Jennifer were still at odds with one another? What the hell was his brother's problem? "Hunter, this is something we both believe in. This is something important. Act maturely. Unless she's done something that you think warrants me eliminating her as the activities director?"

Hunter clenched his jaw and scowled. He looked angrier than Erik had seen him in a long time. "No. It's fine, I'll do the job."

"I'm glad to hear it."

❧

Melanie

Melanie sat in the living room of her old one-bedroom apartment with her laptop open on her lap. The day felt quiet. She had gotten used to the hustle and bustle that occurred in Erik's home. Mary's scuffling step, Hunter and Erik's banter, and Dan's hedge trimmer had become sounds of comfort.

She'd turned on the radio, but it wasn't the same. Oh well, she shouldn't have been wasting her time getting preoccupied about the noise or lack thereof in the apartment anyway. She looked at a few job search engines for chef positions. She had about half an hour before she needed to get ready for her date. Mostly because Sheila had inserted her nose in Melanie's business and decided that Melanie needed company while she got ready. Because there could be some sort of clothing disaster, obviously.

She shook off her annoyance and focused on the websites in front of her. The pickings were slim, but she'd found a couple of commis and chef de partie positions. She found a couple of openings in a nearby resort, one at a hotel in Tempe, and two at upscale restaurants. The two at the resort and the options at the restaurants were appealing. They were probably out of her league, but she wouldn't let that stop her from applying.

She made a list of her preferences and wrote down the requirements for the application processes. For the most part, they didn't look that time-consuming. Her doorbell rang.

She glanced at her phone, wondering if she'd lost track of the time. Nope, it was only 5:30 p.m. and Sheila wasn't supposed to be there until six. She walked to the front door and looked through the peephole.

Sheila's lush features looked oblong through the peephole. "Hello," she called in a singsong tone.

"You're half an hour early." Melanie unlocked the door and opened it up.

Her friend walked in carrying a makeup case and a large shopping bag that appeared to be filled with shoes. "An hour is not long enough to prep for a date."

Melanie shut the door behind her and rolled her eyes. "I'm putting on clothing, not preparing for war. You realize you are here to hang out, not to apply things to me," she said, motioning to the case in Sheila's left hand.

Sheila dropped the bag and case on the floor and sat on the couch. "Fine, fine. They're here so you have options."

She put her hands on her hips. "How many pairs of shoes are in that bag?"

"Eight," Sheila said without batting an eye.

"I only have two feet."

"I didn't know what dress you're going to wear. You are going to wear a dress, right?" Sheila's mouth tightened to a pout. The girl was readying herself for a battle, all over dresses.

Melanie looked away and nodded. Yes, she was going to wear a darn dress. She couldn't remember the last time she wanted to, but she wanted Erik to react the way she did when she saw him shirtless.

"Oh my God. You didn't even argue." Sheila's voice was a reverent whisper.

"Don't start. I'll go put it on, and you can help

me pick shoes. But that's it. You're here to hang out." Melanie walked to her almost empty bedroom to retrieve the dress. It hung on the door of her closet. The short, burgundy, clinging number didn't leave a ton to the imagination up top. It dipped in the front and the straps were about two-fingers width thick, crisscrossing down the back. There was no way to hide a bra in there. Though the dress was on the shorter side, the skirt had some flare so the material didn't climb her behind when she moved in it. She'd bought the outfit a few months ago on a whim, realizing after she took it home that she would probably never wear it. Tonight, she was going to prove her old self wrong.

She took off her clothes and grabbed a lacy, strappy thong. She slid on the underwear and then unhooked the dress from the hanger.

"What's taking so long?" Sheila's voice called from the living room.

"I can't strip as fast as you." She drew the dress overhead and pulled the soft, silky material down her body.

"Cheap shot," Sheila said.

"Yeah, yeah." She put her arms through the straps and smoothed the skirt. The dress fell a little past midway down her thighs. She looked around for her bedroom mirror and realized it was at Erik's house. She walked to the bathroom to make sure the dress wasn't lopsided. She turned on the bathroom light and bit her cheeks. It was...something. She was not used to having this much of herself on display. There was no denying she looked darn good in it though. She walked out of the bathroom and into the living room, where Sheila kicked her feet in the air in impatience. Sheila caught sight of Melanie and froze. "Holy shit."

Uh-oh. "Is it too much?" Melanie cringed and reigned in panic. They had over an hour. They could find another dress.

"Nope, it's perfect. And now I understand why my sister is a lesbian. He is going to drool all over you."

"Thanks, and ew. Help me find shoes, and then I'll go put on makeup."

Sheila looked up at Melanie, her hazel eyes serious. "You really like him, don't you?"

Melanie sighed. Wasn't it obvious? When did she ever wear clothes like this? She even planned to use eyeshadow. She was in deep, and she knew so little about him. It was time to rectify that situation, starting tonight. "I do."

Sheila nodded, and her gaze clouded. "I know most people would tell you to be careful. That he was interested only in a fling, and you haven't known him long. But the truth is you'd get hurt no matter what at this point. So remember who you are and don't be afraid to go after what you want."

Melanie smiled through the lump in her throat. Her friend was the best she could ever hope for. She was so lucky to have Sheila's support. "And if this falls apart?"

"Then I'll help you put everything back together."

Erik

Erik sat in his Audi in the parking lot outside Melanie's apartment complex. He turned off the car and glanced around the back seat to make sure there wasn't any trash or anything out of place. The car looked clean and smelled like a combination of lemon and soap. He wasn't sure why'd he'd even checked—he'd washed his car a couple hours before. He took a deep breath, grabbed the roses off his passenger seat, and stepped out of his car.

The warm spring night air felt oppressive against his dark gray suit. He straightened his black tie and walked toward the staircase leading to Melanie's second-floor unit. His dress shoes clicked against the asphalt.

He saw a few people as he made his way upstairs. Three women holding each other's arms swayed on their heels as they walked downstairs, and a young couple with backpacks on walked down the hall on the second floor. The bass from some terrible rap music boomed from the unit next to Melanie's as he approached.

He knocked on the door and waited. He wondered what she'd be wearing; if she would don the same kind of button-down she always did, if she even had any other kinds of shirts. Maybe the spandex uniform from the diner was the only other clothing she owned. A small smile flitted over his features as he imagined her wearing spandex pants and a shirt with a fire pattern to a nice Italian restaurant. She would wrap her arms around herself the entire evening.

When the door swung open, the smile slid off his face. Christ, she looked gorgeous. She stood in the entryway of her apartment, one hand still on the door and the other at her side. She wore a short burgundy dress that hugged her breasts and her hips. The cloth held her upper body like a glove, curving around her without a seam.

Her skin was luminous, her blue eyes were fringed with black, her mouth was luscious and red, and her hair looked like black silk. She wore high, strapped, black shoes that elongated her smooth legs. He could imagine those long legs wrapped around his waist, her dress riding up her thighs. His nostrils flared, and he inhaled. Seconds in close proximity to this woman, and he was losing control.

He looked over her body and then her face, realizing that he hadn't said a word yet. When he found her eyes, hers were doing the same thing to him. It appeared the suit was the right choice.

"You look incredible," Erik said.

Her gaze snapped up to meet his. "Thanks. I have to get my purse. Come in."

She stepped back, and he stepped in. "These are for you." He handed her the roses.

"Thank you, they're beautiful." Her fingers closed around the bundle wrapped in cellophane, and she brought the blooms to her nose to inhale. "They smell wonderful. I should get a vase."

She turned around and walked to the small kitchen. Her back was bare except for two straps that crisscrossed down to her hips. He imagined slipping the straps off her shoulders to bare her back completely. Then he would...he stopped short and remembered they had a date. Dinner first. He managed to swallow a groan and shut the door behind him. "You can have a seat in the living room if you'd like," she called to him.

He walked down the one small hallway, past the kitchen, and into her living room. The apartment smelled like pie and Melanie: citrusy, warm, and a hint of something sweet. He sat on the light blue sofa with his fingers interlaced, waiting for her. Her heels sounded sharp on the linoleum. They had reservations in about half an hour, and all he could think about was peeling her out of the dress. A dress that he would have never in a million years imagined her choosing, and she wore it damn well.

"Would you like something to drink?" she asked from the kitchen.

"I don't think we have time before the reservation." If he'd built in time for drinks, he would have built in time for seducing her. Damn it.

"Did you bake a pie today?" he asked her, grasping at anything to distract himself from imagining the things he wanted to do to her.

"Yeah, can you still smell it? I made it early this morning." He could hear water running in the sink.

"For anything special?"

"Not really. I felt like baking. I figured I could take it back to your place tomorrow. Since Hunter will be there for dinner, I thought a big dessert might be nice." She walked in carrying a clear vase full of water and the roses. She set the vase by the window and then turned to Erik. Her hands twisted in front of her. She was clearly nervous and doing her damnedest not to show it.

He wanted to feel smug in knowing his effect on her, but he was nervous too. More than anything, he wanted to convince her he wanted a serious relationship with her. There was a lot riding on tonight, and he didn't want to blow it.

21

Melanie

Melanie grabbed her purse off the coffee table in front of Erik, relieved to have something to do with her hands. Not because she didn't know what to do with them, she wasn't that much of a silly innocent on a first date. No, it was because she wanted to take off his tie and unbutton his shirt. She'd never seen Erik in a suit before, and the sight was incredible. He filled out the smooth, gray material perfectly. The cloth fell across his broad shoulders and tapered down to his narrow waist. She knew the muscles that lay beneath, and she wanted to run her hands over them. However, they had a reservation to get to, and this was a first date. It was one thing to have sex after the first date, but before? No way. Didn't matter how many times they'd done it. She wasn't taking her dress off until after dinner...if at all. Her mother would be so ashamed, and Sheila would be so proud. Thank goodness for Sheila.

She pulled her tiny purse over her shoulder. "I'm ready."

Erik nodded, cocked his head to the side, and looked at her, his dark eyes boring into hers. The intensity of his gaze made her shiver. What the heck was he thinking about?

He stood and walked toward her. She was rooted to the spot, her belly quivered, and she couldn't take her gaze from his. He held her trapped without even touching her.

He stopped when their bodies were centimeters apart. She could feel heat emanating off him and could smell him: clean and a little spicy. It was heady to be so near him without touching. His stare held hers still, and she couldn't think.

His knuckles brushed against her thigh, and she could feel him running his fingers over the hem of her dress. Sparks of arousal shot through her at his touch. Her heart pounded in her chest, and her tongue stuck to the roof of her mouth. His knuckles skimmed higher, moving her dress almost to the point of indecency, teasing her, his hand hot against her skin. Her skin hummed under his touch but then his hand withdrew.

"I was wondering if the dress was silk," he murmured. He stepped back, his face serious, but a gleam shined in his eyes. Melanie stood there blinking, her skin burning for more, trying to get a handle on what had happened.

"Shall we?" he asked, wide-eyed and innocent, holding a hand out.

She narrowed her eyes at him. The tease. She smiled sweetly and put her hand in his. Even the small touch sent electric awareness through her. She looked at him out of the corner of her eye, wondering if he reacted the same way, but his gaze was unreadable.

They walked out of the apartment and Melanie locked the door behind her. “Where are we going?” she asked as they descended the stairs.

“The Silver Bistro.” He led her out of the building and toward the parking lot.

When they got outside, she looked out into the bright sky. The evening was the perfect temperature; she didn’t even need a jacket.

“Great.” She’d wanted to try that place, but the restaurant was out of her price range. It was strange, but she hadn’t given much thought to their differing socioeconomic statuses until then, despite that she worked for him. Most of his habits seemed inexpensive, and his behavior was always so pragmatic. He didn’t seem to spend extravagant amounts of money on luxury items—except for maybe his house. She was glad. Money complicated things and made her nervous. Her mother had drilled polite behavior into her since she was young, and at her private school, money equaled pretension and rudeness.

He ushered her to his blue Audi. Oh, Lord. Maybe she was wrong. Maybe he did spend extravagant amounts of money on his stuff. Her heart fluttered in her chest. “This is your car?” She didn’t even care about the squeak in her voice.

Erik unlocked the car and opened the passenger side door. He helped her inside so that the smooth, red leather interior enveloped her. "Yes."

"How did I not know about this car? I've been living with you," she said as he closed the door. Suddenly, she felt out of her league. She took a deep breath to calm down. She'd been living with this man for weeks. They'd had sex repeatedly. Nothing had changed. Other than her developing feelings for him. She put on her seatbelt and ignored her dampening palms. She would have fun, darn it. Dates were supposed to be fun.

Erik walked around the car and got into the driver's seat. "You never go into the garage."

"This wasn't the car you drove when you got me from the diner," she said.

He buckled his seatbelt and turned on the ignition. "Well, that's telling."

"What do you mean?"

"It was the car I drove. You were so drunk, you don't even remember." He drove out of the parking lot.

Melanie bit the inside of her cheek. "I guess I remember all of the embarrassing parts."

She looked over at Erik's profile as he drove. His features were so masculine, hard, and strong. His nose was straight, his lips firm, and his cheekbones were high and sharp. From the way he clenched his jaw, he seemed to be holding in laughter—laughter at her.

Her cheeks burned. Melanie crossed her arms over her chest. "You shouldn't start out an evening by laughing at your date. It's rude."

He nodded and stopped at a stoplight near the highway. "You're right. I apologize. From now on, I'll be the perfect gentleman."

He turned onto the highway and put a hand on her

knee, his palm skimming the edge of her dress and his pinky finger on the inside of her thigh. Her body tingled at his touch. That's what a perfect gentleman did? "I'd hate to see what you would do if you were being ungentlemanly."

His eyes cut to hers for half a second, heat and challenge in his gaze. "I can show you if you'd like."

His hand inched up, pushing her dress until the material barely covered her thong. His fingers were on the inside of her thighs now. Heat coiled low in her core and her panties dampened. Need pulsed through her, and her nipples tightened. All she could think about was those magical, hot fingers moving higher to tend to her growing need. Then he made a turn on the highway, and she remembered they were in a car, on their way to dinner.

She grabbed his wrist and held him still. "I think gentlemanly is best," she said, lust making her voice low and husky.

He inhaled and nodded, placing his hand back on the steering wheel. "You're right. This is our first date. I want it to be special for you. And that doesn't involve getting felt up in the car before dinner."

Melanie stared at him, and her heart did a flip in her chest. He wanted her evening to be special? How was this man, who frustrated her so often and could be so controlling, so sweet? Well, he had nothing to worry about. She did feel special, the flowers, picking an excellent restaurant, being concerned with her feelings; it was all so considerate. Of course, she also enjoyed his hands on her and their physical relationship. "At least... until after," she said.

His eyes widened in surprise, and then he smiled. It was an easy smile, filled with charm and boyish pleasure. Her heart tripped again. He had a wonderful smile, and she loved being the cause of it.

Erik

When they parked at the bistro, the restaurant patio was full of couples. Erik turned off the engine and walked around the car to help Melanie out. She looked amazing in those heels, but he had no idea how she was staying upright. He opened her door and offered his hand.

She smiled in response and accepted his help. Her hand was so small and pale in his. She seemed fragile sometimes, and he felt as if he needed to be cautious of his size in her presence. At least, unless they were arguing, exercising, or having sex, and then she had so much backbone and energy that it made up for her small stature.

She stepped out of the car, and they walked to the entrance of the restaurant. Erik opened the glass door and held it for her to walk through. As they stepped inside, the hostess greeted them. The woman's features were shadowed from the chandelier and sconce lighting. "Good evening. Do you have a reservation?"

"Yes, under Graham," Erik said. He still held on to Melanie's hand. It was such a small gesture of mutual affection, but he found he didn't want to let her go. He was unused to casual touches of intimacy and comfort but decided he liked it.

Melanie squeezed his hand, and he moved his gaze to

her face, realizing that he'd been staring at their clasped hands.

"Right this way, Mr. Graham," the hostess said, grabbing two menus and walking them deeper into the restaurant.

Erik and Melanie followed the woman between tables filled with dishes in various stages of fullness. Well-dressed people filled the restaurant. Noises of laughter and conversation surrounded them as they walked through the place.

The woman guided them to the back, and then out onto the quieter patio that was lit up by candles. Trees surrounded the several small tables outside, creating an air of seclusion and romance to the patio. The hostess stopped at a table near the back line of trees. She set the menus on the table and stepped back.

Erik walked around to where Melanie began to pull out a chair, and he pulled it out for her. "Thank you," she said, sitting.

"Enjoy your meal," the hostess said and left them. The surrounding three tables were empty, and the voices of people farther away carried to them as white noise. The sky was streaked with swirls of orange and pink as the sun set.

Melanie looked over Erik's head. "You timed this well," she said, watching the sky.

"I wish I could say it was planned." He picked up his cloth napkin and set it in his lap. Melanie did the same.

She lifted up her menu and browsed the options. "Have you been here before? Anything you'd recommend?"

"I haven't. I've heard good things. Since you're a

chef, I wanted to make sure the restaurant we went to could live up to your expert opinion."

"I don't think my expert standards would be that high. Should I remind you about the last place I worked at? A diner? Besides, my favorite food is hot wings."

"Hot wings? I would have thought something more sophisticated, like duck confit, or something."

"Knowing me, that's what you would've guessed?"

"Maybe not. Maybe chocolate sauce, or whipped cream," he said, his voice husky.

Red bloomed up her throat and onto her cheeks. She shifted in her seat. He thought she wasn't going to respond, that maybe her innocence would keep her from speaking.

But she surprised him. "I wonder why you would think that. I've never licked whipped cream and chocolate off anyone. I wouldn't mind giving it a try though." She looked up at him through her long, black eyelashes.

His body reacted to her words, and he bit down on his tongue to keep from groaning aloud. She was such an exhilarating mix of sweet and sexy. Before he could respond though, a young, blond waiter walked up to them. He placed glasses of water on the table. "Good evening. My name is John, and I'll be your server tonight. Can I start you off with anything to drink?"

Erik peeled his gaze from Melanie and looked up at the man. "Nothing for me yet," he said.

"Water's fine, thanks," Melanie said.

The waiter smiled at both of them. "I'll give you a minute to look over the menu, and then I'll be back," he said, walking away.

Melanie looked out at the sunset and then back at

Erik. Shadows crossed her face as the orange in the sky faded to darkness. "No drinks?" he asked her, teasing.

"You know, despite how it may have seemed, I can handle a drink. I prefer to pair my drink with my entrée. Besides, you didn't order anything either."

He grinned. "I do the same."

"Hmm." Melanie focused back on the menu.

Erik glanced at his menu, but he couldn't focus on the words spread out along the page. He wanted to know more about Melanie, to talk to her. He wanted to be closer to the woman in front of him. Her legs must've been near his, but he wanted them to be touching. He wanted everything from her, but he needed to prove to her this wasn't just a fling.

"When did you know you wanted to cook?" he asked.

A half grin played at her lips. She looked wistfully at him, the blue in her eyes dancing with the fading light in the sky. "When I was a little girl I used to have tea parties, but because my mom was involved they weren't normal kid's tea parties with plastic cups and Easy-Bake Oven cookies. No, my mom would get out the silver and china, we would invite my friends, and then we would make real tea-time snacks. We'd bake scones and make finger sandwiches. My friends would always be so shocked. They thought it was the coolest thing. I'm sorry. I'm rambling."

"No, you're not. That's a nice story." He didn't know how to reconcile the rude woman he'd met at his home with the picture of a mother that Melanie was painting.

"I know, hard to imagine, huh? My mom can be harsh, but she's also done incredible things for me."

The waiter approached their table again. "Have you

made any decisions? Or do you have any questions?" he asked.

Melanie smiled at the waiter and looked at Erik. "I'm ready to order."

They both chose fish, and Erik picked a fondue appetizer while she picked a beet burrata. He deferred to her for their wine selection and watched a big grin light up her face as she ordered for them.

Melanie

As the waiter walked away, Melanie realized she'd never been on a first date before where the guy hadn't tried to order for her. Her knowledge of food and her tastes had been disregarded on every other first date. Granted, she hadn't been on many, but still. The only one who hadn't disregarded her knowledge, her education, was Erik. He even wanted her to choose. She could feel his respect for her, and she appreciated it. That's what she wanted from a relationship: mutual respect, support, and desire. For the first time since he'd brought up them being in a relationship, she believed it might work.

It was time to find out more about his life, the way he had about hers. She did not want this to be one-sided. She took a sip of her water and looked back up at Erik who was watching her. "How did you get into app development?"

"It was Hunter. The kid came up with a brilliant video editing idea in college. We worked on it together, and it took off after we finished it." A look of pride stole over his features.

"That's cool. I can't believe how supportive you sound when you talk about Hunter. Most brothers I know are competitive and fight all the time."

Erik shrugged and glanced away. "We're lucky we get along so well."

"So, did you guys make the app by yourselves? Coding and everything?"

"Unfortunately, yes. It was a huge pain. Hunter still hadn't decided on a major, and I had a business degree. He spent so many hours researching coding. I used my business degree to help promote and sell it, but we were both in the dark about design. It was all we did for a long time. Hunter wanted to quit a couple of times, but I wouldn't let him."

"Because you believed in him?"

"Because it was a good idea, and I had spent months working on the app. I didn't want it all to come to nothing."

"That's impressive. And you guys were sold on it after that? You both knew you wanted to make apps?" Melanie's mind reeled. She had spent days perfecting recipes, but she enjoyed the almost-instant gratification from cooking. Within a couple of hours, or in even less time, she could see and taste the result of her work and skill. Granted, it took her years to become proficient at cooking, but still, she couldn't imagine spending months on one project like that. She didn't quite grasp that kind of work ethic.

Erik shook his head and chuckled. "Not quite like that. We realized Hunter liked being a creative, and I liked business. After that, we decided to start an app development company, so we could hire people to design them and code them. I never want to even think about coding again."

"How old were you?"

"When we created the company?"

Melanie nodded.

"I was twenty-four and Hunter was twenty."

"Twenty-four? That's so young."

Erik smiled. "I was ambitious."

"No kidding. What did you parents think about all of this?" She could only imagine how proud they must've been of their sons. To achieve so much at such a young age was such an accomplishment.

Erik's eyes clouded. His gaze was still pointed in her direction, but he looked through her. She could feel it; she could feel him going somewhere else. His change in emotions sent a shiver up her spine. Shoot. She hoped she hadn't asked the wrong thing. His parents would come up eventually, and it never occurred to her it wouldn't be an easy subject.

"They passed away before then."

"Oh, Erik, I'm so sorry," Melanie said, her heart heavy. She had complained about her own mother twice to him, and he didn't even have one anymore. Lord, she'd been oblivious.

He waved a hand, and his dark gaze focused back on her. "It's fine, it was a long time ago."

Her eyebrows raised. "Did Stacie...did she raise you guys?"

"Oh, no. Nothing like that. We weren't some sob story. We had a great childhood. Our parents supported us and took care of us. They died in a car crash while Hunter was still in college." He tugged at his sleeves. She hoped she hadn't pushed him too much.

"That's still really hard. I'm sorry. But I'm sure they'd be proud of you. I can't believe how much you and Hunter have accomplished. And this summer camp for foster kids is incredible."

Erik smiled briefly. "Thanks."

22

Erik

Even the delicious looking food in front of Erik couldn't distract him. Guilt flowed through him, thick and hot. He couldn't believe he'd lied so much about his childhood. He'd been unprepared for her questions though. His real dates were so few, he'd forgot the kinds of things people discuss when they're getting to know one another. He should have told her the truth, laid everything out for her to see. He could only imagine how she'd pity him if he said he was a foster kid, that he and Hunter had left their foster home when he was fifteen, and that Hunter wasn't even his real brother.

There was another part to it all. If he told her the truth, and she rejected him, he couldn't bear it. He'd suffered the consequences of being honest before. He didn't want to lose her before their first date ended.

He would tell her everything someday. He needed more time. Hopefully, she would understand. He dipped a piece of the sausage in the fondue and took a bite. The warmth and smoothness of the cheese spread over his tongue first, followed by the spiciness of the meat. The food was fantastic.

He looked up, and Melanie had dug into her appetizer as well. "How is it?"

She swallowed and patted her mouth with a napkin. "Excellent. How's yours?"

"It's great." She smiled, and guilt surged within him again. He had to focus on something else. "Hunter and I are working on coming up with a few socials for the foster summer program so that the kids can meet each other before the practices start."

"That's a great idea. I'm sure everyone will be more comfortable that way."

"I was wondering if you had any food advice for me. I'm getting it catered, but they're open to recommendations."

Melanie's eyes widened in surprise. "You want my opinion again?"

He ran a hand through his hair. Was it really so hard for her to believe that he appreciated her thoughts and opinions? Shit. What had her past relationships been like if she found that surprising? "Yeah, of course. Food is still your area of expertise. Besides, I always want to know your opinion."

She blinked at him and nodded. "All right. Are you having kids of all ages at these events?"

He shook his head. "Sort of. All the kids under

fourteen will be split by area, not age. But everyone fourteen and up will go to a social at the end of the summer. We'll have snacks for that event though."

Melanie nodded thoughtfully. "That makes sense. I'm sure the older kids will appreciate that. What were you thinking food-wise so far?"

Erik chewed on his pretzel. "I had thought of doing burgers and hotdogs. Maybe a barbecue."

"I'm sure they would like that. It's an easy option. But there's another way of thinking about this."

"What's that?"

"Some of these kids probably have plain diets. I'm sure they eat a lot of burgers and hotdogs. What if you did a buffet style with an around-the-world theme? You could have a variety of foods so that the kids would get to experience something new."

"That's a fantastic idea."

"I'm glad you think so." She spread cheese on a piece of toast and took a bite.

Her tongue flicked out to lick a crumb off her lip, and he felt an urgent need to have his lips on hers. They hadn't even finished their appetizer yet, and he wanted to take her home.

She watched him with hooded eyes as he drank his wine. She was noticing him too even though they were in the middle of a meal. Good, he didn't want to be alone in his desire.

He dipped a piece of pretzel into the fondue, and then reached across the table. She parted her lips, and he put the morsel in her mouth. Her lips closed around the piece, a dab of cheese sliding over her bottom lip. He dragged a thumb across it, and then he sucked the cheese off his finger.

Her blue eyes darkened. He wanted to lean across the table and pull her to him. He took a deep breath and reigned his libido in. He needed to talk, to continue their conversation. This couldn't just be sex because she would need more than that. He was starting to think he would too.

"I know we're at the beginning of our first date but I want to ask you out on another one. This is going well after all."

Melanie smirked. "Kind of cocky, don't you think?"

He smiled and dragged a thumb up the inside of her knee under the table. Her body jerked in response. "You don't agree?"

She shifted her knees, but he continued to stroke her leg. He needed to touch her. He missed the smoothness of her skin, the warmth of her body.

"Where would we go?" she asked, ignoring his question.

"I want you to come to the fundraising banquet as my date."

She smiled until his hand snuck a couple of inches higher. She gasped, and her eyelids fluttered. "Erik..."

Her skin was hot underneath his touch. "Hmm?"

Her legs clamped hard on his hand, so he couldn't slide it higher. "You're distracting me."

"I'm sorry, I'll stop." She eased her thighs open, and he removed his hand.

"For now," she murmured.

"For now," he said, agreeing. "Do you have an answer?"

"I can't turn down a good cause, now can I?"

"I wouldn't think so." Tingling spread through his chest at her response. He was thrilled she'd said yes.

Melanie

Melanie was in a haze of lust throughout the rest of dinner. He kept up a seductive barrage of touches throughout the meal. Some caresses were casual and seemed unintentional, and others...others were clearly intended to be teasing. She'd reciprocated in kind: a light brush of her fingers over his knuckles, a hand on his knee under the table. She almost felt guilty because their food became secondary the longer they sat there.

Halfway through dinner, she'd started sitting in positions to better display her cleavage. He knew what he was doing to her and turnabout was fair play. She left to the bathroom after her own teasing, brushing past him on her way away from the table, and noticed the obvious evidence of his reaction to her. She'd sauntered away, certain he watched her legs and ass.

Once she'd gotten through most of her fish, she couldn't taste anything anymore. Erik's hand was on her leg again, and her high-heeled foot nudged up his pants. She had never behaved this way before in public, but she was enjoying herself. She loved watching his throat tighten, his jaw clench, and his eyes become molten.

"Are you still eating?" he said, his voice harsh.

She took the finishing sip of her wine and shook her head. She ran her fingers over her water cup until they were covered in the condensation, and then she ran a finger over her collarbone. Erik's gaze darted to the movement, and his Adam's apple bobbed.

He cleared his throat. "Would you like dessert?"

She smiled mischievously. How much had that polite question cost him? She wondered what he would do if she said yes. She was tempted to find out, to tease him even more, but need was building inside her. Heat licked her insides with every touch and caress. "No, thank you."

He sighed in obvious relief as the waiter approached. "Anything else I can get you? Would you like to see a de—"

"The check please," Erik cut in. His smile to the waiter was belated.

The waiter nodded unfazed and pulled a bill from the pocket in his apron. He placed it on the table in front of Erik. "I'll be your cashier whenever you're ready."

As the waiter spoke, Erik was taking out his wallet. He glanced at the bill before his eyes were back on Melanie, his gaze black and intense. She couldn't look away. He threw down a couple of bills. "Keep the change."

"Thank you, sir. Have a good night," the waiter said, lifting the bill. There was surprise in the young man's voice, and she wondered how much extra Erik had left. She didn't look up though—she kept her eyes on Erik's smoldering ones.

He stood and took Melanie's hand, helping her up. His his grip was tight on her as he led her out of the restaurant. He wanted her. She could feel his desire in the grip of his hand, see it in the straining of his arms through his suit jacket.

When they got in the car, Erik cut his gaze to Melanie. His eyes...oh Lord. The way he looked at her had her squirming in her seat.

"Where are we going now?" She'd meant to sound sultry and seductive, but her voice shook.

"Spend the night with me." Something feminine in her tingled at the rawness of his tone. She wasn't sure whether it was a request or a command, but she wanted to give in. She wanted to be in his arms, she wanted him inside her.

"All right."

He inhaled, and then wrapped his hand around the back of her neck. He drew her to him and kissed her, his lips languidly moving against hers. She breathed in relief at him touching her. He opened his mouth, and she thrust her tongue between his lips, wanting to get closer, wanting to taste him deeper. He moaned in appreciation and reciprocated, swirling his tongue around hers, plundering her mouth. She gripped his shoulders and tugged, trying to haul him closer, oblivious to the console between them.

He leaned back and groaned. "I want you so bad."

"Okay."

Erik grimaced and sat back in his seat. Melanie blinked in a daze. "You're killing me, sweetheart. We're still in the parking lot at the restaurant."

She whipped her head around, her face heating. "Right."

"Do you need anything from your apartment before we go to my house?" he asked, breathing deep.

His kisses made her lose her wits, but Melanie gathered her thoughts. "Pie."

He looked at her, clearly not interested in stopping for pie. "We can get it tomorrow."

The lusty haze started to clear. "You asked." She

sunk into the leather and folded her hands in her lap, waiting for him to start driving.

"Sweetheart, that was a courtesy. With the way you were all over me, there's no way I'm going to stop for pie."

Erik

Erik drove them back to his house in under twenty-five minutes. Traffic was heavy on the highways, but they were able to avoid a lot of it by taking side streets and neighborhood roads. He kept his hand on the inside of her thigh the entire way to his house. He couldn't help himself. The warmth and smoothness of her skin were too alluring for him to let go. He brushed the silky, red cloth back and forth over her leg, loving the whispering noise it made over her skin.

"This isn't fair," she whispered as he drove through his neighborhood.

"What do you mean?" He dipped his fingers under her skirt, and she gasped.

"I can't reply in kind because you're driving."

His lips quirked in a hint of a smile. He drew spirals on her thigh with his forefinger, caressing upward until he found lace. He fingered the edge of her panties. She shuddered beneath his fingers. "Mm, pretty," he said, his voice like silk.

She looked over at him, the blue in her eyes lost to black hunger. "You can't see them," she said on a gasp as he skimmed one finger under her panties and over the crease between her thigh and her sex.

"I can imagine." He stopped at the gate outside his property and waved at the security man in the kiosk beside it. The gate slid open, and Erik almost forgot to step on the gas.

Melanie moaned as his finger trailed closer to her center. He drew his finger in circular motions over her silken thatch.

He drove up the driveway and opened the garage, pulling his car into it. His erection stood against his pants, all too aware of the heat of Melanie's arousal. He had to have her, had to thrust himself deep inside her, but he enjoyed teasing her too much to stop. His finger slid over the seam of her lower lips and was thrilled to be met by so much heat.

"Erik," she whimpered.

She was such an erotic vision against his leather seat. Her skin was tinged with a pink hue and her skirt was so high he could almost see the panties he'd been playing with. He wanted to see more of her. He wanted her to come in his car, so he could imagine her falling apart under his hands every time he left for work.

He unrolled the windows for air and turned off the car. Then he pushed the button to lean her seat back.

"Erik." She panted as he stroked his thumb between her folds. "Erik, what are you doing?"

"Making you come in my car." He unbuckled both their seat belts and shoved up her skirt until he could see his hand through her black, lacy thong. He groaned at the sight of his hand on her, but he wanted to see more. With a swift tug, he pulled her thong aside, so he could see her delicate flesh slick for him. She clenched her thighs closed on his hand.

He spread her legs until he could see pink peeking out at him from between her legs once more. She was so open for him. His cock was achingly hard for her, but he concentrated on the sight before him. He ran his thumb over her swollen bud, and she arched her back again.

"I need to see more of you." He tugged her low neckline until her breasts were freed. The pale globes heaved, and her peach nipples were hard under his gaze.

He almost came at the sight of her. She was a fantasy come true. Her lithe body thrust forward, her breasts hanging out over the crimson of her dress, her legs open against his leather car seat. He lifted his fingers from her feminine center, and settled them on her nipple, flicking gently.

"So pretty," he murmured.

She gazed at him, her eyes wide and skin flushed with a light sheen of sweat. "Please." She whimpered.

"You want to come, sweetheart?" He palmed both her breasts in his hands. He leaned his head down, stroking the stiff peaks with a swipe of his tongue.

"Yes," she cried out.

"Do you have any idea how sexy you look?" he asked before closing his teeth around one nipple.

She shook her head, her hair whipping around her face.

"No idea? With you arching against my hands and my mouth, and that small scrap of black framing your pussy? So fucking sexy." He dragged one finger between her breasts, over her belly, and between her legs, and she whimpered.

He sunk two fingers inside her, and her eyes rolled upward. He pumped her, stroking her clit with his thumb, and she quivered beneath his hands. She was right on the edge; he could see it in her lust filled expression, and he could feel it in the way she tightened around him. He leaned forward, sucked hard on her nipple, and she cried out, her entire body shuddering around him.

He held on to her as she convulsed in pleasure, leaning back to watch her face open in the passion of her orgasm. She was so beautiful, so real, and he was falling in love with her.

23

Melanie

Melanie looked into Erik's dark, fiery eyes, and her cheeks heated in embarrassment. She felt exposed as he watched her in the car, and she realized it was a feeling she enjoyed. There was no judgment in his eyes, no disapproval, just lust, enthusiasm, and...oh boy, she'd been thinking love. She averted her gaze. Looking at him made it impossible for her to get her head on straight. She was getting way ahead of herself.

She slid her skirt back in place and covered her breasts with her dress.

"If we pass anyone in the hall, no one will be able to tell what we were doing," he said. His lips were straight, but his eyes gleamed.

Yeah, right. Because her hair wasn't a mess, and

her dress wasn't wrinkled like it had been thrown on the floor and trampled on. She wasn't worried though. It was late enough that the staff wouldn't be wandering around. She smiled and sat up in her seat.

Erik rolled up the windows of his car, and then he got out, walking around to open the door for her. He reached out his hand, and she took it. She still felt shaky, her legs wobbled, and she wasn't even standing yet. He tugged her out, and she stumbled, but he held her firm and drew her against his chest. She shuddered at the warmth of his body against hers. His long, hard shaft nudged against her lower belly and desire flowed hot inside her again. She wanted him. After a mind shattering orgasm, she still wanted to feel his hard length inside her, filling her up.

She looked up at him. Red slashed across his cheeks, and his eyes filled with smoldering need. He was gorgeous, strong, and brave, and he cared for her. She wanted this. She wanted to be with him.

"To your bedroom?" she asked.

He nodded sharply, and they walked through the garage, down hallways, past the grand room, and into his bedroom. He closed the door behind him and locked it. She stood in the center of the bedroom, looking around at his green comforter and dark furniture. She was filled with anticipation and, if she was being honest with herself, nerves.

But it was her turn to play, her turn to make him crazy, to touch every inch of him. He turned back to her and stalked toward her. She held a hand up to stop him. He cocked his head to the side, and his nostrils flared. "Wait."

He clenched his jaw, and stilled, his body tense, and coiled with energy. “What am I waiting for?”

She smiled and grabbed the hem of her dress, drawing it over her head in one motion. She left her thong in place and her heels on. Erik’s eyes widened, and he looked her over, his eyes dragging over her like a hot caress. He took a step toward her, but she put up her hand again.

His hands clenched at his sides, and Melanie slipped the thong down her hips, her legs, and then she stepped out of the scrap of fabric. He swallowed, his eyes feral, his muscles straining through his jacket. She left the shoes on and walked to him, stopping when her nipples brushed against his jacket. She could see him tense beneath his clothing.

“Melanie, I don’t have a lot of control left.”

“Let’s see how long you can hold out,” she said, teasing. He blinked but didn’t shift otherwise. She was looking forward to taking his clothes off. She tugged his jacket off his shoulders and let it fall to the floor. Then she loosened his tie and pulled it over his head, tossing it onto the bed. Next, his button-down shirt. She untucked the shirt and unbuttoned it, exposing his tan skin inch by inch.

The shirt parted, exposing a swath of smooth, hard skin covered in a smattering of dark blond chest hair. He was temptation personified. She had to taste him. She bent and licked from his navel all the way up his neck, nipping when she reached his earlobe.

“You need to hurry, sweetheart,” he said, his voice guttural.

“But it’s my turn to play,” she whispered.

He growled, and she shivered at the noise. "You get five minutes. I don't want to come before I'm inside of you."

She nodded and pushed his shirt off his shoulders. The garment followed his jacket to the floor. Her heart pounded in her chest as her fingers unbuckled his black belt. Her patience was waning. She wanted him in her hand, and she wanted to watch his face as she touched him. She unbuttoned and unzipped his pants. Then, she stuck her hand down his pants and boxers, barely registering the tight material stretching across his thighs.

She wrapped her hand around the base of his shaft, and he groaned against her neck. He was hot and hard, but his skin was silky smooth, and her fingers just met around his girth. He was so big and long...she felt just how long as she stroked up to the tip.

His sharp inhale was audible in the quiet of the room. She loved his reaction to her, the way he shuddered beneath her hands. It was intoxicating. She rubbed her hands up and down his length, squeezing as she pumped him.

His breath quickened, and he grabbed her hand, stilling her. "Okay, sweetheart, time's up."

"What? It's been like two minutes," Melanie said, her gaze flying to his.

"I can't wait any longer." He nudged her hand away and reached around her, lifting her and kneading her behind. She wrapped her legs around him, and he carried her to the bed.

She would've enjoyed more time, but she had to admit that his hands on her and his loss of control were sexy. He set her on the bed and stood to look at her. Naked except for her shoes, she made no move to cover herself this time. Instead, she basked under the heat of his gaze.

Without taking his eyes off her, he took off his shoes, socks, pants, and boxers until he stood naked before her. He grabbed a condom from the bedside table, ripped the foil packet open, and slid it on. He climbed over her, lying against her so that every inch of them touched. The connection of skin against skin felt amazing. He stilled his rod at her slit, and she strained to meet him.

"You ready for me?" he asked.

"Yes."

He sunk into her inch by glorious inch until she could feel him deep against her womb. He kissed her softly on the lips and began to thrust. The pace was slow, gentle; she could feel every bit of him massaging her insides. Sex felt different this time, the desire built, she could feel herself losing conscious thought to sensation, but there were intimacy and warmth.

She looked into his eyes, trapped in his gaze. The look was so caring, it made her heart flip in her chest. She was falling for this man. Nothing could stop it. Nothing could slow the feeling. Every time he moved in her, she fell deeper.

He brushed a hand over her cheek and kissed her again. He nibbled on her lower lip and a need for release grew inside her. She met each of his thrusts with a thrust of her own hips, holding him deeper inside. He locked his gaze on hers as she writhed beneath him. Her fingers dug into his shoulders, and he caressed her everywhere, sliding his fingers over every part of her he could reach.

His touch felt possessive, primal, and she loved every second of it.

His cock pounded against her most sensitive skin harder and harder until she couldn't take it anymore. He slid a finger around her opening where he was joined with her and she lost it, succumbing to pleasurable oblivion. She shuddered over and over, and he pumped one final time before shouting her name and collapsing on top of her.

Her breathing slowed, and an awareness of her surroundings returned. Erik laid on top of her, and she struggled to draw breath. He kissed her forehead and then rolled off. She stayed where she was, her limbs lazy as satisfaction flowed through her. Then he wrapped his arms around her, tucking her into his side.

"I want to introduce you to Stacie and Hunter as my girlfriend at lunch in a couple weeks when they come over," he said against her head.

Her heart tripped in her chest, and warmth spread through her. "We've only had one date." She needed to make sure that was what he really wanted. She wasn't sure she could bear it if he changed his mind. She needed to know he was ready for a serious relationship.

"We'll have more before then. Be mine, be my girlfriend."

It sounded like a question. She could hear something underlying in his voice, like insecurity, or fear. It almost made her smile. How could he be worried when she was so clearly falling for him?

"Yes." A rush of satisfaction surged through her. Erik was hers, and she was his.

❧

Erik

In the two weeks following their first date, Erik took Melanie to dinner a few times. On days when he had too much work to justify going out, he dropped by home for lunch. They ate sandwiches by the pool, their feet dangling in the water. With no time for sex during his quick afternoon visits, they talked instead. She shared stories about her childhood and he talked about getting his business degree, hoping not to get too close to the topic of his childhood. The more time he spent with her, the harder he found it to tell her the truth about his past. He needed to be sure she wouldn't leave him, the way he'd been left before. Her childhood was filled with sweet stories about her and Sheila. His was filled with the violence he faced in foster homes. He didn't want her to see that part of himself.

She slept in his bed most nights, and he found himself terrified by the comfort she brought him. Her back pressed against his chest, his arms around her, and his mind would empty of every stress, of thoughts about his past, of everything painful. He wondered how long it would take him to rely on her comfort to sleep.

One night they stayed up for hours after they made love. Melanie brought up brownies from the kitchen, and they ate, green covers around them, and chatted until well past three in the morning.

"How is it that you weren't with anyone when you came to work for me?" he asked.

She put the plate of brownies on the bedside table. "I could ask you the same question."

She smiled, but he saw through her change of subject.

"You know that I didn't date. You must have though."

"Yeah. I was in a relationship up until a year ago." She played with the edge of the blanket by her hip.

"And then what? You swore off men?" He nudged her thigh playfully with his knee.

"Just a bad breakup." She laughed, but the sound was tight.

"What happened?"

Melanie

Melanie took a deep breath and she was surprised to find that she wanted to share the story of her breakup with Erik. The past couple of weeks had been wonderful. He'd shown her in so many ways that he wanted this to work. Looking into his deep dark eyes filled with sympathy, she wanted to tell him everything. Even if her past was painful.

"I was dating this guy, Dave. We'd been dating since we were sixteen."

Erik's sharp inhale filled the quiet room. Was he surprised that she'd only had one serious boyfriend? Did she come off unpracticed or prudish? She swallowed her embarrassment and continued. "I know. I've only been with one other guy. It's a little—"

"I don't care how many guys you've been with, Melanie." He took her hand and pressed it to his mouth.

She swallowed and nodded. "We were together six years, and I was ready to start our lives together. I was ready for a real commitment. And I guess he wasn't."

Erik's eyebrows furrowed together. "The idiot. So,

you broke up?"

A painful lump formed in her throat. "He uh...left while I was at work. He left a note. Said he needed to commit to the breakup. That he didn't know who he was. He said that I'd pressured him and—" She couldn't continue.

Erik pulled her to him and hugged her close. The pain melted away in his embrace. "What an asshole."

She shook her head against his chest. "I shouldn't have pushed him." Her voice was muffled against his chest.

"Hey, look at me. What he did was not your fault. He was gutless." He held her chin up with a finger and kissed her on the forehead.

Melanie's eyes burned, but she laughed. "I guess no woman has ever broken your heart like that, huh?"

He paused but then after a minute, spoke. "No."

She wondered if he'd been going to say something else.

"Are you looking forward to lunch with my family this weekend?" he asked, changing the subject.

"I'm a little nervous." She figured she might as well admit it now in case she acted awkwardly.

"You know they already like you."

She tucked a hair behind her ear. "Not as your girlfriend."

He kissed her cheek and turned off the lamp. "They're going to be thrilled."

She fell asleep crossing her fingers. She knew how much Erik respected his brother's opinion, and she wanted his family's approval.

Erik

Erik had never introduced a girlfriend to Hunter before. When he was younger, he'd been protective of his kid brother. When they got older, neither one of them had been looking for long-term relationships. He supposed that this should be easy. Hunter knew and liked Melanie, Hunter had known Erik's interest before he did, and he seemed to approve of them. Erik doubted Stacie would look down on their relationship, even though he was Melanie's employer. She approved of Melanie. Despite all of this, his back was taut with nerves. He wanted everything to go smoothly.

Stacie and Hunter would be arriving any minute. Melanie was in the kitchen taking her anatra al sale out of the oven and dressing her salad with citrus vinaigrette. Erik offered to help, multiple times, but she had refused. She told him that it was still her job, even if she would be eating with them. Then she gave him a look that he didn't quite understand and kicked him out of the kitchen.

She seemed to be much more nervous than he was. They'd spent the morning together, but after they ate a light lunch, she'd told him she needed to get to work and that he couldn't distract her. Leaving her be took all his self-control. He felt like he was addicted to being around her, to feel her in his arms. He had work to get done though, so he'd gone to his office to make a few calls and finalize things for the fundraiser.

Now he was pacing in his office to keep himself from going back into the kitchen again. The doorbell rang through the house, and he jumped at the noise. It was probably Stacie. Hunter always used his key.

He walked down the hallway and through the grand room to get to the front door. He opened it, and Stacie stood in the doorway. Her hair didn't seem to have a single strand out of place, and she wore a navy skirt suit with white heels and a matching white scarf. He opened the door, and she smiled. He gave her a quick hug and then stepped back.

"How are you?" he asked.

"I'm fine, dear, how are you?" she asked.

"Good," he said. He stepped back to let her enter and music filtered into the house from outside. He looked over Stacie's shoulder to watch Hunter's red car roll into the driveway.

"Your brother has good timing," Stacie said, shaking her head in amusement.

Hunter parked next to Stacie's beige Toyota and got out of his car. He pushed his sunglasses onto the top of his head. "Hey, guys," he called out, walking toward them.

"Hey," Erik said, as Hunter walked in the house. Erik shut the door behind him, and the three walked through the living room. "Melanie will be eating with us this afternoon."

"That seems unorthodox for a cook." Stacie teased.

Hunter smirked at him. "Is this a cooking-at-your-table thing?"

Erik raised an eyebrow at them. He would've preferred to finesse this conversation, but they were going to tease him one way or the other. "She's my girlfriend."

"No shit," Hunter said, stopping in the middle of the hallway that led to the dining room.

"And she's still your employee?" Stacie asked.

Erik shrugged. He kept walking for a few seconds, but when he realized neither one of them were following him, he stopped.

"Good for you, man," Hunter said, whistling low. His dark eyes were wide.

Erik clenched his teeth. "Do you have to sound so surprised?"

"Yes."

"This could become...complicated, you know." Stacie's blonde eyebrows drew together.

Hunter and Erik both swung their gazes to her. "He's not that bad. I mean, I know he's rough around the edges, but I'm sure he can handle a girlfriend," Hunter said.

"I don't mean that," Stacie said, waving a hand. "I mean dating one's employee."

"I'll keep that in mind," Erik said. She was right, it was a little weird to date someone that worked for him, but they'd been managing things well so far. He didn't want to concern himself with that right now. He was thankful he could call Melanie his.

"And don't misunderstand me, I do like her, and I'm happy for you. I just don't want you to get hurt." Stacie patted him on the shoulder.

"Thanks. Are we going to go eat lunch, or do we have more to discuss in the hallway outside of the dining room?"

Hunter leaned back on his heels and stuck his hands in his dark-fade jean pockets. "I'm hungry, let's go eat."

The three walked into the dining room as Melanie set out silverware. Burgundy placemats and a pitcher of water sat on the table. She straightened as they approached, and a warm smile spread over her lips. “Hi, Stacie, Hunter. It’s good to see you both again.”

“Hello, dear.” Stacie kissed Melanie on the cheek.

“Hey,” Hunter said on Stacie’s heels. As she stepped away, he hugged Melanie.

“How’s your cooking going?” Melanie asked as they stepped apart.

Hunter shrugged and rubbed the back of his neck. “It’s up and down. I burned my last batch of brownies. I think the oven was too hot.”

Melanie rolled her eyes. “All you have to do is follow the directions and this wouldn’t happen.”

“I was trying to expedite the process,” Hunter said.

Erik bit back his smile. His brother was always looking for a quick way to get things done. “It’s not a merger, Hunter, it’s a dessert.”

“Yeah, sure.” He pulled two wooden chairs out from the table and held one of them out for Stacie. She smiled, sat, and he followed suit.

“Do you need any help, Melanie?” Erik asked as she put out the last napkin on the table.

“I’m fine. I’ll go grab the food, and we can have lunch.” She smiled and walked into the kitchen.

Melanie

Melanie took a deep breath to get the butterflies in her stomach to stop flapping so darn hard. She’d met Stacie, and she’d spent a fair amount of time with Hunter, but she was still nervous. She told herself nothing had changed, but so much had. Approval from the people Erik cared about most was important. She bit the inside of her cheek and looked at the food that sat in serving dishes on the counter.

The golden-crusted duck sat on a silver platter, and the mashed potatoes and green beans filled bowls beside it. The colorful spring salad was on the other side of the counter. Melanie looked down, satisfied with her food. Now if she could just carry the dishes out there without spilling, she'd be thrilled. If only her hands would stop shaking.

She loaded the heavy dishes onto a serving tray and lifted them off the counter. Then she scooted butt first into the dining room to get through the door. She turned back around and put the tray in the center of the table, managing not to shake the table.

"This looks amazing," Hunter said. His stomach growled to punctuate his statement. The other three people at the table swung their gazes to him. "It's been almost four hours since the last time I ate."

Erik grinned at Melanie, the light in his eyes gripping her heart. A look from this man and her body warmed. She was glad he was hers. He pulled out the chair beside him. "I'll serve everyone."

He sliced the duck and gave everyone sides. After Hunter toasted the cook's health, everyone dug in.

"This is delicious." Stacie looked up from several square pieces of cut duck.

"I'm glad you're enjoying it." The butterflies in Melanie's stomach slowed their pain-in-the-butt flapping.

The back of her neck prickled, and she swung her

gaze to Erik. He scrutinized her, and she was tempted to squirm in her seat. He rubbed his thumb over her palm on the table. Tingling spread through her fingers. She picked up her glass of water and swallowed a large gulp. Oh, boy. Erik could not be a distraction at this lunch.

She turned and looked between him and Hunter. "So, is everything set for the fundraiser?"

"Assuming there aren't any last-minute hiccups, yes," Erik said.

Hunter shook his head and grinned. "You sound like that's what you're expecting to happen. Everything's coming together fine."

"Erik's such a worrier." Stacie smiled over her water glass.

Erik's light eyebrows rose. "I think the word you're looking for is 'pragmatic.' 'Worrier' seems extreme."

"She's got you pegged, Erik. But your worrywart tendencies probably saved me, so I can't be too hard on you," Hunter said, teasing.

"Saved you?" Melanie wondered what kind of heroics Erik had in him. It wasn't surprising, but his humility might be. Erik's hand tightened on hers, and he glared at Hunter.

"Hunter—" Erik began, but his brother cut him off.

"I know he doesn't like the word 'save,' but I mean, if not for him, our foster dad would've beaten the...um, heck...out of me when I was ten. Who knows what my life would've been like if he hadn't helped me escape."

The smile froze on her face. Oh, God. Foster kids. They hadn't had parents. They had been foster kids? Her stomach plummeted, and she glanced around the table, looking for confirmation about what Hunter said.

"I'm sorry?" Melanie said, floundering.

"Well you know, our foster dad was drunk and got a hold of a baseball bat," Hunter said.

Melanie nodded dumbly. Emotions warred inside her. There was sympathy, and she wanted to comfort Erik about his past, but then a coldness stole over her heart. He didn't want her comfort, he couldn't possibly, otherwise he would've told her the truth. Lies. Everything Erik had told her was a lie. She felt like the chair had fallen away beneath her, like nothing was holding her up. She turned to him, hoping to see on his face that what Hunter said wasn't true, but all she saw was a flash of his eyes on her, and then he turned to glare at Hunter.

How could she have been so stupid? He'd said from the beginning that he wasn't the type to be in a relationship. He hadn't wanted to open up, so he'd lied. This wasn't a relationship. This was a fling. She knew the signs of someone who wasn't ready to invest in a relationship. He didn't even respect her enough to tell her something that would be, of course, public record. She was so naive that she hadn't even researched him before taking the job. She wasn't sure if she was angrier with him or herself.

"Oh, sorry, I didn't realize Erik hadn't told you that story yet. Don't look at me like that, man, just because you're too humble to share doesn't mean she wouldn't want to know. What'd you do, skip the reason you left foster care and jumped to the part where we ran away?"

Hunter's voice tore Melanie from of her reverie. She had to remember there were still others around. Her heart felt like it was collapsing in on itself. He had lied to her, repeatedly. But she wouldn't fall apart right now.

The back of her eyes burned, and she knew she needed to get out of the room fast.

"Something like that," Erik finally said.

"I should go check on the pie," Melanie said, hoping her voice sounded natural. Her throat was tight, and she felt unsteady, but she made herself stand and walk to the kitchen. She kept her bland smile in place the whole time. At least her mother had taught her how to save face.

Erik

Erik looked between Hunter and Stacie. Both sets of eyes were wide and too perceptive for comfort. His heart pounded in his chest, and his skin felt cold. Melanie's pain-filled eyes tore at his insides, but he could fix this. He could make her understand that he needed time to tell her everything.

"Excuse me," he said. He stood from behind the table and walked into the kitchen.

Her back was to him when he entered. He watched in silence as she pulled a pie from the oven and set it on the counter. Even after she took her oven mitts off, she did not turn around. He couldn't take the quiet any longer.

"Melanie—" he started, uncertain about what to say next.

She slowly turned around to face him. Her blue eyes shone with unshed tears, but as he caught her gaze, her face hardened. Her mouth tightened, and her brows narrowed. He wasn't sure which hurt worse: her pain or knowing she was readying for a fight.

"I should have known you were going to lie to me. You said from the beginning you weren't interested in a relationship. I should have listened." Her voice was as quiet as a whisper, but each word fell on him like a whip.

He didn't know where to begin. All he knew was that he didn't want to lose her. He had to fight for her. "I was going to tell you the truth—"

"When? When I had looked it up for myself on the Internet? When we celebrated our five-year anniversary? Or maybe you never intended us to last that long. When were you going to share the basics of your life? Because that's what they were. The basics. Stuff everyone knows."

Everything was so fucked up, but if he could make her understand, he could fix this. "I didn't want you to pity me. I saw the way you looked at me when I told you my parents were dead. I didn't want you to look at me like that. Especially when you were so impressed when I told you everything else about what I do. Do you know how good it felt to get your approval?" He took a step forward.

Melanie clutched the counter and grimaced. "Yes, because I felt the same way when you were impressed with my cooking. But I told you about my problems, too. I shared everything with you because that's what a relationship is, it's sharing. You should've trusted me enough to tell me the truth."

"I do trust you! I needed some time. Can't you understand that?"

"You don't trust me. You just let me pour my heart out and said nothing about your own past. I knew you weren't ready for a relationship. I knew it. For goodness sake, you said it yourself." She laughed, the sound empty.

Anger welled up inside him. He'd told her again and again that he wanted a relationship. He'd showed her in every way but one. She couldn't even afford him time to get over the problems of his past. "Enough. You know that this isn't about my lack of commitment. You know I want this relationship. You're too scared to see it because of your ex."

"Are you kidding me? We are not having this conversation because of a breakup I had a year ago. We're having this conversation because you lied to me. Again, and again, and again. If Hunter hadn't spilled the beans, you would've never said anything."

"That's bullshit. I would've told you. We've been dating for two weeks, Melanie. Two weeks. Jesus, that's not even long enough to tell you my whole past if I wanted to."

"Well, we've been screwing longer than that. And back then our agreement was honesty. Even before we were dating, the only thing I asked you for was honesty." Her eyes brimmed with tears, and she held the counter behind her as if it was holding her up.

He deflated at the tears in her eyes. She was right; he'd broken his promise. "Let me share with you now, please. I'll make it up to you, I'll tell you everything that happened." He reached for her hand.

She drew her hand away before he could touch her, and his heart hollowed. "How am I supposed to trust you now? I can't be in a one-sided relationship, Erik."

"Please don't give up on us. I want to share everything with you, I was...scared." He'd finally said the word and admitted he was vulnerable. It was out there but now it was probably too late.

Melanie looked away. "I need some time to think."

Erik ran a hand through his hair. He could give her that. He would be able to find a way to keep her. "Okay, that's fine. We'll keep our relationship professional for a few days and then we'll talk."

Melanie shook her head, her black hair swaying over her eyes. "I don't think I should work here anymore. I think it's time for me to go home." Her voice shook.

Every nerve ending inside of him screamed that he should make her stay, but Erik nodded his head dumbly. What right did he have to ask her to stay? But the idea of not seeing her every day made his body cold. "Promise me you'll still come to the banquet. Please. We can talk about everything then. It'll give you two weeks to think." His heart burned from holding in everything else he wanted to say: that he loved her, that he would do anything to make it right.

The threatening tears in her eyes spilled over. "I'll think about it."

He nodded, but his muscles shivered under his skin. He wasn't sure he could believe her when her eyes were saying everything her words weren't—that it was over.

24

Melanie

Melanie smiled through sadness at an older man in a gray suit who made small talk with her at her mother's party. She didn't have a clue what he was saying. She had dragged herself out of her apartment to go to the soirée, as her mother put it, but it hadn't been easy. The only reason she'd gone was that she didn't want her mother too interested in her personal life. She regretted the decision more and more as acquaintances wouldn't leave her alone. She was thankful Sheila and Angie would be there soon.

Sheila had tried to get Melanie to leave the apartment all week, but Melanie didn't want to do anything. She'd wanted to be alone. Getting through each day caused her physical pain. She couldn't stop thinking about Erik, about how much she wanted him back even though he had lied. Sheila didn't seem to think it was the end of the world. She'd told Melanie straight out that she thought they could work out their problems, but Melanie wasn't convinced. Sheila just didn't quite get it. She'd pushed her ex to settle down when he wasn't ready, then he'd left town. She knew better than to force a guy if he wasn't ready. Besides, Erik wasn't even in love with her. What was there to work out if they didn't have a future anyway?

"And the other day, someone brought in a monkey," the older man said, half laughing, half wheezing. His glasses-covered eyes were trained on her, and his eyebrows were climbing. She supposed she'd missed her cue.

"What was wrong with the monkey?" So far, she'd gathered that the man was a veterinarian and that he was in her mom and dad's bridge group.

"The monkey swallowed a key. The woman who owned the monkey said it was part of a show. The monkey was supposed to hold onto the key that unlocked her magic cabinet, but he swallowed it instead," he said, laughing.

Melanie forced a chuckle. She wasn't sure how much longer she could bear being there. She wanted to curl into a ball somewhere and not think. Thankfully, as there was a lull in the conversation, she saw Sheila's warm eyes over the man's shoulder. Thank goodness.

"Excuse me, I see someone I need to say hello to." Melanie nodded at the man.

"Of course. It was nice meeting you," he said with a wave of his hand.

Melanie walked around him and hugged her friend. Sheila's crisp, floral sundress rustled against Melanie's blue one. Melanie took a step back and looked over at Angie who stood beside Sheila. Angie wore a long skirt and an embroidered shirt that didn't quite cover her midriff. It was the second time she could ever remember her wearing a skirt. The bandage wrapped around Angie's left arm tipped her off to the reason behind the clothing choice. The poor girl's leg was still healing from the glass table accident.

"How are you?" Sheila asked.

"I'm okay." The smile Melanie managed was stiff. "How are you guys?"

"Just great. My leg looks like a piece of sausage, and I can't put any weight on it. Where's the alcohol?" she asked.

Melanie's eyes widened, but she resisted the urge to say anything. She glanced at Sheila, but she didn't say anything either. Before she could decide how to respond, Angie rolled her eyes and limped away. "I'll find the damn whiskey myself."

Her sister left, and Sheila shook her head. "I thought that the injury might wake her up, but she's angrier than ever."

"I'm sorry," Melanie said. She could only imagine how Sheila felt. Her sister was out of control.

Sheila looked down to pick at the hem of her dress. She was quiet for a few seconds but when she looked at Melanie, she smiled. Melanie could recognize a fake, but she didn't say anything. Who was she to call out her friend for using the same techniques to fend off unwanted conversations that she did?

"Can we walk? I feel like I could use some air," Sheila said.

"Me too." Melanie led them through the back door, out the courtyard, and down the sidewalk beside her parents' house.

"You stopped responding to my texts the past couple of days," Sheila said.

Melanie's white flats padded against the sidewalk. "I didn't want to talk."

"You miss him." It wasn't a question.

For a second, Melanie was tempted to lie, but she wasn't sure why. It was obvious she did. She couldn't keep her mind off him, she missed his arms around her, and she felt like pieces of her heart were flaking away each day they were apart. But how could she trust him? And what did trust matter if there was nothing there but sex? She loved him, and he couldn't even tell her about his life.

"It doesn't have to be over, you know. Why don't you go to the fundraiser?"

"What would be the point?"

"You guys could work this out and get back together."

"I'm not sure he's ready for a relationship."

"You're not going to find out if you're not in one with him."

Melanie didn't respond. They walked through the neighborhood. Neither one of them spoke for some time. The sun was setting, and reds and oranges traced the mountains in the distance.

"Should we head back to the house? We've been gone for quite a while," Sheila said.

"Yeah, my mother probably isn't too pleased." They

turned back down her parents' street.

"Does she know what happened with Erik?"

"Nope. I don't think I'll tell her. If it is...over, I don't want to tarnish it with conversations with my mother." The words tore at her heart. The idea of her time with Erik being over was crushing.

They walked through the gate at the side of the house and into the courtyard where people milled around by the table of refreshments. Her father lit the grill, a stack of raw hamburgers on a plate to his right, her mother stood behind the cake, cutting pieces, and Angie was approaching fast, her limp now more of a drunken sway. She had a big smile on her face, and she was headed for Diane.

"Oh shit," Sheila said.

"She's got that smile for the cake, right? Please tell me she really loves chocolate cake." Melanie's eyes widened in horror. They jogged toward the table, hoping to intercept Angie. Melanie had no idea what was about to happen, but it was hard to imagine it could be good.

They were about five feet from the table when Angie swung her arms around Diane's middle and planted a wet one on her neck. Diane let out a shriek, and the piece of cake on her plate flew into the air. It landed on the table with a loud splat and bits of frosting flung at surrounding guests. Angie was undeterred, she held fast to Diane. "Now, now, Sarah, you certainly liked it fifteen minutes ago."

Melanie stood, shocked to complete stillness, watching things unfold. Sheila rushed forward to grab Angie but didn't make it there before another woman with a similar beige dress to Diane's walked up to Angie and poked her in the shoulder. She swung her head to the other woman and blinked blearily at her. "Sarah?"

"What are you doing?" the woman asked.

Diane gripped Angie's arms and shook them loose. "Release me at once."

"Let her go," Sheila said.

Angie looked at Sheila and lowered her arms. "Who am I holding?"

"Diane," Sheila said, cringing.

"Oh, shit," Angie said.

Melanie smacked her forehead with her palm. She knew she shouldn't have gotten out of bed that morning.

Erik

Erik stood in the dressing room at a men's boutique that Hunter had dragged him to. The banquet was five days away and Hunter pointed out he would need to wear clothing to the event. He was fine wearing a suit he already owned, in fact, he only wanted to go because he was hoping to God, and the devil for that matter, that Melanie would show. Hunter persuaded him to shop anyway.

Erik supposed it didn't matter where he was or what he was doing, he couldn't sleep, and his work went at a snail's pace, he was so distracted with thoughts of Melanie. He couldn't bear to believe that he might've lost her for good.

He slipped the black jacket over his dark gray button-down and checked the cuffs. Everything fit fine.

"Are you ever coming out?" Hunter called from

outside the dressing room.

"I wasn't planning on doing a fashion show for you." Erik eyebrows furrowed.

"And I don't want one," Hunter said, and Erik could practically hear the eye roll that accompanied the other man's tone. "But the tailor needs to check the suit."

Erik sighed and unlocked the door. He stepped out, and an elderly woman with a pincushion on her wrist grabbed his hand and dragged him to carpeted steps with a small platform surrounded by mirrors. She muttered under her breath about vain men as she shoved him up the steps. Erik swung his head toward Hunter who stood behind him, shaking his head in silent laughter.

"Isn't she great?" Hunter asked, his voice low.

Erik glanced down at the small, hunched, old woman, but she hadn't looked up. Her shawl hung loosely around her shoulders, and she folded the hem of his pants up. Erik raised an eyebrow at his brother.

"She can't hear well."

Erik nodded. "Why did you drag me here?"

"I didn't have a choice. You leave home only to go to work, you won't talk to me, and Stacie says you haven't called. You heartbroken makes you even more of a stubborn asshole than usual."

"I'm not heart—" he started, but he couldn't bring himself to finish the statement. It was true and pathetic. How long had he known her? A few weeks? This was ridiculous.

"Why don't you go talk to her?"

"I promised I would give her some space." He'd done many things wrong in the short time they'd known one another. He could at least do this one thing right and respect her wishes.

"For how long?"

"She said she would think about coming to the banquet."

"A quarter-inch. It'll be done in a day. Everything else seems fine," the woman down by Erik's knees, said.

"Sounds great," he said. She looked up and squinted her eyes at him. "Sounds great," he said again louder.

She nodded and tottered away. "Take them off and give them to me...once you're dressed, mind you. You wouldn't believe the number of men who try to strip right here in front of me. Do I look like a urologist?"

Erik's eyebrows shot straight up his forehead. "No, ma'am."

The woman shook her head and muttered to herself as she walked to the front of the store where a few younger men milled around sports coats. "Looks like a bunch of hooligans."

Erik stepped from the platform and looked at his brother.

"Told you she was great," Hunter said, beaming.

"I should've worn something I already had." Erik stepped back into the dressing room and removed the suit.

"Do you have a contingency plan?" Hunter asked through the door.

"A contingency plan?"

"If she doesn't show up."

Erik cringed at the words. He'd given the possibility thought, of course, but to hear it aloud was painful. Still, it didn't matter because he always had a backup plan. She'd asked for space for two weeks, and he was going to give her that time, but after he would go after her. She deserved to know the whole story, and he deserved a chance to tell her the truth. He wasn't going to let their relationship end after a few weeks because he'd been an ass.

Melanie

Melanie stared at a drawer full of exercise clothes in her bedroom as she talked to Sheila on the phone. "I think the interview went well."

"No salt problems? No domineering bosses?"

Melanie stifled a groan. Melanie thought about Erik enough during the day without her friend bringing him up in every conversation they had. "No, the head chef is a woman."

"When will you hear back?"

"A couple of days." Melanie was crossing her fingers for this job. She'd be working at a resort under a well-known chef who seemed interested in sharing her craft. That was too rare these days. She hadn't enjoyed anything since leaving Erik's house until the interview. It was nerve-wracking too, of course, but also exciting.

"That's great," Sheila said.

"It really is. But that's not why you called me." Melanie fingered a couple exercise shirts. Maybe she could go for a run later. Work out some of her romantic frustrations. It hadn't worked in the previous days, but she figured it would at some point. Could she feel this terrible forever? God, she missed him.

"No, it isn't. Look, she wants to apologize."

"Sheila, I care about you and Angie, but I can't be around her anymore. I told you, I can't talk to her anymore." Sadness gripped Melanie's heart, but she stayed firm. She supposed it had been a long time coming. Angie had a problem, and Melanie couldn't be around her when she was drinking. Erik's comments on the subject echoed in her head. She hated when that man was right. She hated that he was on her mind all the time. She wanted badly to be back with him, for sex, flirting, hell, she'd even take fighting. But to what end? It would be kicking the can down the road.

"She's made a couple mistakes," Sheila said.

Melanie registered the tone that tugged on her heartstrings so much, but she had to be strong. What an awful week and a half. "I care about her, but I can't be around her when she's drunk. She needs help for her alcoholism."

"Mel, she isn't an alcoholic."

"How many times are we going to have this conversation? Sheila, when is she not drinking? She's hurt herself, you, and others. I'm not going to sit here and act like nothing's happening."

"Maybe you're right. She's so fucked up. She tore out some of her stitches the other day when she went out. She doesn't even know how it happened. I don't know what to do."

"I think it might be time to talk to her. She's going to need help. I know you care about Angie, but you're not going to be able to take care of her."

"I don't know that she'll do anything about it."

Melanie shut her drawer as the doorbell rang.

"Maybe not, but it seems worth it to try to broach the

subject. This is your sister's health we're talking about. Shoot, someone's at my door." Melanie walked toward the front of the apartment.

"Thanks for being honest."

"We can talk more about it later, ok?"

"Sure. But hey, Mel, I still think you should go to the banquet."

She ignored the comment. "I gotta go. Bye."

Melanie hung up her cell and looked through the peephole to see Hunter standing outside. She stood staring for a minute, a little cross-eyed, wondering what the heck he was doing at her place. Sure, they were friends, but she wasn't sure she could handle the pain of being around anything that reminded her of Erik. She'd been counting down the days to the banquet—three left—and she still wasn't sure if she should go. Her resolve not to was weakening. Whether Erik loved her or not, she loved him, and maybe that was enough to give it a shot? Maybe if she acted relaxed and didn't push too hard, they could build a relationship over time. She was pathetic.

"Melanie? Can I come in? I have your baking dish," Hunter's said through the door.

"Oh, yeah, sorry. Come on in." She opened the door.

Hunter's broad form filled the doorway. He wore jeans, a black T-shirt, and a stylish pair of multi-colored Nikes. He looked over her, his dark eyes filled with sympathy. He pulled her into a one-armed hug with the baking dish hanging down by his hip.

"Hey, Hunter," Melanie said, muffled against his chest. She wanted to take solace in his comforting behavior, but her survival instincts told her to be strong.

She stepped back and stretched her lips into a forced smile. "Let's get you something to drink."

She walked toward the kitchen and Hunter followed. They rounded the corner and walked into the small, but bright, kitchen. She grabbed a glass from the cabinet and looked back at Hunter. "How did the apology cake turn out?"

"I don't think it tasted great, but she seemed to appreciate the gesture." He looked down at the ground and smiled.

"Yeah?"

"Yeah." He cleared his throat. "We hooked up."

She laughed and filled a glass with water. "I warned you that my cooking might land you a spouse."

His eyes widened in alarm. "Oh, no. No way. It was a one-night thing."

"Maybe you followed the recipe wrong." She gave him the glass and thought back to Erik's one-night deal with her. She didn't buy Hunter's answer.

He thanked her and took a sip. His dark hair curled around his ears and tan forehead. His appearance mocked her previous naive belief that Hunter and Erik were related. Besides their dark eyes, they had nothing in common. The pain of Erik's lies slithered through her again.

"I can't believe I was such an idiot." Her voice cracked, and she hated herself for it, but as soon as it did, she couldn't help the tears that fell.

Hunter put the dish on the counter, walked up to her and gave her another hug. "Mel, you're not an idiot."

"Yes, I am. You both look nothing alike. I could have Googled him for goodness sake. Who doesn't Google their employer?"

"Someone trusting and good. Someone like you." He half carried, half dragged her into the living room and helped her onto the couch.

"The worst part is that, even though he lied, I still miss him so much. What's wrong with me?" She hiccupped and leaned back against the armrest. She rubbed the cuff of her green button-down over her eyes to wipe away the tears. It was too embarrassing to cry in front of the guy's brother.

"Nothing. You care about him. Look, I know my brother was a dumbass, and he fucked up, but he cares about you too. He misses you like crazy."

Melanie hated the weakness that allowed his words to comfort her, but they did anyway. "Really? How do you know?"

"He won't do anything, he won't talk to me or Stacie..."

"Did he send you here?" Melanie asked, suspicious of Hunter's appearance.

"No. He's all about 'respecting your desire for space and time.'"

"Then why are you here?"

"Other than the fact that we're friends, and I owe you that dish back?"

Melanie grinned but shook her head. "That's your brother's dish, you know. And three days before the banquet? C'mon, be honest."

Hunter smiled sheepishly and looked at his hands. "All right, fine, I'm here because it's three days before the banquet, and I figured you hadn't made up your mind yet one way or the other."

"I see, so you are here for your brother."

"I doubt he would appreciate me being here."

"I'm sure you're right about that," Melanie said, her stomach knotting at his words.

"When he took me out of that house when I was eleven, I didn't know what it would mean for our future, but he did. He was fifteen and knew that by saving me, there would never be any turning back. I'm not saying his life was great jumping from foster home to foster home, but when we left, he knew there would never be another foster home—"

"Hunter, I'm not sure why you're telling me this." Learning about his past was interesting, but wasn't this Erik's story to tell? If he had wanted to be with her, wouldn't he have told her all of this?

Hunter looked up but didn't respond to what she said, his dark eyes were clouded and unfocused. "He has never told me anything about his life before that point. Ever. Not a thing. I have no idea what his first fifteen years were like, and I've been with him for almost that long. As far as I know, he's never told Stacie either."

Melanie's mouth dropped open, but she didn't care enough to close it. She couldn't imagine never talking about her life with anyone, pretending that her past didn't exist. Erik must feel so alone.

"When a kid goes into foster care, it's so common for bad shit to happen to them. A lot of us are more than a little screwed up. I don't know what happened to Erik, but I doubt it was anything good. You're the first girl he's ever introduced to me. You're the first girl I've ever seen him really care for. I know this isn't easy, but if you love him, you should give him a chance. If you don't, don't come to the banquet on Saturday because the sooner you cut this off, the less he'll suffer in the long run. And he doesn't need any more pain."

Melanie

Melanie sat with Diane at a local coffee shop around the corner from the country club where her dad was playing golf. It was mid-morning the day before the banquet, and Melanie was still uncertain about what to do. She could admit to herself she loved him, but she wasn't sure her feelings would be enough. Hunter's words hung over her head, but she didn't know what to make of all of it. To distract herself, she was trying to smooth things over with her mother after the debacle with Angie.

They sat at a small, wood table in mismatched chairs surrounded by eclectic, unmatched furniture. The milk frother hissed, sounding over the conversations at nearby tables. Diane sat stiffly in a green pencil skirt and a white blouse, sipping a cappuccino. Melanie chugged her iced coffee, hoping it would perk her up from her constant emotional low.

"How are all your friends after the party?" Melanie asked, bracing herself for a world of criticism.

Diane pursed her lips. "They thought it was very... progressive of me to take interest in a woman with such issues."

"I'm sorry about what happened."

"I know it wasn't your fault, dear. I invited Angie."

Melanie's eyes widened in surprise at her mother's

reaction, but she didn't say anything. She nodded and took another gulp of her coffee.

Diane straightened and narrowed her eyes at her daughter. "All right, who is he?"

"Who's who?"

"The man that's turned my assertive, talkative daughter into a moping child."

Melanie's stomach dropped. Was her heartbreak that obvious? Even her mother noticed—how embarrassing. She forced a smile. "There's no one, or at least there isn't now."

"What did he do?" Diane scowled.

Melanie sat without speaking uncertain what to say.

"Come now, tell me. The devil will take you if you lie by omission."

Melanie sighed. "He lied to me."

"About what?"

"Does it matter?"

"Don't sass me. You know it does. Despite your SAT scores, I know you're not this dense."

There was the critical mother she recognized. Melanie fought an eye roll. "He lied about his past."

Diane gripped Melanie's hand across the table. "I don't know the specifics of what happened. I don't know who this man even is. But I have been married for over twenty years, and I have sixty years of life experience, so I do know a couple of things about people and people in love."

Melanie lurched forward in her seat. "How do you know I'm in love?"

Diane looked down her nose at Melanie. "Only love can make someone this miserable. You were no pleasure to be around during my soirée either."

"Doesn't that make love sound wonderful?"

"I also know that when I went to see you at your employer's house, you've never looked happier, and you were covered in cuts and bruises."

Melanie shook her head. "I wasn't in love back then."

"Maybe you were on your way to falling in love," Diane said, waving a hand. "In any case, my point is that sometimes, when you're with someone you love, you want them to see only the best side of yourself."

"I'm honest with everyone."

"Melanie, dear, what in your past might scare people away?"

Her mother had a point. Melanie may not have had the best relationship with her mother, and she may have struggled to figure out who she was when she was younger, but she had never done anything that would make her think for a second that someone might no longer love her because of her past.

"I'm not telling you what to do, dear, I just want you to be happy. When you fall in love, you want to put the best part of yourself out there, and sometimes your past isn't conducive to that," Diane said, clasping her hands together.

Melanie grinned. "What would you know about that, mother?"

"Absolutely nothing," she said, her eyes wide.

Her mother sipped her cappuccino in silence. If even Diane could tell how unhappy she was, maybe she wasn't ready to let go. Melanie didn't know how Erik felt about her, or why he lied, but maybe it was worth it to find out. She loved him, and she didn't want to give up on love so soon. If he would open up to her, they could have a future. She would just have to go to that banquet to find out if he was ready to share his past with her.

Erik

Natural light and the glow from chandeliers hovering over dozens of crystal-covered tables filled the country club. Soft music from a band sounded over the hum of animated conversation. The ballroom was filled with people in evening wear; colorful hems swirled around women's ankles, and men were draped in suit jackets of subdued grays and browns. And Erik barely noticed any of it.

The banquet had started half an hour ago and still, there was no sign of Melanie. It was time for the toast, and he was thankful he had written it all down because he wasn't sure he could speak from memory right then. He hoped Melanie was going to show up for his speech, he'd thought about her as he'd written it. She made him realize that he was tired of hiding from his past. Maybe one day he would have an opportunity to share it with her. She at least deserved to know the truth about his childhood, about who he was.

Erik stepped up to the microphone beside the band, a crystal champagne glass in hand. The band brought their song to a close, and the room quieted. All eyes turned to him and he took a deep breath.

He thanked his guests for coming and then spoke publicly about his personal life for the first time in his life. "For the longest time, I was ashamed of being a foster kid." He looked over the crowd and registered Hunter's eyes widening in surprise. Erik couldn't help but smile before continuing. "I moved from foster home to foster home, and despite how common that is, as a child, it felt like rejection after rejection. I faced a lot of violence, a lot of neglect, and eventually, I ran away from foster care with my brother. We crossed state lines, running from our past, trying to get rid of our scars. It took me a long time to understand I wasn't a bad person because bad things happened to me. Someone close to me helped me realize that. It's difficult to see yourself when you carry around so much of your past.

"This program for foster kids is designed to help them see themselves more clearly. We'll create good experiences so that the bad ones aren't the only things shaping these children's lives. Thanks to your generosity, these children and young adults will enjoy everything young people should: creativity, confidence, and community. Let's raise our glasses to the kids," he said, and then he saw her. Melanie walked through the crowd, draped in a simple blue gown that matched her eyes. His heart leaped in his chest at the sight of her. She'd come to the banquet, and she was breathtaking.

"Cheers." He took a sip of his champagne. Everyone else did the same, but he had eyes for only her, and she stared back. Blood roared through his ears as he stepped away from the band and back down to the tables. Hunter brushed past him, preparing to give his own speech.

Erik glanced at Hunter, uncertain if he should stay and watch, or go to Melanie. He wasn't sure how much longer he could wait; he needed her in his arms. He needed the reassurance she would accept his apology and was there to be with him.

"Just go, man, I'll tell you how it went later," Hunter whispered in passing.

Erik nodded and then walked to Melanie, who stood by a table near the front of the room. Half of her hair was pinned back, her blue eyes stood out in a small sea of sparkling eyeshadow, and red bloomed on her cheeks as he stepped in front of her. She opened her mouth to speak, her hands tapping against her champagne glass, but before she could say anything, Erik grasped her upper arm and led her out of the ballroom and onto the balcony.

Melanie

Melanie's heart thundered in her chest. Erik's hand on her arm felt so reassuring and sent a shiver of awareness through her. She missed his touch more than she'd thought. Such a simple gesture and she felt like she'd come home. His speech echoed in her head. He hadn't been specific, but she could only imagine the pain he'd endured as a child. She wanted to hold him, to comfort him, but she had to know she was what he wanted first.

They stood on a small balcony overlooking a low-lit rose garden at the country club. The sun had set, but the stars were bright overhead. They were alone outside; the ongoing toasts gave them privacy. The evening was perfect. The warm air rested on her bare arms and exposed back.

She looked at Erik and tried to get her nerves under

control. For calming her nerves, that was the wrong choice. His dark, smoldering gaze was trained on her, his face was hard and unreadable, and he was beautiful. He stood over her, his large form filling out his dark suit, and his warmth and masculine scent surrounded her. She had no idea where to start and he was limiting her ability to speak.

“Did you hear my toast?” Erik asked, his voice barely louder than a whisper.

“Yes, the whole thing. It was wonderful.”

“Thank you.” His widening grin was open and guileless. She loved to see him smile.

“You’re welcome.”

He trailed a finger over her hand that held the champagne. “I know I messed up, but I’d like to make it up to you. I’d love another chance.”

Melanie took a deep breath. She wanted him back in her life so much, but she couldn’t ask him to let her in unless that was what he wanted, unless he was ready to open up. “Erik...I want to make sure this is what’s right for you.”

Erik took her hand in his. “I understand why you might think it’s not, but it is. I want to be with you, I want us to be together.”

Melanie heard the words, but she wasn’t sure she could believe them. She shook her head, backed up, and her back bit into the columned railing.

Erik stepped forward. “Let me tell you a story, please? I want to explain...everything to you.”

“It’s okay, you don’t have to explain anything if you aren’t ready to share yet.” Melanie strained her voice to keep it from wobbling.

"I want to explain now." He set his drink on the railing. "You make me want to share."

"Okay."

Erik smiled in obvious relief. "By the time I was seven, I'd already been in three different foster homes. But that year, things seemed different. I met my new family, and they seemed wonderful. The woman who was supposed to be my foster mom, Hannah, was kind and generous, and she had another foster child, a little girl named, Tara, who was so sweet and laughed all the time. Hannah took me aside after I'd been staying there a few days and told me she wasn't like other foster parents. That she didn't give up children. She said I could tell her anything, that I could trust her, and that I could stay with her and Hannah as long as I wanted. And I believed her," he said, his voice cold.

Melanie's heart fell. This wasn't going to be a happy story. She'd known from the beginning, but the idea of Erik as a little, vulnerable boy in trouble was heartbreaking. She stood and listened, not wanting to interrupt his story.

"I'd been living there a year when she got a new boyfriend. He was nice at first, but Tara stopped laughing when he was around. It took me a while to figure out what was going on, but one night when Hannah was asleep, I heard Tara crying in the room by mine. I thought she had a bad dream, so I went to wake her, but when I walked in...Hannah's boyfriend already there."

"Oh my God." It was beyond horrible. She could've never imagined what had happened.

"He had finished and got up to leave, so I ran to my room. I should have confronted him and checked on

Tara but..." His voice turned rough.

Melanie clasped his fingers. "You were seven. He was a grown man, there was nothing you could've done."

He looked into her eyes, his gaze filled with anguish. "In the morning, I told Hannah. After that, she took me back. She had the guy arrested, and Tara was safe, but she couldn't look at me anymore. I know it was worth it because Tara was safe again, but part of me...I didn't want to go back to foster care."

The weight of the guilt and rejection he was carrying around must have been backbreaking. Melanie shook her head. Her throat was constricted but she had to speak. "You were a child. Of course, you wanted to stay with Hannah and Tara. You did the right thing."

He nodded and gripped her hand. "When I moved into the home where Hunter was, I was pretty messed up. I was withdrawn. I didn't trust anyone, and I didn't want to help anyone, but that one kid, Hunter, got under my skin. I tried to protect him. Melanie, trust is hard for me."

"I'm not going to reject you. I love you." She was so full of sympathy and awe for the incredible man in front of her.

Erik's eyes filled with light, but then he scowled. "You don't have to pity me."

Melanie shook her head. "You're ridiculous. I think you're incredible with your strength, your goodness. This isn't pity. This is amazement. Look at all you've gone on to do and accomplish. I love you, Erik."

"I love you too, Melanie. I've known since before you left, but I didn't want my past to get between us." He stroked her cheek, sending a shiver down her spine.

"You're past is a part of you. I love all of you."

"Give me another chance. I want to share my past with you. I want to try again."

"If you're sure."

"I've never been more certain."

"Then I'm going to stick around for as long as you want me." Melanie stepped closer to him, craning her neck to look up into his eyes.

"That's going to be a long time because I don't ever intend to let you go."

He wrapped his arm around her back and drew her flush against him. Her heart pounded in her chest as he bent his head and kissed her. His tongue swept inside her mouth, and she lost all thought until clapping broke out in the ballroom. She tore her mouth from his. "I think the toasts are over. You'll be missed. We better go in."

Erik groaned but smiled down at her. "Fine, but we'll finish this later."

A shiver of desire shot through her. "Tonight?"

He grinned, his dark eyes gleaming. "Tonight. And then again every night after."

He took her hand, and she followed him inside, ready to move beyond their pasts and to begin their life together.

Acknowledgments

Thanks to my workshop group, Lyndsie, Kaylia, Surabhi, Kurt, and Maya, who have the skills and patience for looking deeply into my blind spots. Thanks to Fran for making me look forward to writing the next draft. Thanks to my editor, Kylee, and the Wanderlust team for helping to make this project what I'd always hoped it could be. Thanks to my family for the moral (and physical, spiritual, financial, mental, etc.,) support, Max, Venise, Max, Ben, Judy, Scott, and Gabe. And to my spouse, Levi, who extended that moral support into the wee hours of the morning. Because writing a book was simultaneously my entire life and separate from it, thanks to my friends who knew when to distract me from this project and somehow knew when to ask about it, Kirsten, Asleif, Gwen, Heather, Becky, and Jeff. A special thanks to Robert and Martha.

About the Author

Carley Mercedes is a romance writer who lives in Missouri with her husband. A sucker for love and happy endings, she started writing HEAs when she was in high school. With a need for caffeine and bookshelves stacked to the ceiling to inspire her, she writes best in libraries and coffee shops. She's happy to be a writer cliché, but when she's not working, she enjoys painting, plays racquetball, and travels.

You can find out more about Carley's work at: http://carleymercedes.com.

CPSIA information can be obtained
at www.ICGtesting.com
Printed in the USA
BVHW081454270819
556814BV00006B/1322/P